Beyond the Horizon

A Journey of Love

RAM CHANGADE

NewDelhi • London

BLUEROSE PUBLISHERS
India | U.K.

Copyright © Ram Changade 2025

All rights reserved by author. No part of this publication may be reproduced, stored in a retrieval system or transmitted in any form or by any means, electronic, mechanical, photocopying, recording or otherwise, without the prior permission of the author. Although every precaution has been taken to verify the accuracy of the information contained herein, the publisher assumes no responsibility for any errors or omissions. No liability is assumed for damages that may result from the use of information contained within.

BlueRose Publishers takes no responsibility for any damages, losses, or liabilities that may arise from the use or misuse of the information, products, or services provided in this publication.

For permissions requests or inquiries regarding this publication, please contact:

BLUEROSE PUBLISHERS
www.BlueRoseONE.com
info@bluerosepublishers.com
+91 8882 898 898
+4407342408967

ISBN: 978-93-6783-583-8

Cover design: Yash Singhal
Typesetting: Namrata Saini

First Edition: May 2025

About the Author

Ram, an engineer by profession and writer by passion, earned his M.Tech in Software Engineering from BITS, Pilani.

His love for storytelling began early, evolving from scribbles in notebooks to the publication of his debut novel, Beyond the Horizon.

Writing became his refuge, offering clarity, connection, and meaning.

Drawing from lived experiences and a deep understanding of human relationships, Ram's narratives are rich in emotional honesty and cultural depth.

His transformative travels through Latin America infused his stories with new perspectives, shaping themes of identity, connection, and change.

Known for blending imagination with emotional truth, Ram writes about love, loss, and self-discovery in ways that resonate universally.

His storytelling bridges cultures and invites readers to feel, reflect, and connect. When not writing, he enjoys observing life, reading, and sketching ideas for future novels.

Ram's journey is a testament to passion, persistence, and the belief that every story has the power to touch hearts and transcend boundaries.

Connect me at:

Email: changaderam@gmail.com

Instagram: ramchang7384

Website: www.beyonddhorizons.com

Contents

Chapter 01: Echoes of the Past 1

Chapter 02: The Casino—Embracing the Unknown 9

Chapter 03: Beyond the Comfort Zone….........................18

Chapter 04: The Beginning of Something Beautiful.........35

Chapter 05: A Walk to Remember 71

Chapter 06: A Game of Chance, A Game of Habit........141

Chapter 07: When Forever Had a Deadline...................168

Chapter 08: Love Finds a Way—Or It Doesn't.............178

Chapter 09: When Dreams Say Yes................................193

Chapter 10: Santiago: Where the Dream Begins............201

Chapter 11: Not My Kind of Coffee 230

Chapter 12: The Art of Walking Away 250

Chapter 13: When the Heart Finds Home 265

Chapter 14: The Stranger's Story 277

Chapter 15: The Night She Became a Star 286

Chapter 16: A Visit to Sikh Seva Sabha…......................293

Chapter 17: Beyond the Horizon....................................301

Chapter 01

Echoes of the Past

We often find ourselves looking back, realizing that our past shapes our future. It takes courage to leave behind what we know and step into the unknown, but it is in these moments that we truly begin to live.

3rd June 2015

It was 10 a.m. In five hours, Krishna would step aboard the world cruise he'd long dreamt of—not as an explorer, but as a casino dealer. He sat in his room, eyes drifting over the neatly packed bags. A quiet relief settled over him. Everything was ready—down to the smallest detail. That level of organization wasn't his style, but he knew exactly who to thank.

Shiva.

His elder brother had always carried responsibility like second nature. Krishna couldn't help but chuckle at the thought. "I always thought engineers were disorganized, rushing to do everything at the last minute," he teased. "But you're the exception, brother. Thank you for being the planner in our lives."

Shiva, standing nearby with an air of calm efficiency, nodded, but the weight on his face betrayed a heaviness he had been hiding.

His gaze swept the room—chaotic poker nights, the echo of laughter, and bonfire memories etched into the walls. His heart weighed with the realization that he was about to leave it all behind. His friends had come to see him off. Despite the jokes and laughter, a sense of finality lingered in the air. They knew Krishna too well—never one to settle, always chasing life's unpredictable roads.

There was more to this departure than just leaving Goa. It was about Shiva too.

Krishna admired the calm fire behind his brother's determination. Shiva had always been focused—burning with an intense desire to achieve his dreams. Working for a world-class IT company had been his wildest dream and to his credit, he had made it happen. His persistence had paid off, but it had come at a cost. Shiva had sacrificed much of his personal life to reach this point. His gaze was fixed firmly on the future, on building something lasting, something tangible. Krishna danced with chaos, while Shiva carved his future with quiet, unyielding discipline.

Krishna, by contrast, never cared for the destination. He was a traveler in every sense, someone who embraced life's twists and turns with open arms. For him, success wasn't measured in achievements or titles, but in the experiences that dotted his journey. He lived each moment fully, always curious, always ready to learn. Krishna trusted his instincts, whether abandoning his education for Shiva or diving into the casino world. Despite their differences, they understood each other. Two brothers, two paths, bound by something deeper than ambition or ideology.

As the clock ticked closer to departure, Krishna received a thoughtful parting gift from Shiva—a brand-new Bhagavad Gita and a mala from the ISKCON temple. It was a quiet, spiritual gesture, one meant to guide him in the uncertainty ahead.

"Chant this," Shiva said, his voice quiet, demonstrating the mantra, "Hare Krishna, Hare Krishna…"

Krishna listened, murmuring the words, though his mind was elsewhere. He knew that Shiva's gesture was more than just spiritual—it was an expression of love, a hope that Krishna would find his way in the world, no matter where his path led him.

Yet, beneath Shiva's calm exterior, something was brewing. As the hour drew near, Krishna sensed a shift in his brother's demeanor. Shiva had always been the strong, silent type, but today, he seemed... distant. His words carried a weight Krishna hadn't noticed before.

Finally, unable to bear the silence, Krishna asked, "What's wrong, Shiva? Aren't you happy to see your brother going abroad?"

The question opened a floodgate. Shiva, who had always been so composed, began to unravel. His voice cracked under the weight of the guilt he had been carrying for years.

"It's my fault, Krishna," he confessed. "If I hadn't fought with you that day... you wouldn't have left Pune. You wouldn't be leaving us now."

Krishna frowned. "Shiva—"

"You gave up everything for me," Shiva cut in. "You were always cleverer than me in everything."

"If you were at my place, you would have been in a better position than me, we both know this. But instead, you sacrificed your academics so I could learn. You stood by me when no one else did. And when you needed me... I turned away."

Regret thickened his voice. "Everyone thinks you left Pune by choice. But we both know it was because of me. Because of that fight. And you never even told the family. You never made me feel the weight of what I did. How can you be so cold?

I know I hurt you, but it hurt more that you never made me feel it.

That guilt stays with me, brother. I've always been self-centered. Let me make it right—will you forgive me?

Your brother has everything now.

You don't have to leave to be successful. You love the market, don't you? Stay. I'll be right here, supporting you.

I was scared that day," Shiva admitted, "I thought we had to start over again. I thought it was the only way to build our dream."

Krishna let the words settle. He had never blamed Shiva, but he could see now—his brother had carried this guilt alone for years.

The air between them thickened with unspoken pain. Krishna had never held a grudge, but Shiva, always so driven, couldn't forgive himself for pushing his brother away. He poured out his regrets, admitting that he had been selfish, focused only on his dreams, blind to Krishna's needs.

Shiva acknowledged Krishna's sacrifices and his own shortcomings as an older brother, expressing remorse for not being there when Krishna needed him the most. Tears welled up in Shiva's eyes as he begged for forgiveness, admitting to Krishna's selflessness and his self-centeredness. Overwhelmed with emotion, Shiva poured out his regrets, burdened by guilt and remorse.

Krishna let him speak, let the emotions spill out. When the silence finally stretched, Krishna spoke softly, his words filled with warmth.

"Shiva, my brother, what I did was my duty as your brother. Anything that can happen will happen. If our fight led me here, then I have no regrets. Every choice I've made led me here and I'm grateful for it.

Our dreams are yet to come true, and together, we'll make them a reality."

As they embraced once more, Krishna whispered, "Maybe our fight was just a catalyst, guiding us to where we're meant to be." The tension between them dissolving into something softer, something unspoken.

Krishna's philosophy was simple: live every moment fully. Whatever life threw at him, he embraced it. His thirst for learning was unmatched. He is always eager to explore new ideas, meet new people, and dive into the unknown.

He didn't know where his life would lead him, but it never bothered him.

And for Shiva, who measured life in goals and achievements, that simplicity was both mystifying and admirable. He had always been in awe of Krishna's ability to live in the moment, to walk paths that hadn't been forged yet. It was a freedom he had never known, bound as he was to his own ambitions.

With the packing finally complete, Krishna took a sigh of relief. But Shiva reminded him, "Not yet. Packing is not complete until we have all the delicacies made by Mumma.

One bag was filled with Laddu, snacks and other treats lovingly prepared by their mother.

Calling home, Krishna felt emotion rise in his chest. Mumma, their mother was restless and tearful, expressing her fears about Krishna's upcoming journey. She gave hurried instructions to Krishna, reminding him to stay safe and vigilant. She could not hide her tears as she bid farewell to Krishna, her fears for his safety weighing heavily on her heart.

"Mumma, please don't worry. I'll return safely soon," Krishna reassured his mother, trying to comfort her as she expressed her concerns about his upcoming journey.

"If you cry, your tears will stay with me throughout the trip. Would you like that?"

"Nah nah, I'm not crying my son. I'm just a little scared, thinking about how you'll manage over there," she replied, her voice trembling with emotion. "But I'm proud of you, my boy."

His father checked in, making sure Krishna had all the logistics in place. One by one, Krishna spoke to every family member, trading reassurances. Finally, with a heavy heart, Krishna ended the call, promising to update them as soon as he boarded the cruise.

Despite their reluctance, the family knew Krishna's determination. He would go through with his plans anyway.

As they headed for Mormugao Cruise Port, Krishna's thoughts turned inward. Goa wasn't just a place—it was laughter, friendship, and the wild thrill of adventure. The casino world had been an unexpected chapter—one he had never anticipated yet embraced with open arms. The friends he had made, the camaraderie they shared, it all felt like a lifetime bundled into a few short years.

Shiva and Krishna both wore success, but in entirely different shades. Krishna had always lived in the present, unbothered by thoughts of the future. It had been the same since the day he gave up his education to support his brother. It was the same when he walked away from Shiva. The same when he stepped into the casino world, chasing luck instead of certainty. And it's same even today when he answers to the call of destiny.

He never knew where his path would lead—only that he'd walk it anyway. That was his magic. He never followed the usual path—he forged his own and left a trail behind. Shiva's success was measured by his unwavering focus and determination to achieve his goals.

Krishna, on the other hand, embraced life with curiosity and zest. He embraced each opportunity as it came, navigating through life's twists and turns with an open mind. Success had no shape in his mind. He welcomed the road as it came, curious about every bend rather than fixated on the end. Krishna found fulfillment in living in the moment and seizing every opportunity that came his way. He didn't walk to reach a goal. He walked to feel the road beneath his feet—and that's why he loved the journey.

If anyone had told Krishna that one day he would go to Goa, work in a casino, and become one of the most skilled casino dealers, he would not have believed it.

Four years ago, he never imagined he'd have the world of gambling at his fingertips. That's life's quiet trick—you only see the full picture when you glance over your shoulder.

Krishna admired Shiva's dedication and persistence, acknowledging that his brother's focused approach had paved the way for his success. Meanwhile, Shiva admired Krishna's ability to find joy in every experience, even if it meant venturing into the unknown. They were the perfect complement for each other.

Despite the uncertainty of where life would lead Krishna, His adventurous spirit never wavered. He embraced each new path with enthusiasm, trusting that his journey would unfold as it was meant to.

Krishna felt a sense of gratitude for the friendships and memories they had created. And as they bid farewell to Goa, he knew that no matter where life would take him, the bond between him and his brother would remain unbreakable.

Chapter 02

The Casino—Embracing the Unknown

> *Life is a gamble, and the greatest rewards come from embracing the unknown. It is in taking risks that we discover our true potential and learn that success is not just about winning, but about daring to play the game.*

Higheline Casino is one of the leading casinos in Goa. They had hired four interns from MBA background. Krishna was the only one without any degree.

Since it was a nightclub and casino, their workday started at 6:00 p.m and stretched deep into the night. Everyone was busy—except Riya and Krishna. Riya hated the idleness. If Krishna hadn't been there, she wouldn't have lasted.

Krishna, however, refused to let the lack of work frustrate him. His indomitable spirit and infectious enthusiasm kept him going. He never hesitated to put in extra hours. He used to arrive at 5:30 in the evening, despite the ten-hour shifts.

Riya, on the other hand, struggled to find her footing in the competitive environment, feeling overwhelmed by the pressure to prove herself.

"Are you out of your mind? Is this what you're here for?" Riya snapped, frustration bubbling up as she watched Krishna move from table to table, effortlessly engaging with people.

Krishna turned his attention towards Riya, a grin playing on his lips.

"What happened, Riya?" he asked, noting the distress in Riya's eyes.

She exhaled sharply. "I see no reason to be here. People are so selfish. They don't want to talk to new faces. They cling to their comfort zones like castaways to driftwood." She gestured towards the reception area where a young girl sat, seemingly engrossed in her tasks, oblivious to the world around her.

"I've been waiting for work details from her forever. If they don't want us, why did they even hire us?" Her agitation grew with every word she uttered.

"It's torture, pure and simple," he muttered, her frustration threatening to boil over.

Krishna, however, remained unfazed.

"Hey, relax," He leaned back in his chair. "You think this is the worst time? That it's torture?"

Riya frowned. "Isn't it?"

Krishna chuckled. "It's an opportunity. An opportunity to observe and learn from the environment around us." Riya's confusion was palpable.

"But sitting idle, with no purpose... it feels torturous," she countered.

Krishna's eyes twinkled with understanding. "Your reason is your perception," he elucidated.

Riya's brow furrowed in confusion. "What do you mean?" She asked, her voice tinged with uncertainty.

Krishna took a moment to gather his thoughts before responding. "You came here with certain expectations," he began, "expectations of success, respect, and validation."

Riya nodded slowly, her mind drifting back to the dreams she had harbored when she first embarked on her journey in the hospitality industry.

"You believed that your college degree and good academics would pave the way for your success," Krishna continued, "but the reality is far different."

Riya's heart sank as Krishna's words hit home. She had indeed believed that her qualifications would guarantee her success in the private sector, but now she saw the flaws in her thinking.

"Success isn't handed to us on a silver platter," Krishna explained gently. "It's something we have to work for, something we have to create for ourselves."

Thoughtful silence hit the floor for a moment.

"Where are you from? How did you end up here?" Krishna asked while breaking the silence. Riya's shoulders sagged slightly as she recounted her journey from Bihar to this unfamiliar place. "I come from a small town, my family values education and encouraged me to pursue my dreams," she explained.

"I thought this internship would be a steppingstone to success, but now I'm not so sure."

Riya open-up about her background and aspirations. She had joined the hotel management program with hopes of gaining exposure and experience, but now felt disillusioned by the reality of the workplace. She watched, torn between admiration and frustration.

"How can you stay so positive?" She blurted out, unable to contain her curiosity any longer. "We're stuck in a dead-end job with nothing to do, and yet you seem content."

Krishna chuckled softly, his eyes crinkling at the corners. "It's all about perspective, my friend," he said. "Life is what you make of it. Instead of dwelling on what we don't have, why not focus on what we do have?" he explained.

"We may be idle now, but there's so much to learn if we open ourselves up to it."

As Krishna spoke, Riya's skepticism began to wane. His words painted a picture of opportunity amidst the apparent stagnation. "Success isn't about where you start, but how you make the most of your journey. And right now, we're in the perfect place to learn and grow." Krishna continued...

"If you open your eyes, you will not get platform better than the casino," Krishna proclaimed, his voice carrying a note of urgency. Riya nodded, feeling a sense of clarity wash over her.

"Look around you—success, fame, love, frustration, fantasy, glory, glamour—everything around you," Krishna urged, gesturing to the bustling casino around them. Riya followed his gaze, seeing the world with new eyes.

"If you ride on the tide of human emotions, you will never turn back," Krishna warned, his words a sobering reminder of the dangers that lurked in the shadows. Riya nodded solemnly, vowing to remain steadfast in the face of adversity.

"Everyone is telling you something. You just need to learn how to listen, observe, and read between the lines." Krishna advised, his words a call to action. Riya nodded in agreement, realizing that there was much she had yet to learn about the art of communication.

"Do you know why this is the best time of your life?" Krishna asked, his eyes sharp with insight.

Riya shook her head, eager to uncover the secret that lay hidden within his words.

"Because you are not a successful person yet. Once you reach that height, you cannot come down," Krishna revealed, his words a revelation to Riya's understanding of the world. She nodded, a flicker of humility in her gaze— success was far more layered than she'd imagined.

"You are an intern. You can do anything. You can be anyone. You can become a waitress and know when people order their drinks," Krishna urged, his words a challenge to Riya's perception of the world around her. Possibility, she saw now, held a power she had barely begun to understand. She nodded, the thought settling in.

"See that girl serving order. She can tell you what the state of mind of any person is." Krishna continued, his words a testament to the power of observation. Riya nodded in agreement, realizing the importance of paying attention to the subtle cues that revealed the true nature of those around her.

"Look around at other people. Observe them closely and you'll start to hear what their presence is saying." Krishna advised, his words a reminder of the wealth of knowledge that surrounded her. Riya felt a sense of wonder wash over her as she marveled at the intricacies of human behavior.

"Look around. Someone's waiting to make a new friend." Krishna urged, his words a challenge to Riya's perception of the world around her. Her nod came with a newfound appreciation for how deeply connection shaped their lives.

"Look down, and you'll see—the girl with the red purse is waiting to meet someone," Krishna observed, his words a testament to the power of intuition. The subtle beauty of human interaction struck her afresh. She nodded, absorbing the moment.

Krishna's tone sharpened. "That guy in the three-piece suit?" He's going to lose big today. Krishna remarked, his words a challenge to Riya's perception of the world around her. She gave a quiet nod; struck by how little she understood the chaos beneath life's surface.

"You know why the Higheline Casino is one of the best in Goa?" Krishna asked, his words a challenge to Riya's perception of the world around her. She nodded thoughtfully, a new awareness dawning—success ran deeper than she imagined.

"Have you ever thought about why Friday nights are silent? Why music starts at 9 and why one beer is complementary?" Krishna questioned, his words a puzzle waiting to be solved. Riya furrowed her brow, pondering the significance of these seemingly mundane details.

"Have you ever thought about why Saturdays are disco nights?" Krishna continued, his words a challenge to Riya's perception of the world around her. She nodded slowly, awed by the hidden patterns shaping everything around her.

"It's not random. Everything—the music, the free drinks, the event timings—has a psychological reason behind it."

Riya saw it now. The structure beneath the chaos.

"Higheline casino is the best in Goa because it is not static. Behind everything, to every event, there is a psychological reason," Krishna explained, his words a challenge to Riya's perception of the world around her. She nodded, humbled by the vast labyrinth of the human psyche.

"The management has a precise estimate of how much they'll earn each night from concerts, the casino, and drink sales."

Krishna revealed, his words a challenge to Riya's perception of the world around her. She nodded, finally sensing how deep the mechanics of money and strategy could run.

"This is the best time to learn as much as we can." His words resonated deeply with Riya as she reflected on her journey thus far. She realized that her lack of success had been a blessing in disguise. This is our opportunity to absorb, adapt, and grow.

"If you take it a little bit positively and survive here, you will never look back," Krishna assured her, his voice filled with confidence. Riya felt a renewed sense of purpose course through her veins, as she embraced the challenges that lay ahead.

As Riya absorbed Krishna's words, a transformation began to take root within her. The once-desolate landscape of idleness now teemed with possibilities, each moment pregnant with meaning and insight. She looked around, her senses heightened, as if seeing the world through new eyes. The walls of the casino seemed to whisper secrets, and even the framed image of Lord Balaji bore a knowing smile.

She felt like God was watching over her, guiding her on her journey towards success.

Feeling a newfound sense of determination coursing through her veins. She had spent too long dwelling on the negatives, but now she saw the world through a different lens—a lens of opportunity and possibility.

Scanning the casino, she saw stories everywhere—in every face, every flickering light, every roll of the dice. She just needed to open her eyes and listen, really listen.

As she looked out at the bustling casino floor, she felt a sense of excitement bubbling up inside her. She was ready to embrace the challenges ahead, to seize the opportunities that lay before her, and to write her own story—one filled with success, happiness, and fulfillment.

She had been so focused on the destination that she had overlooked the beauty of the journey itself. Krishna opened Riya's eyes to a new perspective on their situation. He challenged her to see beyond the surface frustrations and embrace the unique opportunities that their job at the casino presented.

Krishna's words struck a chord with Riya, prompting her to reconsider her approach to their shared challenges. She realized that success wasn't just about meeting expectations or following a predetermined path—it was about embracing the uncertainty of the journey and finding fulfillment in the process. With Krishna's encouragement, Riya began to see the casino not just as a place of work, but as a world of endless possibilities waiting to be explored.

She learned to listen, observe, and engage with her surroundings in ways she had never imagined before, discovering hidden insights and connections that had previously eluded her. As Riya's perspective shifted, so did her attitude towards her work. She approached each day with a renewed sense of purpose and excitement, eager to uncover the secrets and mysteries that lay beneath the surface of the casino's glittering facade. With Krishna by her side, Riya embarked on a journey of self-discovery and growth, learning valuable lessons in resilience, determination—and what success truly means.

Together, they proved that even in the absence of a mentor, they could find their own way and forge their own path towards greatness.

Chapter 03

Beyond the Comfort Zone...

Growth begins at the edge of our comfort zone. It is only by stepping into unfamiliar territory that we uncover our strengths and realize that the greatest adventures lie beyond the boundaries we set for ourselves.

They raised their glasses in a long overdue toast. The room buzzed with energy, a farewell party for Krishna. Shiva had come from Pune, joining Ali, Jai, and Riya—who were already warm with drinks. Krishna and Shiva stuck to their soft drinks, but that didn't dull the laughter, the stories and memories.

As they reminisced, memories of their time with Krishna flooded the room. They laughed about the good, bad, and downright reckless moments they'd shared. But underneath it all, a quiet realization settled in—Krishna was leaving.

Shiva raised his glass, his voice steady but weighted. "I've learned so much from you, brother. I have learned what it means to keep the family. I am proud of you. We all are. Please come back soon." Krishna looked at his brother, unable to find the words to respond.

Riya, in a moment of clarity, amidst the haze, struggled to stand. "I need to say something," she announced.

"Say it from there, we all are listening to you," Jai urged her to remain seated.

"Hey, come on! I'm not high today!" she shot back, before turning to Krishna. "I'm going to miss you, my friend." her voice tinged with emotion.

Krishna smiled, acknowledging the depth behind her words.

Riya took a slow sip of her beer, her voice growing more measured. "You remember how we met? We weren't friends then—we were rivals, thrown into the chaos of the casino, trying to prove ourselves."

"We were both thrown into this world without guidance, without anyone to mentor to us," she said, recalling their early days of uncertainty and frustration.

Instead of support, they faced indifference and hostility from their colleagues, who seemed more interested in maintaining their own status than in helping newcomers like them.

In their first few days they hadn't known why the casino hired them. Every day, they had to go to the casino to observe people.

"Those were the days full of torture. Until that day I used to think how lucky people who don't have anyone pushing them to work. We were nobodies, ignored, dismissed. Until one day, I had no choice but to talk to you," She smirked at Krishna, "And here we are."

She shared how Krishna's positive attitude and tireless work ethic had inspired her during those difficult times. Despite the lack of direction, Krishna had taken the initiative to learn and adapt, becoming a beacon of hope for those around him. Riya's eyes turned moist as she expressed her gratitude for Krishna's presence in her life. She recounted how he had helped her navigate the challenges of their workplace and had encouraged her to embrace every opportunity for growth.

Krishna listened intently, his heart swelling with pride at Riya's transformation. He realized that their journey together had been about more than just survival—it had been about supporting each other and growing together.

As Riya finished speaking, Krishna reached out and hugged her, an unspoken promise that distance wouldn't change what they had built.

"Thank you, Krishna," she whispered.

"You don't need to thank me," he said. "You made your own success. You always had it in you."

One by one, the party wound down. People sprawled wherever they could, too exhausted—or too drunk—to move.

Shiva thought he'd woken up early—it was already 11:00 AM, and the house was in disarray.

Riya, Ali, and Jay were nursing hangovers from the heavy drinking while Krishna maintained his composure.

They made their way to nearing restaurant, nursing teas and breakfast, the weight of the night still lingering in their minds.

Krishna went about his usual routine at the casino, ensuring that everything ran smoothly in the casino, he couldn't help but overhear snippets of conversation between jay and Ali, two of his closest confidants. They spoke of last night's events, of laughter and camaraderie.

But amidst the chatter, Krishna's mind was elsewhere, grappling with the weight of Mr. Roy's words. The casino owner had paid him a visit that morning, offering words of wisdom that echoed in Krishna's mind.

"My casino is always open for you," Mr. Roy had affirmed, his eyes gleaming with a quiet intensity.

"Don't limit yourself. Go, explore... Experience and feel. Do the things you haven't done before."

Those words lingered with Krishna as he went about his day, the weight of them settling in his chest. For too long, he had confined himself to the familiar comforts of routine, afraid to venture beyond the boundaries he had set for himself.

But as he looked around at the bustling energy of the casino, at the people whose lives had been touched by its magic, Krishna felt a stirring within him. Maybe it was time to heed Mr. Roy's advice, to embrace the unknown and see where it led him.

And as he gazed out at the world beyond the casino walls, Krishna felt a sense of liberation wash over him. In that moment, he knew that no matter where life took him, the casino would always be a place of transformation and possibility.

"Can I ask you something?" Krishna's voice quivered slightly. Mr. Roy raised an eyebrow with curiosity. "Of course, Krishna. What is it?"

"Why didn't you stop me?" Krishna's question hung in the air.

Mr. Roy's lips curled into a smirk as he chuckled heartily. "Stop? Why should I stop you, my boy?"

Krishna's brows furrowed, his frustration bubbling to the surface. "Wasn't I important to our casino?

The laughter from Mr. Roy only intensified. "Oh, Krishna, you never fail to amuse me."

Deep down, he knew his next question would be met with mockery, yet he couldn't silence the voice inside him.

"Would you stay if I asked you to stay?" Mr. Roy's voice was steady, his eyes locked onto Krishna's.

"Certainly not," Krishna said, his voice dropping to a whisper.

"I know, I wouldn't have stayed," Krishna admitted, the resignation heavy in his words.

"I can't be selfish. Do you know the story of the frog living in the well?" Mr. Roy's voice was calm, his eyes searching Krishna's for understanding.

"No," Krishna responded, intrigued by the unfamiliar tale.

"There was a frog who lived in a well," Mr. Roy began, his voice steady. "It was born and brought up there, living a happy and successful life. One day, another frog from the sea fell into the well."

Krishna listened, something about the story striking a chord as Mr. Roy painted the scene with his words.

"The frog from the sea exclaimed about the vastness of the ocean, but the frog from the well couldn't comprehend anything beyond its limited perspective," Mr. Roy continued. "To the frog in the well, its world was all there was; it couldn't fathom anything greater."

As the story unfurled, a pang of recognition echoed in Krishna's chest. He pondered if he resembled a frog in a well, content within the stone walls of a familiar surroundings, remaining oblivious to the vastness of the world existing outside.

"If your sea is so big, you are lying to me. Nothing can be as big as my well," the frog from the well protested, echoing Krishna's own doubts.

"But the frog from the sea urged the frog from the well to venture beyond its narrow confines, to explore the vastness of the world that lay beyond," Mr. Roy explained, his words resonating with Krishna.

"I don't want you to be the frog in the well." Mr. Roy said, his gaze steady.

The world is vast and full of opportunities. There is much for you to learn beyond the confines of your familiar surroundings.

Krishna nodded slowly, absorbing the words.

Determination surged through Krishna as he realized the truth in Mr. Roy's words.

Mr. Roy leaned back, a knowing smile tugging at his lips. "I'm not doing charity here. I'm investing in you.

Because when you come back, you'll bring something bigger with you."

Krishna exhaled, feeling something shift within him. He had spent years building himself inside these walls. Now, it was time to step beyond them.

And maybe, just maybe, he'd find his ocean.

At the bustling terminal, amidst the hustle and bustle of travelers and luggage, Krishna stood with a sense of quiet contemplation. It was a rare sight to see Krishna so silent, his usually vibrant presence subdued by the weight of his emotions.

Three suitcases and a backpack marked the beginning of his new journey, a journey that stirred emotions he rarely allowed himself to feel.

Shiva stood next to him, his arms crossed, eyes unreadable. The bond between the brothers had never needed words, but today, silence felt suffocating. Krishna glanced around, the weight of the moment pressing on his chest. The uncertainty of what lay ahead clawed at him—a rare, unsettling feeling.

As he surveyed the terminal, thoughts of the future swirled in Krishna's mind, momentarily paralyzing him with fear. For the first time in years, he felt a pang of uncertainty, a fear of the unknown that threatened to engulf him. But amidst the chaos of his thoughts, a voice echoed in Krishna's mind—the voice of Mr. Roy, a mentor whose wisdom had guided him through many challenges.

"Any decision made at this moment will push you beyond your comfort zone. There are many talented people who never progress because they hesitate to leave their comfort zone." The words echoed vividly in Krishna's mind.

The memory of Mr. Roy's words stirred something within Krishna—a determination to step out of his comfort zone, despite the fear that gnawed at him. He knew that staying in his familiar surroundings would only lead to stagnation, a fate he was unwilling to accept.

As Krishna bid farewell to his friends and Shiva, gratitude welled up within him. Krishna embraced his brother tightly, promising to return soon. As he stepped onto the platform, the weight of his luggage in tow, Krishna felt a surge of anticipation mingled with apprehension. He was ready for the challenges that lay ahead, prepared to embrace the discomfort of the unknown in pursuit of growth and opportunity.

"Okay, guys," Krishna announced, breaking the heavy silence that hung between them. "I'm ready to go."

Shiva enveloped his brother in a tight hug, a silent affirmation of their bond. "Come back soon," Shiva urged, his voice tinged with emotion. "We'll be waiting for you."

"Thank you, guys. Life wouldn't have been so wonderful without you." Krishna said, turning to his friends, his voice thick with emotion.

"Our time together will stay with me forever."

"Yes, my friend, we'll be here, waiting for you. Until then—sayonara!"

As he walked closer to the Cruise, the laughter and well-wishes followed him, a reminder of the love and warmth he was leaving behind. With one last glance at his brother, Krishna stepped into the unknown, ready to chase new horizons and embrace the discomfort of growth.

He watched the buildings of Murmugao Port Terminal fade into the distance, Krishna knew that this was just the beginning of a new chapter—one filled with uncertainty, but also with the promise of adventure and growth. And with that thought in mind, he took a deep breath, steeling himself for what lay ahead.

Now, as he prepared to embark on a new journey, he understood the perils of stagnation. "The story of the little frog was so true," Krishna mused, his mind drifting back to the tale Mr. Roy had shared. "Had I spent a few more years here, I wouldn't have been able to come out of it for sure."

With a deep breath, Krishna resolved to embrace the discomfort of the unknown. "New journeys look uncomfortable at first," he acknowledged, grateful for the wisdom imparted by Mr. Roy.

"Thank you, Mr. Roy," he whispered silently, acknowledging the guidance that had brought him to this moment of departure.

Krishna's pulse quickened as he stood before the towering terminal, its glass facade gleaming under the evening sun.

As he walked up the gangway, he caught glimpses of the ship's interior through the large glass windows. When he finally set foot inside, he had to remind himself that he was on a cruise, not inside a luxury hotel. The gleaming crystal staircase spiraled toward a magnificent chandelier, its glass prisms catching the light and scattering it in a thousand directions. The lobby pulsed with quiet grandeur, the soft hum of voices mingling with the distant melody of a piano.

A massive screen displayed information about the ship—12 decks, a crew of 900 catering to 4,500 guests, and a wealth of amenities. Krishna's gaze swept over the details. The tallest slide at sea, world-class restaurants, a sprawling casino, theaters, pools, and a rock-climbing wall—it was overwhelming. More than that, it was exhilarating.

Krishna stood at the boarding gate, staring at the massive white vessel before him. The Harmony of the Seas loomed like a floating city, its ten stories rising above the deep blue water. He had seen pictures, read about it, but standing here, about to step aboard, felt surreal.

Anticipation surged through him—this journey was bound to be different. Stepping inside, he was greeted by the terminal officer, who briskly cross-verified his documents and tickets.

"Good afternoon, sir! I hope you have a wonderful time on board. Could you please tell me the cruise reservation number?" He asked, her voice filled with genuine warmth and hospitality. Krishna fumbled for his ticket, his fingers tingling with anticipation.

"Is this your first journey?" The officer inquired formally.

"Yes, first time on a cruise. How'd you guess?" Krishna blurted, his voice a mix of nerves and excitement.

"We see it all the time, Mr. Krishna," he said, a mischievous glint in her eyes as she scanned his documents.

As he handed over the document, he couldn't shake the feeling that this journey was going to be more than just a cruise. It was going to be an adventure, full of surprises and unexpected moments, waiting to unfold with each passing waves.

He rounded a corner near the park's iconic fountain, something unusual caught his eye.

A charming little stall stood on the ground floor, amidst the vibrant scenery. The stall was adorned with a beautifully crafted, oversized sign that read, "Free Photoshoot – Pay Only If You Like It."

Krishna approached the stall. The 3D Thermocol couple statue was ingeniously crafted, its metal wires twisting together like an elegant piece of scientific art. Sunlight reflected off its surface, making it impossible to ignore.

Behind the stall stood a photographer, a man in his late thirties with an inviting smile and a welcoming demeanor. He was adjusting his camera, a professional instant pic cam mounted on a sturdy tripod. As Krishna got closer, the photographer looked up and greeted him warmly.

"Hey there! I see my sign caught your attention. I'm Leo," he said, extending his hand.

Krishna shook his hand and smiled. "Hi, I'm Krishna. Your sign is impressive! I could not resist coming over. What made you design it like that?"

A spark of excitement flickered in Leo's eyes.

"I used to be an engineer myself before I pursued my passion for photography full-time. The Thermocol couple Statue represents a junction of two different worlds for me; Engineering and art. Plus, it tends to attract people with a curious mind, like yourself."

Krishna nodded, appreciating the thought behind it. "That's brilliant. So, how does this photoshoot work?"

"It's simple," Leo explained. "I take your photos for free, and if you like them, you can pay whatever you feel they're worth. If not, no hard feelings. It's my way of spreading joy and capturing moments without any pressure."

Intrigued and impressed by the unique concept, Krishna agreed to the photoshoot. Leo guided him to a picturesque spot where the autumn leaves formed a vibrant backdrop. The shoot began, Leo's skill behind the camera quickly became evident. He had a knack for making his subjects feel at ease, capturing candid moments and genuine smiles.

As Leo clicked away, he and Krishna chatted about their mutual love for world exploration. Leo shared stories of how he transitioned from a corporate job to following his passion; Krishna found himself inspired by the courage it took to make such a change.

Once the shoot was over, Leo invited Krishna to review the photos on his laptop. As the images appeared on the screen, Krishna was amazed at how beautifully Leo had captured the essence of the park, the play of light, and Krishna's own personality. Each photo seemed to tell a story; Krishna found it hard to pick a favorite.

"These are incredible," Krishna said, genuinely impressed. "You've got a real gift, Leo."

"Thank you," Leo replied with a humble smile. "I'm glad you like them. So, how much would you like to pay?"

Krishna thought for a moment and then handed Leo a generous amount. "Consider this an investment in your passion. You've inspired me today, and that's worth every penny."

Leo accepted the payment with gratitude. "Thank you, Krishna. It means a lot. And remember, if you ever need a photographer or just want to chat about World Exploration, you know where to find me."

The encounter had been more than just a photoshoot; it was a reminder of the importance of following one's passions and the beauty of unexpected connections. The giant thermacol 3D statue had indeed done its job, bridged the worlds of art and science, and created a memorable experience for everyone who crossed its path.

The photographer, a jovial man with a keen eye for creativity, wielded his Fujifilm instant peak camera with flair. His unique proposition? An irresistible photo illusion that made people appear as if they were floating in water. It was a whimsical sight to behold, and the photographer's infectious enthusiasm drew in the crowds.

People could not resist the temptation. Families, friends, and even solo adventurers lined up, eager to experience the magic of his photography. The photographer guided each group with meticulous care, positioning them just right and ensuring their poses were picture perfect. With a swift click of his camera, he captured moments that seemed straight out of a dream.

The cleverness of his business lay not only in the unique photo effect but also in the irresistible charm of the experience. As the instant photos developed, laughter and delight spread like wildfire.

"Wow, this is incredible!" A young woman exclaimed, holding up her photo, for her friends to see. "I have to have this!"

Indeed, most people didn't hesitate for a second. The allure of the amusing and beautifully crafted photos made them reach for their wallets without a second thought. They happily handed over a few bucks to take home a cherished memory, a snapshot of joy.

The photographer's business acumen shone brightly. By offering the initial click for free and relying on the captivating results to secure payment, he ensured a steady stream of customers. It was a simple yet brilliant strategy, turning casual passersby into paying customers with ease.

With passing time, the photographer's stall became a hub of laughter and mirth. His Fujifilm instant peak camera clicked away, capturing moments of pure happiness. The ingenious setup, the delightful photos, and the effortless charm of the photographer created a perfect recipe to create memories.

In the heart of Central Park, a clever photographer transformed an ordinary day into a cascade of smiles and unforgettable memories. His business thrived not just on the promise of a unique photo but on the joy and laughter he brought to everyone who stepped in front of his lens. Indeed, it was the best business idea—a testament to the power of creativity and the simple pleasure of a well-captured moment. People were spinning their bucks without a second thought. That photographer was surely a clever businessman.

Click for free and if you like the pic, then pay for a hard copy. Indeed, the best business idea.

As Krishna walked to his hotel room, a stunning woman approached, balancing a tray with three glasses and two bottles.

"Good evening, Sir, which one shall I make for you?" Merlot or pinot noir?" asked the girl. "No thank you,", "Krishna replied". "It's a welcome gift Sir, from cruise line, you don't have to pay anything for this complimentary drink."

"If I don't take something complementary, how can I justify being an Indian?" Krishna murmured in his mind.

"Anything in mocktails?" He asked. The waitress routed Krishna to the nearby cafe for mocktails.

Odyssey Café, with its grand glass walls, was set up with a library theme. The café offered a wide variety of coffee and occasionally a glass of beer. It was filled with an assortment of specific coffees and teas, along with access to newspapers and the internet. People were chatting over coffee, while two groups played cards and trivia games. Krishna sat in a comfortable leather chair, bypassing the Italian, Mexican, and cocktail menus to order his favorite—lemon black tea.

Nothing unwounds him like a steaming cup of lemon black tea. The waiter arrived with a small, automated machine to scan Krishna's sign and sail card to record his complimentary drink in their system. He enjoyed his tea while observing the scene outside, watching the unfathomable sea.

He was having a relaxing time, enjoying a sip of tea, when he noticed a beautiful girl sitting in the far-left corner of the café. She was an ethereal vision, captivating and serene.

Her beauty carried an ethereal grace, as if time itself paused to admire her. To Krishna, it felt as if the world had momentarily paused to admire her presence. She didn't glow—she ignited. A slow, radiant blaze that burned into him, quiet and permanent. Like art that doesn't ask for attention but takes it anyway.

A slow burn of anticipation settled in his chest as he looked at her.

She wore denim blue bottoms, a yellow top and grey-tinted glasses. Two empty beer bottles rested beside her with the book in her hands—"The Fault in Our Stars."

Krishna had read it when he was in Pune. "I wish she could be my partner in this journey," Krishna murmured unknowingly.

As he descended a staircase, a pianist played Yiruma's River Flows in You, the familiar notes pulling at something deep inside him. He had first fallen for the piano through the music of a South Korean-British pianist, for a moment, he considered approaching the man, asking him to play it again. But he hesitated, then shook off the thought and made his way to his cabin.

His room was more than he had expected—sleek, modern, and fully equipped. A plush bed, a minibar, a small but elegant en-suite bathroom, and a balcony overlooking the endless ocean. He stepped outside, just in time to see another ship arriving at port. The sheer scale of it all made him pause. Three times the size of the Titanic, he thought. The comparison was staggering.

Krishna placed his backpack in the closet and sank onto the bed, exhaustion beginning to settle in. He was about to drift off when the doorbell rang.

Krishna opened the door to find a man grinning at him.

"Hey, brother! Sorry I'm late!" a cheerful voice called from the other side.

"I was supposed to meet you in the lobby, but we took a quick walk to Morjim Beach instead. Had to see your country's beauty first," the man added mischievously.

Krishna smirked. "Hope you enjoyed it. If you'd met me earlier, I would've shown you a few more places to hang out."

He remembered from the briefing—Alex was not just a fellow dealer, but also his roommate for the cruise. The guy had an easygoing energy, the kind that made people feel instantly at home.

They settled in quickly, chatting about the cruise, the casino and their upcoming work. By the time the conversation tapered off, Krishna found himself surprisingly at ease. The journey had barely begun, but something told him it was going to be unforgettable.

Chapter 04

The Beginning of Something Beautiful

Every new beginning holds the promise of something beautiful. It is in the moments of uncertainty and change that we find the opportunity to create a life that is truly our own.

Krishna arrived at the casino with Alex at exactly 6:00 p.m. — too early for a place that thrived in the late hours.

"You're early today," one of the security guards said, raising an eyebrow at Alex.

Alex grinned. "Blame him." He gestured toward Krishna. "Meet our newest family member—Mr. Krishna."

Krishna nodded in greeting as they stepped inside. The casino unfolded before him—glittering, sleek, and full of potential. The two-story space pulsed with vibrant LED lights, reflecting off mirrored surfaces. A sweeping staircase led to the upper floor, gleaming beneath the LED lights. The ground floor had 58 slot machines, their screens flashing hypnotic colors. To the side, a single escalator ran parallel to the glossy staircase.

Upstairs, seven tables ruled the floor—three for roulette, four for blackjack. His domain. A high-roller room sat tucked away in the corner, discreet and exclusive. A café sat adjacent, offering drinks, snacks, and a steady supply of cigarettes to those who needed both luck and caffeine to survive the night.

A small stage stood at the heart of it all—a spotlight glowing in the haze of wine, cards, and hushed wagers. Since the cruise was still docked, the casino remained closed, giving the crew a rare moment to breathe. Alex, always the life of the party, was thrilled to have a like-minded companion.

"At sea, people get restless," Alex mused as they walked toward the bar. "Seasickness, boredom... They need someone to talk to when the cards stop flipping."

"Krishna!" A booming voice cut through the ambient chatter.

He turned and spotted Mr. Gabriel's unmistakable grin. A slow smile spread across Krishna's lips. "I was just thinking about you."

"Think of the devil, and he appears!" Gabriel laughed, clapping Krishna on the shoulder.

Gabriel, the casino manager, commanded the room—charismatic, sharp-eyed, and effortlessly in control. Krishna had only seen him once before, on a video call during his interview.

"Come, come." Gabriel waved him toward the stage. "Time to introduce you properly."

A handful of crew members drifted closer, curiosity flickering in their eyes. Gabriel clapped his hands together. "Ladies and gentlemen, we have someone special among us tonight—straight from India. I've heard a lot about this man." He turned to Krishna with an amused smirk. "They say what he can do in a casino back in Goa, no one else can. He's not just a dealer—he's an artist. A man who believes gambling is not just a game, but a way of life. A chance—" Gabriel paused, letting the word hang in the air.

"A chance everyone should take."

He turned back to the crowd. "Let's welcome the best from Goa to one of the finest casinos at sea. Krishna!"

A polite round of applause followed. Gabriel gestured for Krishna to step forward.

Krishna took a deep breath, steadying himself. The stage was not exactly his comfort zone, but he had been in high-pressure rooms before. He adjusted his posture, met Gabriel's eyes, and nodded.

"Thank you, Mr. Gabriel," his voice measured but firm. "And thank you all for the warm welcome."

"A casino is unlike any other place. Here, people arrive from every walk of life—happy, broken, some chasing dreams that slip through their fingers like sand. Every bet they place is a hope, a battle, a belief that maybe—just maybe—tonight is their night."

He let that thought settle before adding, "But no matter the game—blackjack, poker, roulette—the kings of the table are always us."

A few chuckles and nods of approval.

Then, mid-sentence, he stopped.

His gaze locked onto someone—in the crowd.

At the far end of the room, just beyond the roulette tables, stood a girl.

A girl he had seen before.

The same glossy red lips. The same luminous skin, glowing under the soft casino lights. The same dark, smoldering eyes framed by impossibly long lashes.

His breath hitched and time paused as he looked at the girl.

The sounds of the casino faded into the background—Gabriel's voice, Alex's laughter, the distant hum of conversation. All of it blurred, insignificant.

It was her. The girl from the café.

His pulse hammered against his ribs.

For a moment, he forgot where he was.

Then—she was gone.

Slipping through a door at the back.

Krishna exhaled sharply, snapping out of his trance.

"Pulchritudinous," he murmured, almost to himself.

"Pulchri-what?" Alex frowned.

Krishna smirked, patting his friend on the shoulder. "Beautiful."

Alex chuckled. "Damn, man. You got it bad."

Krishna didn't answer.

His mother's words whispered in his mind.

"When you meet the one, your heart will tell you before your mind even understands it."

For the first time in a long time, Krishna—the calculated, pragmatic dealer—felt completely, utterly lost.

It was Friday. Krishna had just wrapped up a grueling week. The past five days had been a whirlwind, with every moment tightly scheduled. It was not easy making his mark; everything was fast-paced and fully packed. He had gotten used to being busy, arriving early, and staying late. One thing always nagged him: from the security guard to the cashier, even the bouncers, everyone spelled his name wrong—Kisna instead of Krishna.

He often wondered if the people in the UK and US were conspiring to slowly transform his name, as if by silent agreement.

Mr. Gabriel, his team manager, was a different breed. Krishna had seen his share of leaders and managers, but Gabriel stood apart. He wasn't just a boss; he was a leader in the truest sense, a man who led from the front.

"Great leaders don't just create followers," Krishna mused to himself, "they create other leaders. Gabriel was definitely one of them."

The cruise had already sailed ten miles from the port. People were slowly making their way to the casino. Mr. Gabriel stood near the entrance, assigning tasks to the team. Since they had just left the port, they weren't expecting a large crowd tonight. Only two blackjack tables would be open. Alex was assigned as the primary pit boss, overseeing the tables, while another pit boss was on standby. Four dealers were scheduled—two for blackjack, one for roulette, and one rotating between games.

Every casino followed a rotation system, shifting dealers between tables after an hour to keep their focus sharp. It wasn't just the players who dealt with bad luck; dealers did too. If a dealer felt the cards weren't in their favor, they could request a break. After all, the casino's goal was to win.

Gabriel approached Krishna, handing him a nameplate. "You're on Table #2," he said with a nod.

Krishna glanced at the table assignment—blackjack. His game.

There was something thrilling about being a dealer. It was the only job where you played without the risk of losing. As he settled in, he turned to the pit boss, a lingering question on his mind. "Why does the casino only open after we're ten miles away from the port?"

The pit boss smirked and said, "Simple. There are casinos on land, so local authorities want passengers to spend money there before gambling at sea."

Krishna nodded, but his attention drifted toward the casino café. His eyes searched for the woman he had seen earlier. The one with the intoxicating smile.

Alex noticed and smirked. "Looking for someone?"

Krishna didn't hesitate. "Who is she?"

Alex chuckled knowingly. "Natalia."

Before Krishna could ask more, a group of young gamblers approached his table. They looked inexperienced, eager but cautious.

He got into position, showing his hands back and forth—the standard protocol before dealing. The first few rounds were light, with players placing small bets, feeling out the game. But as the night wore on, the atmosphere shifted. The hesitant newcomers thinned out, replaced by seasoned gamblers. The pit was alive now—cheers, groans, the clink of chips stacking higher.

By 1:30 AM, the cruise was fully alive. The lounge upstairs had a live band performing old jazz numbers, but down in the casino, it was all about the cards. The small bets had climbed to $10, then higher. Krishna's table was the hottest spot in the room, drawing in more players, some even waiting for a seat.

He was in his element now. His hands moved with machine-like precision, flicking cards with effortless grace. There was no hesitation, no reaction to wins or losses, only the smooth, calculated rhythm of a master at work. When he played, the game itself seemed to blur into motion. No distractions, just the cards and the numbers unfolding like a story only he could read.

"Excuse me," the young man seated in front of Krishna, called out.

"Yes, Sir. How can I help you?" Krishna's heart skipped a beat as he heard the soft voice. Natalia the waitress, with a dazzling smile asked.

"One beer and a sandwich, please," the young man ordered.

"Yes, sure, Sir," she replied, her eyes meeting Krishna's once again. In that moment, Krishna felt as if he had known her for ages. She looked into his eyes with a faint smile.

He barely noticed as the game continued, though his hands moved on instinct. The cards, the bets, the cheers—they all faded behind the silent conversation happening between their eyes.

Finally, he exhaled and turned his hands up, signaling his break. As he stepped away, the murmurs of the crowd swirled behind him. Among his colleagues, whispers followed. He had made $130, second only to the record of $180 for a single night as a tip. Not bad for his first shift, especially since the casino had opened late.

The manager, watching from the pit, exchanged a glance with Emilia, "He's good," he muttered. "Really good."

Alex, now free from his own table, found Krishna near the smoking area. Krishna took a sip of coffee while Alex lit a cigarette beside him.

"You were on fire today," Alex said, exhaling smoke. "If you keep this up, Gabriel might have to shut down a few tables or fire the rest of us."

Krishna smirked. "Relax. Not every night's a Sunday. Besides, I got lucky—both times I dealt blackjack."

Alex laughed. "We don't mind if you get blackjack every day. But if you do…" he nudged Krishna with an elbow, grinning, "she'll have to keep serving at your table all the time."

"Good evening, Gabriel. How are you today?"

Gabriel looked up from his tablet, his face lighting up with a familiar warmth.

"I'm doing great! How about you, buddy?"

"Doing good too, thank you." Krishna smiled, appreciating Gabriel's informal approach. He prefers being addressed by his first name, insisting that it break down walls and made people feel more connected.

Gabriel leaned back in his chair, his easy-going nature always apparent. "Looks like you've had one hell of a week."

"Yeah," Krishna chuckled, "it's been intense, but I'm getting the hang of things. Slowly."

Gabriel agreed with a nod. "I've noticed. You're doing well. Remember, it's not about rushing. It's about staying consistent."

Krishna appreciated that about Gabriel. He never pushed for perfection, just steady improvement.

As the minutes ticked by, they continued to talk, the tension of the week easing away in the casual conversation.

Gabriel glanced up at Krishna "I see you come early every day, young man. Why don't you roam the cruise a bit? You're not enjoying the journey, are you?"

Krishna smiled, leaning back subtly. "It's nothing like that, just habits. Also, I noticed that I am not alone in these solo adventures, you come here often too. Does that mean you are not enjoying the journey either? Krishna said with a playful challenge gleaming in his eyes.

Gabriel shook his head. "No, I enjoy the cruise wholeheartedly. It's the challenges here that keep me going.

You could say this is my way of embracing the journey. Planning each day perfectly and making sure everything runs smoothly—that's what makes me happy. Seeing the smiles on everyone's faces brings me joy."

Krishna nodded, his hands still shuffling cup of coffee. "Same here. I love what I do, maybe that's why I'm up early every day, ready to be what I'm meant to be."

Gabriel grinned. "Well, I guess we've got something in common, then."

"That we do," Krishna agreed with a hint of admiration in his tone. "But we've got some differences too."

Gabriel raised an eyebrow. "Like what?"

Krishna laughed softly, leaning back in his chair. "I never drink."

Gabriel joined in the laughter. He glanced at his watch, noting the time. There was still an hour left before the crew would join them. The café was empty, just the two of them sitting on high stools in the corner, chatting.

"Tell me," Gabriel asked, taking a sip of his coffee, "how did you develop this habit of starting early?"

"I got this habit long ago, back in my childhood," Krishna said, his voice carrying a hint of nostalgia. "Every morning, before the sun even stretched over the horizon, my father would wake me up. The air would be crisp, carrying the scent of damp earth and fresh hay. I'd stumble out of bed, still half-asleep, but the moment I stepped outside, the cold breeze against my skin would jolt me awake.

My father and I would walk to the cattle shed; our breath visible in the chilly dawn air. The cows, still drowsy, would shift lazily at our approach, their warm, musky scent filling the space. I'd help tie them properly, stroke their heads to calm them, I watched as my father worked with practiced hands. Eventually, I learned to do it myself—the steady rhythm of milking, the sound of warm milk hitting the metal pail, the occasional impatient huff from a cow.

It wasn't just about the work. It was a ritual, a moment of quiet understanding between me and my father. He wasn't a man of many words, but in those mornings, he taught me patience, discipline and respect for life's routines.

That habit never left me. Even now, no matter where I am, I find myself waking up early, as if my body still remembers those mornings. It's like the day doesn't feel right unless I greet it before everyone else does."

You know, I believe that nine hours of work can get you everything you need. But if you want to excel at something, it's what you do after those nine hours that matters most."

Gabriel nodded thoughtfully; his tone appreciative. "You're fortunate to have learned that so early. Some people spend their entire lives chasing that wisdom. And when they finally grasp it, there's often no time left—or hardly any time at all."

Krishna nodded, gazing into his coffee cup. "I guess I'm lucky in that sense. But it's a lesson that sticks with you. Work isn't just about the hours you put in, it's about the passion you bring to it."

"Exactly," Gabriel agreed, a quiet admiration in his voice. "It's not just about showing up; it's about showing up fully."

The two shared a moment of silence, both reflecting on their journeys, before they carried on with the conversation, each appreciating the others company.

"Gabriel, do you work at a university of leadership or something?" Krishna asked with genuine curiosity. "Your leadership skills are phenomenal. How does everyone respect you?" He paused, clearly impressed. "How do you manage all these people? I'm surprised everyone is so happy. I want to be like you."

Gabriel smiled; Krishna's enthusiasm was evident; it was the kind of compliment that resonated deeply.

"Tell me," Krishna continued, "how can I become an exceptional leader like you? I feel motivated just being around you. What makes you so different from all of us?"

Gabriel looked at him thoughtfully for a moment, as if weighing his words carefully.

"Let me tell you one thing, Krishna?"

Krishna nodded eagerly. "Yes, please."

Gabriel began, "On your very first day when you introduced yourself to me, I felt comfortable with you right from that moment. Had you ignored me or brushed me off, you wouldn't have been any different than anyone else. But that connection—we made it right then."

Krishna sipped his coffee and nodded. "I agree, Gabriel. First impressions are important. They play a huge role in shaping how one perceives the other."

Gabriel's face lit up with a smile. "Well, if I told you who I am and how I got here, it would be a long story.

Krishna listened intently as Gabriel paused, his tone turning more reflective. "I will tell you my story when the time is right. But what I can tell you now is that I wasn't born a leader. It's something I earned, something I built over time."

Krishna's curiosity was piqued, and he leaned in closer as Gabriel continued.

"There was a time I nearly gave up. I still remember the day I walked into my boss's office with a resignation letter in hand. I was ready to leave it all behind." Gabriel stopped; the weight of that moment evident in his voice. "But my boss asked me to reconsider. And what I got in return that day changed the course of my life."

Krishna was surprised. What could have happened on that day that changed Gabriel's life so drastically? He grew even more curious, trying to piece together what had made his mentor the leader he admired.

Gabriel noticed the look in Krishna's eyes. "The tool that helped me become the leader I am today isn't some secret formula. It's about resilience and introspection, about understanding every experience as a lesson."

Before Krishna could ask more, Gabriel glanced at his watch. Their conversation had to wrap up—there were other matters to attend to. Krishna, sensing this, thanked him for his time.

Gabriel smiled warmly and placed a hand on Krishna's shoulder. "Remember one thing—introspect everything that happens to you and around you. If you look deeply, you'll find the universal law behind everything. There's a theory that governs all things, and once you understand it, you'll know how to navigate your life."

Krishna nodded, feeling the weight of those words sink in. "I'll keep that in mind."

"Follow this every hour," Gabriel added, standing to leave. "Do it mindfully and it will change your life."

As Gabriel excused himself, Krishna sat back in his chair, the weight of the conversation hanging in the air. He swirled the last sip of coffee in his cup, his mind drifting back to his first meeting with Gabriel. He remembered the warmth in Gabriel's handshake, the way he welcomed him openly.

Krishna asked himself quietly, "What makes me respect Gabriel? He realized that was the right question to start with."

The other day, Krishna had felt humiliated when Gabriel told him to serve customers as a waiter—for three straight days. A master dealer reduced to service tables. It stung. Krishna had spent years mastering his craft. Now, here he was, balancing trays instead of cards. He wouldn't have done it if Alex hadn't nudged him to follow orders.

At first, Krishna saw Gabriel as nothing more than a dictator, someone misusing his power to push people around. But he had no choice—no one else seemed to. Everyone did what they were told without question. That was Gabriel's way. Instead of keeping people locked into one job, he rotated them constantly, making sure the core gambling tables—blackjack, roulette, poker—were handled by experts. Everything else? Fair game.

Natalia worked alongside Krishna as a waitress, but he couldn't meet her eyes. He felt embarrassed, stripped of his status. That entire day, his mood was written all over his face. No jokes, no small talk, not even a simple goodbye when he left. He didn't join the others for dinner. He was fuming.

The second day? No different. When Gabriel assigned him the same task again, Krishna didn't react—no argument, no protest. Just silence. But inside, he was livid. No one had ever humiliated him like this. Even as he smiled and greeted customers, he knew it was forced. His heart wasn't in it.

Yet, something gnawed at him. On this very first day as a dealer, he had pulled in $130 in tips. And yet, for all his effort as a waiter, he hadn't received a single dollar bill as a tip being waiter. Waiters usually made more than dealers in tips—so why was his box empty?

Krishna had always prided himself on his work ethic, but this time, he had failed to connect with anyone. His diligence, usually his strength, wasn't impressing anyone, it frustrated him.

Gabriel's words echoed in his mind. "Your tips don't define you, but they show who you really are."

Krishna put on his best smile the next day, determined to change things. He greeted customers warmly, served with enthusiasm, but the tips still didn't come. It bothered him. It wasn't about the money—it was the lack of appreciation.

As the night dragged on, Krishna found himself feeling more at ease, though the frustration remained beneath the surface. His earlier anger and humiliation began to fade as he watched Natalia serve the guests with a smile. For the first time, he looked her in the eyes. Something shifted within him. It was no longer about him being the best dealer or the one with the highest tips. There was something deeper here—something he hadn't seen before.

"What would you like to drink, sir?" a voice asked from behind him. It was familiar.

Krishna turned. His breath caught.

Gabriel stood there, holding a tray with two glasses of soda.

Krishna froze. His pride cracked, then collapsed entirely. He stared at Gabriel, unsure how to react.

Gabriel met his gaze with calm expression. No mockery, no superiority. Just understanding. There was no humiliation in his eyes—only quiet confidence.

"Let's take a break," Gabriel said an hour later. By then, the casino had quieted down. Past 1 a.m., the crowd thinned, leaving only a few stragglers looking for sandwiches or pastries.

They stepped outside. Gabriel lit a cigarette and leaned against the wall.

"You weren't at your best today. I was surprised to see your tip box empty."

Krishna exhaled. "I don't know what I was doing wrong."

Gabriel held up a twenty-dollar. "See this? Small but significant." He took another drag.

"Your problem isn't skill, Krishna. It's perception. You think knowing something is the same as learning it."

Krishna's expression darkened. "What do you mean?"

"You know how to deal cards, how to read people, how to play the game. But knowing isn't enough. Applying what you know is what matters."

Krishna stayed quiet, digesting the words. Gabriel continued.

"You respect me because of the image you created in your mind. But why did you create that image? Because on your first day, I made you feel comfortable. That's the first rule—treat people the way you want to be treated."

Krishna nodded slowly.

"Remember what you said about Goa?" Gabriel asked. "What I can do, no one else can. But that wasn't you talking—that was your pride. And what did that get you? Friends? No. Despite how impressive you were on your first day, no one approached you. They admired you, but they didn't connect with you. Because they saw the arrogance in your eyes."

Krishna swallowed hard.

"You were at your best when dealing," Gabriel continued. "But who were you when you were a waiter?"

"But I smiled," Krishna defended.

Gabriel shook his head. "Curving your lips isn't smiling, Krishna. It has to come from the heart."

Krishna looked away, ashamed.

"It's enough for today," Gabriel said, finishing his cigarette.

Inside, the casino was winding down. Emilia counted cash and chips at the counter. The pit master checked each table, making sure every chip was accounted for. A few chips were always missing—some guests kept them as souvenirs, a superstition that casinos didn't mind. It meant those guests would come back.

Gabriel left Krishna with words that lingered. "Knowing is one thing, but learning from it, that's where the real growth is. If you really want to master this, you must love the process—not just the outcome."

Krishna inhaled deeply. Three days of humiliation had humbled him. No matter how high you rise, if you don't stay grounded, you'll fall. And if you reach the top alone, with no friends to celebrate with, is it really success at all?

Krishna felt something shift inside him. He had been chasing the wrong thing. Back home in Goa, he was a king in his own world, revered and respected. Here, he was just another dealer. That was humbling. But maybe, he realized, that humility was exactly what he needed to find his place again.

As the night came to an end, Krishna met Natalia's gaze once more. This time, he didn't look away.

An electrifying shock surged through Krishna's body, starting from his stomach, winding through his intestines, finally settling in his heart when he saw Natalia again.

Natalia and Emilia sat across from each other, carefully laying out their cards, their expressions intent. He watched as Natalia and Emilia playing a game with cards, their movements deliberate and careful, as if they were handling something as precious as ancient documents. Krishna found it oddly satisfying to observe. Natalia's face was a canvas of joy, her expressions bright and animated. When a favorable card came her way, she jumped up with both hands in the air, letting out an excited, "Yay!"

Unable to resist any longer, Krishna knocked on the door and, with a playful glint in his eye, asked, "Can I join you?"

Emilia looked up, a smile spreading across her face. "Hey Krishna, it's our pleasure! Please, join us," Emilia said warmly.

Krishna thought Natalia would at least glance his way, but she remained still, eyes locked on her cards, hands steady.

"Seems like your friend doesn't want me to join you," Krishna teased, his eyes fixed on Natalia.

Natalia quickly responded, a hint of unease in her voice, "No, nothing like that. But we're not card masters," her voice carrying a faint hint of hesitation.

"Anyone can become a master," Krishna reassured her. "Even masters were beginners once."

"Tell me what you were playing. Count me in—I'll be a player. I'll play by your rules," Krishna said with a grin.

Natalia relaxed slightly and explained, "It's a game of luck. I'll deal one card to each of us, I'll keep dealing until you ask me to stop."

"If you ask for another card and your total goes above 11, you're out. The winner is the one who gets 11 or closest to it."

"Okay, got it," Krishna replied with a cunning smile.

In a way, it felt like the very first step towards the game of blackjack—a simple version of a game that would one day evolve into something more complex and widely known. Blackjack.

The one who invented blackjack must have gone through this stage of evolution, Krishna mused. The way Natalia was shuffling the cards was almost comical—so slow that he could easily tell which card was on top. But he didn't say a word; he was too busy enjoying the sight of her smiling face.

"What a mesmerizing face!", Krishna mused. One could lose a hundred times just to see that happiness, to see her winning.

"Well, our faces shouldn't reveal what's in our cards," Krishna remarked, glancing at the girls. "That's the very first unwritten rule in a casino." He could almost guess which cards they had, their expressions giving away more than they realized.

Natalia, such a happy soul, couldn't hide anything from her face. Her expressions said it all—one could read her entire life just by looking at her. This was completely opposite to Krishna. He had become a master at concealing his emotions, his face a cold, unreadable mask. Over time, he had forgotten that he even had a heart and that it beat wildly.

"Let me guess, you've got a seven?" Krishna teased, his eyes sparkling with mischief.

Natalia's eyes widened in surprise. "How did you know?"

"It's written all over your face." Krishna replied. Emilia laughed mischievously at the remark.

"How do you win every time?!" Natalia complained, her voice tinged with frustration.

"How can I win? It's a game of luck, Luck just happens to be on my side all the time," Krishna replied proudly.

"I'm here. That's why you're winning. How could it be otherwise?" Krishna asked in playful tone.

"Arguably," Natalia said, raising an eyebrow.

"It's because he must be watching my every move. But if that's the case, I'm happy you're the reason for my wins!" Krishna argued back, laughing.

"Okay, you be the dealer this time. Let's see who has the luck now," Natalia challenged, passing the deck of cards to Krishna.

He had been waiting for this moment. Handling cards was his strong suit. His heart raced as he took the cards, his fingers moving faster than anyone could track. In a flash, he mixed the cards with a speed that left them bewildered.

Krishna began performing tricks, his hands moving with precision and flair. He laughed, shook his head in amusement and marveled at his own abilities—all while Natalia watched in awe, trying to figure out his secrets with her skeptical mind.

"Please, teach me! How do you do all this? How can someone be so fast?" Natalia pleaded with curiosity.

"It's not rocket science. Anyone can become perfect with practice," Krishna replied casually.

"Can I become as fast as you?" She asked, her voice filled with hope.

"Yes, you can be even faster than me if you practice," Krishna mumbled, his voice soft but encouraging.

"You teach me, then," she replied, her voice light.

"If practicing the right way makes the difference, then I'll be perfecto."

"Perfecto? What does that mean?" Krishna asked, curious.

"It means, "Perfect"" she said with a laugh.

"Alright, time to go. It's already 6:30 AM," Krishna said, looking at his wristwatch.

"See you. Vamos hasta mañana," she said, waving as she turned to leave.

"What does that mean?" Krishna asked, intrigued.

"See you tomorrow," she replied with a smile, disappearing from his view.

As her eyes met his one last time, Krishna felt a strange sensation in his heart—something unfamiliar, yet deeply stirring. This was the first time he had experienced such a feeling. Many things were happening for the first time in his life, and he knew he was on a journey—one he would remember.

"The journey is going to be a memorable one," Krishna murmured to himself.

"Where is she from?" he wondered.

She wasn't from the US or the UK—her accent and choice of words hinted at a different origin. Many of her words were unfamiliar, neither Asian nor Western in origin.

As he walked, Krishna noticed Alex had a few pegs of wine along with Michael and Hugo, the other two colleagues who worked Alex's shift.

"I've never seen him turn in for the night without a drink," Krishna mused, a hint of amusement flickering in his thoughts.

Normally, Krishna would join them with a cup of his favorite black coffee, but today, he wasn't in the mood. Instead, he was lost in thought, replaying the day in his mind. That smile of hers lingered, tugging at the corners of his lips, forming something unspoken.

Thinking back to the casino, Krishna felt a quiet warmth rise within him—her presence still fresh in his mind.

"Good morning, guys! How are you doing today?" Gabriel's voice cut through the hum of conversation as he stepped confidently onto the stage. The audience responded with a chorus of cheerful greetings and applause. The collective energy of the staff was palpable.

He paused for a moment, letting the question sink in. "It's the last Friday of the month—a special day for me. Is it the same for you too?"

The crowd responded with a mix of nods and murmurs. Gabriel's eyes twinkled with satisfaction. "Yes……., the buzz here on the floor is unmistakable. In the casino business, we treat Friday as the real start of the weekend, rather than the weekend itself."

Gabriel took a breath, knowing the impact of his next words. "To kick things off, I want to make today special. I'm starting with something that's a bit of a tradition here—our Employee of the Month announcement."

He glanced around at the gathered staff, who were now leaning in with interest. "Every month, we celebrate someone who stands out from the crowd. It's always a tough choice, but this month, we have someone who really made a difference."

The room grew quiet as Gabriel continued. "Now, before we reveal the winner, I want to hear your guesses. Who do you think it might be? We'll take a few moments for you to ponder and share your thoughts."

Gabriel starts every day with something special. Everyone in the room knew that these meetings were never dull, Gabriel's unique approach to leadership always kept them on their toes.

"Before I reveal the name," Gabriel continued, his voice steady and measured, "I want to remind you all why we're here today. It's not just about numbers or targets. It's about recognizing the effort, the passion, and the commitment each of you brings to this team. We're not just co-workers; we're a family, and every single one of you plays a crucial role in our success."

He let his words hang in the air for a moment, allowing them to sink in. Gabriel had always been a firm believer that motivation stemmed from recognition, and he was meticulous in ensuring that each of his team members felt valued.

The staff began to murmur and guess, their voices a mix of curiosity and excitement. Krishna, amid the speculation, couldn't help but think, I would have been an obvious choice had Gabriel not kept me off the casino floor and stuck me with waiter work.

The buzz in the room pulled him out of his head. Gabriel raised his hands for attention.

"Alright, let's give a big round of applause to our Employee of the Month! She's not here just to please people; she's here to amaze them with her exceptional service. Please welcome Miss Natalia!"

Natalia stepped forward with bright eyes, a grin spreading across her face.

Gabriel continued, "Natalia exemplifies what it means to go above and beyond. Her smile and dedication make all the difference, no matter what the task."

Krishna observed Natalia, feeling a pang of mixed emotions. She's so happy about this award, as if she's won the highest accolade. It's hard not to feel a bit envious, especially since I've been caught up in my own frustrations. He realized that while Natalia found joy in her role, he had been struggling to find contentment in his own duties.

Gabriel's words struck a chord with Krishna. "I urge all of you to give your hundred percent, no matter what you're doing. It will make a difference."

Krishna nodded to himself. "I need to appreciate where I am and what I'm doing. Maybe it's time to shift my perspective and find joy in the present moment, rather than dwelling on the past or worrying about the future."

Gabriel wrapped up the meeting with the week's plans, guidelines, and a few tokens of appreciation. His way of conducting meetings was unique—he blended recognition with constructive feedback so seamlessly that it never felt like criticism. He had a knack for pointing out areas that needed improvement, but he always did it with a touch of kindness, making everyone feel valued rather than criticized.

The night shifted into high gear as the floor crackled with the electricity of live music and the crowd's roar. The wine and mocktails flowed freely, adding to the ambiance. Natalia was busy serving the crowd, her smile never wavering.

It was 9:00 p.m. His table had only two players, he noticed that they were engaged, albeit slowly. New players often came in early, eager to learn rather than to win big.

One of the players, Lucas, was betting cautiously with $10 increments, showing the typical behavior of a novice. Krishna watched as Lucas's hand trembled slightly with each new bet. It was a reminder of how important it was to support and guide newcomers, just as Natalia did with her exceptional service.

With renewed determination, Krishna focused on his role. He knew that no matter where he was or what he was doing, it was his attitude that would make the difference. The night was busy, as he looked around, he found a new appreciation for the small moments and interactions that made his job worthwhile.

Krishna was a bit taken aback when he heard that he would be taking charge of the blackjack table today. He wasn't too thrilled about it, especially since he had just started to find some enjoyment in serving people the day before. Looking into the eyes of the customers, smiling genuinely—these small actions were his first steps toward humility.

The casino floor buzzed with activity as the night kicked into full gear. A live band played in the background, filling the air with energy, while wine and mocktails flowed freely. The atmosphere was intoxicating, encouraging the visitors to spend more freely.

Natalia was busy as usual, her tray loaded with wine, sandwiches and drinks. She caught Krishna's eye from across the room and flashed him a warm smile. Krishna, now stationed at his table no 2, near the giant pillar—felt a mix of emotions. The casino was already packed, yet his table had only two players. They were playing slowly, a typical sign of newcomers who arrived before the usual rush after 10 p.m. These players were more interested in learning the ropes than winning big.

The rocker's hand was still warming up with $10 bets, while another group of players had started cautiously with $5 bets. Krishna could tell, the group was still getting the hang of things. The table was filled with novice players, each one trying to figure out their strategy.

Cynthia, who was playing the role of the monitor tonight, watched the table closely. Krishna found himself observing the subtle changes in the players' facial expressions, particularly around Lucas. He listened to the conversations, noting how they discussed their cards and strategies. Blackjack is such a fascinating game, Krishna thought to himself. I've always believed that the dealer has a better chance of winning than the player. But maybe it's not worth dwelling on probabilities all the time.

As the night progressed, Krishna noticed the dynamics at the table shifting. The players grew more confident, and the bets began to increase. Cynthia kept a close eye on the action, but Krishna was more interested in the human element—the tension, the excitement, and the subtle interactions that revealed so much about the players.

Krishna couldn't help but reflect on how much he had changed in just a short time. From dreading the idea of working on the casino floor to finding a new appreciation for the job, he realized that there was more to this role than just dealing cards. It was about connecting with people, understanding their motivations, and, in some way, guiding their experience.

As he continued to watch the game unfold, Krishna felt a quiet satisfaction. He was beginning to see that his work, whether serving drinks or dealing cards, had its own unique value. And in that realization, he found a sense of purpose he hadn't felt before.

His thoughts drifted to a familiar question that had nagged at him ever since he started working in the casino: Why does the casino always manage to make money at the end of the day?

Of course, He knew the answer. All the card games—blackjack, roulette, craps—were meticulously designed to give an edge to the casino. It wasn't much, just a few percentage points, but it was enough. Even that one extra percent was enough to tilt the scales in favor of the dealer.

Over time, that slight advantage meant that most people walked away with lighter pockets, no matter how well they played.

Krishna's eyes drifted to Alex's table. Lucas, a young man who looked to be in his early 30s, was playing with a group of friends. They were all laughing and having a good time, but it was clear that Lucas was on a roll. Young man's face lit up with excitement as he won hand after hand. He's probably winning, Krishna thought, noticing the way group of the friends were cheering him on and, subtly, watching with a hint of envy.

It's funny, Krishna mused. No matter how good your friends are, when they start pulling ahead, it stings a little. Even though his friends were happy for him, Krishna could see that they were losing while Lucas was winning one-sidedly. It was a sight Krishna had seen countless times—the thrill of victory on one side of the table, while quiet disappointment on the other.

The young man began to bet higher with each passing win. It might be his day, Krishna thought, or maybe it was just the law of probability playing out. Luck, or perhaps what some call the "principle of favorability," seemed to be on the young man's side tonight.

Krishna remembered the first time he heard about the "principle of favorability." It had seemed strange at first, but the more he saw, the more he started to believe it. After all, he had seen it happen so many times—people winning big on their first visit to the casino, only to spend the rest of their visits trying to recapture that initial rush.

Beginner's luck, he thought with a chuckle. It was as if the universe opened the door for you, letting you taste success before you even realized what was happening. But the wise knew better. They recognized that such opportunities were often traps, a lure to keep you coming back for more.

Krishna couldn't help but laugh at the thought. How many times have I seen it? He had watched players dive deeper and deeper into the game, chasing that elusive win, much like investors chasing a booming stock market, only to get checkmated before they realized what had happened.

As Lucas continued to play, the monitor—a seasoned dealer, Cynthia—kept a close watch on the game. Even dealers, Krishna knew, had their streaks of luck. When a dealer's luck ran out, the monitor would often swap them out, trying to break the cycle for the players' sake. Cynthia, noticing the one-sided nature of the game, decided it was time for a change.

Krishna watched at the monitor, Cynthia, made the call to switch dealers. Though it was a small game, the change was necessary. Like all players, dealers had their own streaks of luck, and when a dealer started losing too much, it was common practice to bring in someone new. The goal was to keep the game unpredictable and fair, ensuring that neither the players nor the house had too much of an advantage.

When Daniel handed Krishna the note, asking him to replace Alex, Krishna knew it was time for him to step in as the dealer. He approached the table with a calm, confident demeanor, raising his hands and showing his palms to the players—an essential procedure to prove that his hands were empty, and nothing was being hidden. This ritual was a critical part of casino protocol, ensuring that everyone at the table knew the game was being played fairly and without any manipulation.

Krishna took his place behind the table. The energy in the room was palpable. It was well past midnight; the casino was at its liveliest. The liquor was flowing, the music was pulsing, and the lights cast a vibrant glow over the bustling crowd. The night had grown to its fullest, and the atmosphere was electric, with every seat at Krishna's table occupied by eager players.

People were packed around the table, some waiting for a spot to open up, others simply watching the action unfold from behind the players' chairs. The tension and excitement were almost tangible as Krishna dealt the cards, his movements smooth and precise, honed by countless hours on the floor.

The young man, still riding his earlier wave of luck, seemed undeterred by the dealer change. His friends watched with a mix of anticipation and cautious optimism, cheering him on as he continued to place his bets. Krishna couldn't help but notice how the dynamic had shifted at the table—players were more focused, their expressions intense as they calculated their next moves.

As the night wore on, Krishna found himself fully immersed in the rhythm of the game. The cards, the chips, the subtle exchanges of glances and smirks—it was all part of the intricate dance that played out in every casino. And though the odds always favored the house, Krishna knew that each player at the table believed, at least for a moment, that they might be the one to beat those odds.

The minutes ticked by, and the game continued. The casino was a living, breathing entity, its pulse quickening with every bet, every win, every loss. By the time the clock approached 2:00 AM, the crowd showed no signs of thinning. The players at Krishna's table were fully engaged, their focus unwavering as they played hand after hand, trying to outwit the dealer and each other.

Krishna remained steady, his hands moving deftly as he dealt the cards and managed the bets. He could feel the eyes of the crowd on him, watching his every move, waiting for the next card to turn. The energy was infectious, and for a moment, Krishna forgot about everything else—the long hours, the late nights, the monotony of it all.

In that moment, nothing else existed—only the game and the shifting energy of the players.

As the night pushed on into the early hours of the morning, Krishna knew that the casino, like every other night, would eventually win. But in these fleeting moments, as the players leaned in closer, the tension thickening with each deal, it was easy to believe that anything was possible.

When Krishna stepped away from the blackjack table, his tip box was full, a small victory in his otherwise tense evening. He stretched his hands out and walked off the floor, grateful for a moment's peace. Alex, the veteran of the team, joined him as they headed to the smoking area just to cool down.

"Why is this casino always so crowded?" Alex complained, taking a deep drag from his cigarette and exhaling with frustration. "It's exhausting to work here every single day."

Krishna sat on a chair by the balcony, his gaze drifting toward the blackjack table and the stage where a live band played. "People come here to enjoy themselves, to spend money," he replied with a shrug. "That's just how it is. You work hard, but they're here to have fun."

Alex sighed. "Yeah, I know people come to spend. But why only this casino? I heard from Eric that the South Casino empties out completely around 4 AM."

"Eric? He's a dealer from the South Casino, right?" Krishna asked, still gazing across the casino.

"Yeah," Alex confirmed, crushing his cigarette.

"I think the credit goes to Gabriel. He's the real reason this place thrives."

"Gabriel's a true manager," Krishna said, nodding. "He plans everything perfectly—from the staff to the decorations to events like this dance night."

"Exactly," Alex agreed. "Just imagine if instead of this rocky disco band, they had classical music on a Friday night. Do you think this crowd would be here?"

Krishna chuckled as his eyes were drawn toward Table number 2, where Natalia was serving drinks and sandwiches with her usual bright, alluring smile.

He couldn't help but admire her dedication to her work. Her graceful movements, her infectious energy—it left him momentarily speechless. Every time he saw her, something inside him stirred.

"Yes, you're right," Alex continued, deep in thought. "Gabriel knows how to keep things fresh. It's not about pleasing people; it's about amazing them."

Krishna nodded absentmindedly, his attention still on Natalia. She was moving through the tables, completely in her element, her eyes focused, but then—those same eyes met his. They locked onto him, and for a moment, time seemed to slow down. Krishna couldn't pull away. His heart raced, his throat dried up, and he was at a loss for words.

"What?" Natalia's expression seemed to ask from across the room, though she said nothing.

Krishna felt a strange, unexplainable sensation in his chest.

His stomach tightened, not in pain, but in a way that felt new—an emotion he couldn't yet name. When he closed his eyes, her face flashed in his mind, and without realizing it, a smile spread across his lips—a smile unlike any he had experienced before.

Whatever conversation he had been having with Alex was long gone, floating away with the smoke from Alex's cigarette. "Let's get back to work," Krishna muttered, not really paying attention.

Inside, the band had shifted to a new rhythm. The tables were packed, people dancing and celebrating. Dollar bills and liquor flowed freely, as though money and time were endless.

The band paused. Suddenly all the casino staff gathered on the stage. Alex motioned for Krishna to join them. "It's our group dance," Alex explained, tossing away his cigarette.

"You go ahead," Krishna replied, hesitating. He was shy when it came to dancing, especially in front of a crowd. But more than that, his thoughts were still on Natalia.

Nati, as everyone called her, had joined the dance floor. The song was upbeat, the crowd wild, and even the pit box managers had joined in. It was a celebration—a spontaneous, joyful moment where everyone let loose. Krishna had never heard the song before, but its rhythm resonated in his chest, especially as he watched Nati dance with effortless grace. She was captivating, more beautiful than ever.

Krishna stayed in the smoking zone, watching from a distance. Nati was dancing with a group, moving in sync with the music, her face glowing under the dim casino lights. Their eyes met again. This time she signaled him over with a playful wave.

Krishna's heart skipped a beat. He knew he should go, but his body wouldn't move. He raised his glass of juice in acknowledgment, offering a smile that felt hesitant. She responded with a slight tilt of her head and mouthed, "Thank you," inviting him once more to the dance floor.

For a fleeting second, Krishna imagined himself dancing with her, like a scene from a movie—a slow, romantic dance, just like Jack and Rose in Titanic. But then reality sank in. He didn't know how to dance, not like that. The only dance he was familiar with was the Ganpati dance back in Pune, a lively but clumsy celebration that couldn't compare to the elegance of Nati's moves.

Instead, he lifted his glass again, offering a small nod. "Go on," he mouthed. "Enjoy the moment."

Nati smiled, her eyes shining as she danced, while Krishna stood on the sidelines, caught between admiration and hesitation. Though they were fifteen feet apart, the connection between them felt clear, as if they were having a silent conversation, one not bound by words or distance.

Krishna couldn't take his eyes off her. Every glance, every movement she made stirred something deep within him. It wasn't just attraction—it was something more. Something that made his heartbeat faster every time he saw her, something that made time slow just a little whenever their eyes met.

He stayed there, watching her dance, knowing that this feeling, whatever it was, it wasn't going away anytime soon.

Chapter 05

A Walk to Remember

Happiness is not about what we have, it's about how we perceive what we have—free from comparison, expectation, or envy. In that realization, a quiet smile crept onto his face. It was a lesson he was glad to learn.

"Let's get ready, Krishna. It's time to go," Alex said, yanking the blanket from Krishna's face with a playful tug.

Krishna groaned, half-asleep, gripping the last shreds of his dream. Nati's smile floated on the edge of his fading dream. He wanted to stretch the dream, to hold onto it a little longer, but Alex's wake-up call snapped him out of it. He blinked, struggling to pull himself into the present.

Alex rarely woke up before him, and why wouldn't he? Saturdays meant a break for the crew. The ship was docked at the shore, and they wouldn't be departing the port until Sunday night. Two whole days of work lay ahead, but for now, there was time to explore.

Alex stood ready; backpack slung over his shoulder. "Come on, Krishna," he said with a grin. "It's time to get up and get ready. Today's the day."

Krishna stretched, feeling the excitement starting to build within him. This was his first real opportunity to step off the cruise, into a foreign land without the pressure of work. Working on the cruise, especially in the casino, comes with its benefits—one of which was the chance to explore the world when the ship docked. The casino crew was one of the few groups on board who got some downtime when the ship was in port. Maritime law shut down casinos when ships neared the shore.

The whole point of cruising is to give people a chance to experience something new. You can't call it a world tour if people spend all their time in the casino like they would at home. The cruising business thrives on providing people with a diverse, dynamic experience.

Krishna's excitement grew as he looked out at the city waiting for them on the shore.

After all, Cruising is all about stepping out of your routine, feeling alive in a way you can't when you're stuck in the same place. Every port is an adventure waiting to happen.

With his backpack slung over his shoulder, Alex strolled into Café Tranquillo, the spot on the cruise where both complimentary and premium coffees were served. The name suited Alex perfectly. He lived life like the café's title—Tranquillo, relaxed, unbothered by the rush of the world around him. Even though they were already late, Alex had no tension about it. Sometimes he reminded Krishna of an old friend back in Pune—someone who also believed in living life on the edge, with everything done at the last moment, but always calm, never showing a hint of worry or urgency.

Alex could talk to anyone. He didn't need to be close to someone to open-up.

In fact, anyone who crossed paths with him became his friends in no time. It was his nature—he was effortlessly likable, the kind of guy who didn't need an introduction. His easygoing attitude made it impossible not to warm up to him.

Alex ordered two coffees and then motioned toward the exit. "Let's head to land," he said, handing Krishna his cup. "You know, when you're out on the water all the time, it's easy to feel a little seasick. That's why the shore calls to even the biggest ocean lovers."

Krishna nodded, taking a sip of the coffee as they made their way toward the exit. Downstairs, a group of friends from the cruise was already waiting for them. They called out loudly, their voices echoing across the deck.

"Come on, champs! We've been waiting for you for half an hour. hurry up!" They laughed and waved, a lively bunch of crew members, mostly from the casino. Krishna could see why working on the cruise, especially in the casino, was such a unique experience. Not only did they get to explore new places, but they also met so many adventurous people along the way. The friends they made were explorers at heart, always ready for the next wild adventure.

As Krishna and Alex descended the gangway, Krishna couldn't help but smile. This was the best part of life on a cruise—being surrounded by new faces, new experiences and the excitement of the unknown just beyond the shore.

Alex had a theory for everything. As they neared the escalator, he rambled on, but Krishna's mind was elsewhere.

Just as they reached the glass wall of Café Tranquillo, his heart skipped a beat. There she was! Natalia.

She was sitting in the same seat where Krishna had first seen her. The setup was eerily similar. She was still reading "The Fault in Our Stars!" the same book she'd had that first day. The only difference was a coffee cup instead of beer bottles.

Her face, framed by her black-rimmed glasses, looked more beautiful than ever, almost glowing under the café's soft light. Krishna felt a rush of emotions. Was she not coming out for the outing? he wondered. Doesn't she feel seasick being in the ocean for so long?

His heart pounded. His eyes followed her every move through the glass wall as they descended the escalator. Alex was still talking. Krishna had no clue what Alex was saying anymore. Nati was slipping out of his sight, and he couldn't bear it. His mind was screaming at him to turn around, to stop, to do something.

Suddenly, Krishna made up his mind. "Alex, you guys go ahead. I'll catch up later," he said quickly, his words almost drowned out by the whirlwind of his thoughts.

Alex stopped mid-sentence, surprised. "What? Where are you going? Aren't you coming?"

"No, I mean yes... I'll come, just not right now," Krishna stammered, his words tumbling out in a rush. "I just remembered something. I'll catch up with you guys."

Without waiting for Alex's reply, Krishna turned and started running back up the escalator—against its flow. The moving stairs seemed to mock him, slowing him down with every step. For a moment, he thought, following your heart is never easy. But then, another thought flashed in his mind: Nothing is impossible for a willing heart.

The escalator's relentless speed was no match for his determination. His breath came in heavy gasps as he neared the top. People coming down the opposite escalator were gliding effortlessly, looking at him with amusement, some even laughing at his frantic effort. But they didn't understand—they had no idea why he was doing this. They couldn't feel the urgency in his heart, the pull that drove him to act.

When Krishna finally reached the top, his chest was heaving, but he didn't care. He scanned the café again. There she was—Nati. Her eyes, previously fixed on her book, lifted and met his through the glass. For a split second, their gazes locked. His heart skipped again, a rush of adrenaline flooding him.

But then she did something unexpected. With a faint smile, she turned her attention back to her book, as if nothing had happened.

Krishna stood there, feeling both exhilarated and foolish at the same time. He waved his hand weakly, but she didn't look up again. For a moment, he questioned his own impulsiveness.

"What am I doing?" he thought. But deep down, he knew the answer. Following your heart might be crazy, but sometimes, craziness is the only way to feel alive.

Hey, good morning, Krishna broke the ice with a greeting.

"Hola, Krishna. Good morning! What's up?" Natalia replied with ease, her smile warm and inviting.

"The fault isn't just in our stars, is it?" Krishna said, smirking as he nodded toward her book.

Natalia tilted her head, caught off guard. Krishna had read The Fault in Our Stars? That was unexpected.

She looked at him for a moment, her eyes twinkling with curiosity and happiness. There's something about finding someone who shares your interests that brings a certain kind of comfort, an instant connection.

"Books are powerful, they reveal more about a person than we realize. What we read usually reflects our mindset, our inner world. Not always, but often enough.

"Maybe the fault isn't in our stars, Krishna, but in ourselves." She sipped her coffee, staring at the swirling liquid as if searching for answers in its depths.

Krishna adjusted the strap of his backpack, coffee cup balanced in his other hand. He grinned at her. "I've met Miss Philosopher," he teased.

"And I've met Mr. Gambler," she shot back sarcastically, folding the book in her hands with a playful smirk.

"It's a wonder to see you here," he said, taking a seat across from her. "This is the day we all wait for—especially the casino crew. When the cruise hits the shore, it's no work, just new faces, new places and exploration. But here you are, an exception to the rule. Don't you want to join us? Back on the land?"

Natalia chuckled, a small, knowing smile playing on her lips. "Actually, yes. But these days, I find more comfort in my new company," she said, gesturing toward her book with a small, knowing smile. It was clear she wasn't as comfortable with the rest of the crew, preferring the solace of her own thoughts.

There was something different about her today. Until now, Krishna had seen Natalia as an elegant, vibrant girl— her beauty was undeniable, accentuated by her radiant smile.

But today, there was a calmness about her, a warmth, like the quiet wisdom of a goddess Saraswati herself.

The way she embraced the world of words, the calm serenity she exuded, was spellbinding. Yet, there was also a tinge of melancholy, as if she was retreating into a world of her own making.

Krishna found himself comparing her to Hazel Grace, the introspective protagonist from her book. But no, he thought, this isn't a girl defeated by life or pain. She's far from sick or depressed.

"Certainly, you can't say the girl is depressed or sick," Natalia said, picking up on his thoughts, her tone both thankful and lightly argumentative, as if she sensed his internal musings.

Krishna laughed. "I'm not saying that".

"I'm just saying the beauty of the world is meant to be felt. What kind of traveler would lock themselves away in the lines of books, missing the real world right outside?"

Natalia paused, her smile fading into a thoughtful expression. "Well, it's different for everyone," she replied slowly. "For you, maybe exploring the beauty of nature means joining the crowd, seeking adventure out there in the world. But for me…" She looked down at her book. "For me, sometimes the best journeys happen between the pages. Sometimes, the most profound exploration is within."

Krishna leaned forward, intrigued by her words. "So, this is your adventure then? These pages with cup of coffee?"

Natalia nodded. "Maybe right now, yes. I don't need the crowds or the noise. The journey I'm on isn't about outshining anyone, it's about understanding myself."

Krishna, still processing her words, nodded. "I get that. Maybe that's what makes you different from the rest of us. You're not just out there exploring places—you're exploring yourself."

She smiled faintly. "Maybe." Then, with a glimmer in her eye, she added, "But that doesn't mean I don't enjoy a good adventure every now and then."

The weight of his own thoughts began to press down on him. Natalia's words had a way of lingering, echoing in his mind, blending with the rhythm of the ocean and the hum of the ship.

Natalia smiled, her eyes drifting toward the vastness of the ocean. "Walking along the balcony, watching the waves rise and fall— You can see nature's beauty in the way the sea shifts its colors, how the sun illuminates it, and finally, how it disappears beneath the waves at day's end."

She paused, letting her words settle between them like the gentle lapping of the waves.

"Haven't you ever been lost in the rhythm of the tides? The sound, the rhythm... beauty is everywhere. You just need to step out of your own perception and definition of it."

Krishna fell silent, his mind absorbing what she said. Her words hung in the air, making him feel like she was revealing something deeper about the world and herself.

It wasn't just the words; it was the calm conviction with which she spoke. She saw the world differently in a way, that made him question his own perspective.

He sought beauty in motion, in energy—but Natalia discovered it in stillness. In moments of quiet reflection. He admired her ability to find beauty in stillness, even if he couldn't fully grasp it.

For a moment, they stood together, the silence settling between them—easy, unforced. The only sound was the rhythmic lap of waves against the ship's hull.

At last, Krishna broke the silence, amusement flickering in his eyes, a smirk teasing his lips.

"Whom am I talking to?" A great man once said, "Never cross paths with a philosopher—you might not see the world the same way again."

He chuckled at the memory of her saying that. It was true. She had already started to change his idea of what reality could be. A reality where beauty wasn't just found in the thrill of the casino, or in the rush of the land excursions they were about to embark on, but in stillness, in moments of reflection. He wasn't used to this kind of thinking, but it intrigued him.

Natalia chuckled, raising an eyebrow. "Is that so?" She made a mock-serious gesture, bringing her hands together in a playful Namaskaram. Laughter spilled between them, dissolving the weight of their conversation.

"All right then, see you at work," Krishna said, trying to keep things light. But his legs had felt heavy as he walked away, a silent hope tugging at him that maybe—just maybe—she'd change her mind and join them.

"It was nice talking to you. Go on, feel Hazel's pain—she's waiting for you in those pages. Meanwhile, the land is calling me with its own set of amusements."

"See you at work," Natalia replied with a gentle wave, her eyes following him as he prepared to leave.

Her gaze held an unspoken understanding, as if she, too, wished the conversation could stretch a little longer.

Krishna's feet felt heavy as he turned to walk away, his heart torn between the pull of his friends waiting on shore and the desire to stay a little longer with Natalia. He glanced back one more time, hoping against hope that she might change her mind, that she'd close her book and join him in the day's exploration.

"See you around, Krishna," she murmured, her voice carrying the quiet finality of a closing chapter.

With a final wave, Krishna headed toward the exit, his heart lingering behind even as his feet carried him forward.

Her presence lingered in his thoughts, an unshakable whisper at the edges of his mind.

He had a feeling this conversation wasn't the end—but perhaps the beginning of something he didn't yet fully understand.

Krishna reached the stairs that would lead him back to his friends, he glanced back one last time. Natalia was still there, sitting at the table, her eyes drifting back to the book. She looked so serene, like she had found a kind of peace most people spent their whole lives searching for. Part of him wished he could just stay, sit across from her, and lose himself in the quiet wisdom He could hear their voices drifting up, full of energy and excitement for the day ahead.

But as he placed his hand on the railing, he let the cool breeze wash over him. The sound of the waves, rising and falling, seemed to mirror the steady hum of his own thoughts. He could see what she meant. There was something undeniably beautiful about the simplicity of it all. His mind wandered back to Natalia. What if he could bring a piece of her world—the quiet, reflective part—into his own? What if, for once, he let go of the need to chase excitement and embraced stillness instead? He knew it wouldn't be easy. His whole life had been built around action, around being in the thick of things. But maybe, just this once, he could try something different.

With a final glance at the horizon, Krishna started down the stairs. The land awaited, alongside the laughter and the noise of his friends. But the quiet conversation he had just shared would stay with him, like a quiet melody in the background, reminding him that there was more to life than the thrill of the moment.

Sometimes, the real beauty is found in between the excitement—in the pause, in the reflection. He smiled, remembering his playful farewell to Natalia. But amusement didn't feel as important now. Sure, he was excited to explore, to step onto new soil and experience the novelty of a foreign land. But a small part of him was already yearning to come back, to return to that quiet moment with Natalia, to the soft edges of her words and the subtle challenge she posed to his view of the world.

As he would rejoin the group, he couldn't help but wonder: Would Natalia join them later? Would she let herself be pulled away from the stillness she cherished so much? Maybe, just maybe, she would. Or maybe, he would find himself returning to her world sooner than he thought. Either way, the day was just beginning.

Krishna stepped forward, but part of him stayed with Natalia. He glanced over his shoulder, hoping she'd call out to him.

Then came her voice—soft, teasing. "Hola." It halted him mid-step.

For a second, he thought she might follow.

When he turned, she was still seated, book resting closed in her lap, her expression betraying an unspoken conflict.

She wasn't ready to leave her solitude, yet her gaze clung to Krishna, as if torn between comfort and curiosity.

Krishna hovered at the edge of the moment, waiting.

I've been traveling for five months now," Natalia began, her voice low but certain.

"Throughout my journey, I've learned one thing: it doesn't matter if you're on land or water—if you don't have a companion to share the journey with, it all becomes... dull."

Krishna listened intently, processing her words. Was she hinting at loneliness?

He raised an eyebrow. "So, are you saying you don't have a companion? Or that I don't qualify?"

Natalia smiled faintly.

"Are you offering to be my companion?" She countered, with a playful glint in her eyes.

"I didn't say that" Krishna laughed, shaking his head.

"Instead... why don't you join me? I'll show you parts of the cruise you haven't even explored yet. You'll be amazed by the sunset from here, the way the waves hum their endless songs. I bet you haven't experienced the cruise like that before."

She paused, her eyes searching his for a sign.

"You have two choices—one familiar, one uncharted. Which do you take?"

Natalia's heart fluttered. The logic of her own argument echoed in her mind. She was starting to waver. If you're going to explore the cruise all the way to Miami, why not take this last chance to explore the land?" Krishna urged, stepping closer.

She bit her lip, clearly torn. "But I didn't plan for this... I am not prepared."

"Who needs a plan?" Krishna grinned widened.

"The best adventures start when you stop looking for directions."

He extended his hand toward her, an invitation not just to join him but to break free from her self-imposed isolation. "Come on, Hazel Grace. Amsterdam—or, well, something close enough—is waiting for us."

Natalia's eyes lit up at the familiar words. After a beat, she slipped her hand into his. "But... will we even make it off the cruise? It's so late," she said, half-laughing as she stood, quickly stuffing her belongings into her bag.

"It's never too late," Krishna said with a wink, setting down his empty cup before they sprinted toward the escalator.

Natalia still couldn't believe what was happening—she had gone from sipping coffee alone in the café to dashing off on a spontaneous land adventure in mere minutes. She held onto Krishna's hand; she couldn't help but smile.

Maybe this was what she'd been missing all along—companionship, spontaneity, and the beauty of the unexpected.

Nearby, a pianist played something slow and sultry—maybe "Crazy Love"—as they hurried to the disembarkation point.

By the time they reached the excursion area, the once-bustling spot had settled into an unusual quiet.

The other passengers had already gone, leaving the excursion manager's desk completely deserted.

The manager, who seemed a little too relaxed, took note of Krishna and Natalia as they checked in, marking them as the last to venture out for exploration.

The dock, usually buzzing with guides pitching last-minute deals had died down, leaving only a few stragglers, like Krishna and Natalia.

But luck was on their side. Thanks to Alex's last-minute arrangement and their own impulsiveness, exploring the city together was suddenly within reach. Alex had arranged one last pickup for Krishna.

Krishna had exuded confidence throughout the ordeal, but deep down, uncertainty tugged at him. He hadn't been sure if their last-minute adventure would pan out. As they finally climbed into the waiting taxi, they both let out a collective sigh of relief.

Natalia broke into a laugh, her eyes gleaming with excitement. "That was crazy, wasn't it?"

Krishna chuckled, feeling the adrenaline still buzzing through his veins. "Yes, it was. But we're doing it."

Their laughter echoed in the stillness of empty place. The streets were quiet now, Natalia sank into the seat, a slow smile spreading across her face.

"I was prepared not to come, you know. But here we are, on the edge of this wild adventure. A moment late and you'd have missed it completely. Wouldn't you have regretted it?"

Krishna shook his head with a smile. "No regrets, Natalia. I did everything I could to make it happen. Whether or not it turned out the way I wanted—at least I tried. Isn't that the point? To try, even when you don't know how it will end?"

Natalia's eyes sparkled as she looked at him "You're right. At least you won't wonder what could have been." She then turned her gaze towards the taxi driver, waving excitedly. "Señor, could you snap a photo for us?"

She handed her phone to the driver, who sighed but took it anyway.

The taxi was parked on a busy street, he wasn't eager to step out and start snapping pictures. But when Natalia smiled sweetly, he couldn't refuse. Her energy had a way of pulling people in, making them want to say yes.

"Come on, Krishna, join me!" Natalia called out, her hand reaching for his.

Krishna hesitated, caught between logic and instinct. It hadn't been long since they first spoke—few days, at most. He still felt the strangeness of their newfound connection. But when her fingers laced through his, pulling him close, the hesitation melted away.

Despite their brief acquaintance, there was a comfort in her presence, an ease in the way they fell into step with each other.

They posed together, laughing as they made silly faces and struck exaggerated poses. It was playful, spontaneous and entirely different from the calm, composed Natalia he had first seen on the cruise. He hadn't expected her to be this open, this carefree. She had shed her earlier reserve like an old coat, revealing a side of herself that thrived in the moment.

The taxi driver, once reluctant, was now fully invested in his role as their impromptu photographer. He adjusted angles, gave them directions and even suggested. Krishna and Natalia continued to pose, making the most of this unexpected, impromptu photo shoot.

As the last few photos were taken, Natalia leaned into Krishna, still holding his hand.

"These will be the photos we will remember the most," she murmured, her voice steady with certainty.

Krishna nodded, glancing at her with a smile. "Yeah, they are. This... all of this... it's something we'll remember for a long time."

For a moment, they stood still, hand in hand, both realizing the weight of what she had just said. This wasn't just about the photos —It was about the spontaneity, connection and the fleeting beauty of unplanned moments that become the ones you cherish the most.

As they climbed back into the taxi, A subtle shift settled between them, unspoken yet undeniable. They had stepped into a world of unknowns together and, in doing so, had forged a connection—something deeper than just a shared laugh or an impromptu adventure.

The pickup area was mercifully free of congestion. As the cab moved smoothly over the bridge, Krishna gazed out of the window, his thoughts caught between curiosity and anticipation. Natalia, seated beside him, alternated between looking at Krishna and watching the world pass by outside. The soft hum of the engine and the rhythm of the city beyond the glass created a peaceful backdrop to their unexpected adventure.

"Would you like some cold water, ma'am?" The driver interrupted the silence, handing over two small water bottles from a cooler in front.

"Thank you," Natalia replied warmly, taking the bottle.

Krishna took one too, smiling at the driver's kindness. "So, how's the city? What places would you recommend we should visit?" Krishna asked him with curiosity.

The driver's eyes sparkled, eager to showcase his city. He launched into a passionate explanation about its rich cultural heritage, from its historical landmarks to hidden natural wonders. As he spoke, there was no shortage of enthusiasm; he seemed genuinely excited to introduce them to the best his city had to offer.

Krishna found himself glancing back at Natalia. As the driver continued to talk, Krishna couldn't help but wonder—who was this girl beside him? They had just embarked on this adventure together, yet they knew almost nothing about each other. They hadn't even exchanged proper introductions beyond their names. His curiosity grew, the questions swirling in his mind.

"So, what would you do once you're done with this journey?" Krishna asked, turning to Natalia, his eyes full of interest. He wanted to know more—everything, if possible.

Natalia hesitated for a moment before answering, as if trying to decide how much to share. "Well, I'm Natalia," she began, her tone soft but clear. "My loved ones call me Nati. I'm a psychiatrist by profession."

Krishna's eyebrows shot up in surprise. "Wait, what? A psychiatrist?" He couldn't hide his curiosity. "Sorry for interrupting you, but... how come you're working here? On a cruise?"

The Nati he'd seen in the casino—lively, effortless—didn't match the composed, analytical image he had of a psychiatrist.

He had seen her expertly navigate the demands of working on the cruise, always serving customers with a warm, diligent smile. She carried herself with such ease in the casino's chaos, yet here she was, revealing a completely different side of herself.

Natalia smiled, amused by his surprise. "Yes, I've completed my bachelor's in psychology. I just need to submit my final project next year to finish. But... I've always had a passion for exploring the world. It was a dream of mine—once I finished my degree, I'd take some time off to travel. This cruise was part of that."

Krishna's curiosity deepened. "But Natalia... if you wanted to explore the world, why didn't you travel by air, maybe with your friends? Why did you choose to work on a cruise?"

The question hung in the air for a moment; then, Natalia's expression softened. "You can call me Nati," she said with a small smile, reminding Krishna that she had let him into her inner circle, even if only a little. It made him feel slightly uncomfortable, but there was also a warmth in being trusted so quickly.

"Well, Nati," Krishna continued, "I just don't get it. You could've gone anywhere, traveled however you wanted. Why this?"

She let out a quiet laugh, shaking her head. "You're right. Flying was an option. I could've traveled with friends. But solo travel, without familiar faces… it's liberating. You don't get out-of-the-box experiences when you're surrounded by people you already know."

Krishna nodded, understanding her perspective. He knew how confining it could be to travel with people you've known your whole life, how it sometimes feels like you're stuck within the boundaries of shared expectations.

"And there's another reason," she continued. "Money matters. I didn't want to burden my family with the expenses of my passion. Working on this cruise allowed me to travel and to explore without feeling guilty about the costs."

She glanced out of the window, her voice softening. "Besides, in psychology, they say if you want to truly observe human behavior, go on a cruise for six months. The vastness of the ocean, the isolation… it brings out something raw in people. You can't hide behind appearances for long. You start to see who people really are."

Krishna was silent for a moment, absorbing what she said. It made sense. Being out on the open sea, day after day, would strip away any façade. The deep blue ocean had a way of revealing what lay beneath the surface, both literally and metaphorically.

"So here I am," Natalia added with a slight shrug. "On this cruise, halfway across the world, working while I explore."

Krishna nodded, impressed by her resolve. "It sounds like you've got it all figured out. You're doing what you love, on your own terms."

Natalia smiled. "I wouldn't say I have it all figured out. But I'm trying to find my way, just like everyone else."

As they neared the heart of the city, Krishna looked at her again, this time with newfound respect. There was more to Natalia than he had initially realized. Beneath the surface, she was driven, thoughtful, and curious, qualities that mirrored his own hunger for adventure.

"Well, Nati," he said with a grin, "let's see what the rest of the day has in store for us. I have a feeling this adventure is just getting started."

Once she started, it was like a floodgate opening. Natalia had that rare gift—she could talk for hours without losing anyone's attention.

Krishna found himself listening intently, completely drawn in by the energy of her words.

"Well, that means you feel the real faces of people aren't as good and kind as they seem," Krishna remarked thoughtfully, reflecting on what she'd just said.

Natalia raised her eyebrows slightly with smiled. "I didn't say that."

"You didn't say it, but your words suggest it," Krishna countered, a playful smirk forming on his lips.

They both fell into a comfortable silence after that, each lost in their own thoughts. It was a kind of pause that didn't feel awkward, rather allowed their minds to process what was unspoken.

The hum of the city filled the quiet space between them. Krishna broke the silence, his curiosity piqued again. "So, how about your native town? Where are you from?"

Almost at the same moment, Natalia turned to him, her voice light with curiosity. "What about you?"

But before either could answer, the driver cut in, taking a sharp right turn and announcing with a grin, "Here's your destination."

Both looked out of the window at the hotel looming ahead, in unison, they said, "So early?"

It was a strange observation, considering they'd nearly missed the chance to come ashore at all, yet the drive felt like it had passed in the blink of an eye. Time had slipped away, lost in the easy conversation and the quiet moments that followed. They'd arrived late, yet somehow, it didn't feel that way. They were only beginning to glimpse into each other's worlds.

Alex and the others were still in the reception area, going through the formalities of checking in. The process seemed to drag on, with security checks and documentation taking time. The hotel itself was grand, its reception area spacious and polished, with two receptionists working through the crowd, their smiles never fading despite the rush.

When Alex spotted Krishna and Natalia walking in, he wasted no time. He hurried over, his eyes wide in mock exasperation. "Where have you been?" He asked. "We've been waiting for you; we had no choice but to leave without you."

Krishna, knowing this was typical Alex, smiled calmly. "I know, thanks for leaving the message with the excursion coordinator," he said, trying to sound as casual as possible. Natalia was just behind him, walking a bit slower. She seemed hesitant, maybe a little unsure about joining the group.

Emilia, who had been lounging on one of the plush sofas, perked up when she noticed Natalia. She stood and approached her with a grin. "Oh, look who finally decided to show up!"

Alex, of course, couldn't resist. He saw the opportunity and jumped in. "Now I remember why you ditched us!" He teased, shooting Krishna a mischievous look, clearly trying to stir things up.

Krishna flicked a glance at Natalia, hoping Alex's jab had missed her. The last thing he wanted was for her to feel uneasy.

As everyone gathered around the reception counter to check on the room allocations, Emilia kept chattering away, asking Natalia what had made her change her mind and join them.

Natalia lifted a hand, a quick gesture toward Krishna— silent confirmation that Emilia was a bit much, isn't she? Krishna couldn't help but laugh softly, giving Natalia a thumbs-up in return. It was a silent, shared moment of understanding between them.

Emilia turned, catching Krishna's laugh. She seemed oblivious to the silent exchange between him and Natalia. "Where were you, Krishna? We thought you wouldn't join us!" She said, her voice laced with a mix of curiosity and light accusation. "I kept telling Alex to wait for you, but of course, he didn't listen."

Krishna smiled but kept his response light. Instead, he glanced at Natalia, who looked amused by it all.

Krishna, feeling the weight of Emilia's words, gave her a smile but didn't engage too much. He just glanced over at Natalia, who seemed amused by the whole interaction.

They both knew Emilia would have been the first to walk away if it came to that. Krishna smiled but kept his response light. Instead, he glanced at Natalia, who looked amused by it all.

Nati sighed and stepped forward as the receptionist called her next. Most of their group had already scattered to their rooms by the time she was done, leaving only Nati, Emilia and Krishna at the reception. Once all the paperwork was wrapped up, the receptionist guided the three of them to their rooms.

The hotel was impressive, with an artistic design that gave it a unique character. Each floor had high ceilings and beautifully adorned rooms, reflecting the grandeur of the place. They arrived at Emilia's room first. It was a cozy, well-decorated space, complete with a small induction stove, a double bed, and a quaint little balcony. While compact, it was neat, vibrant, and thoughtfully designed. Emilia seemed content with her setup, admiring the arrangement.

Next, they moved to Krishna's room, number 28. As soon as the door opened, it became clear that Krishna's accommodations were a notch above Emilia's. His room was vast, with a spacious living area, a separate kitchen, and a master bedroom. It had an air of luxury and comfort, much to Emilia's immediate dismay, though she kept her thoughts to herself for the moment.

While Krishna explored his space, the receptionist showed Nati her room number 29, right next to Krishna's. After the receptionist left, Nati walked over to Krishna's room, visibly upset.

"Krishna, my room isn't nearly as nice as yours," she said, her tone tinged with frustration.

Her childlike innocence in voicing her disappointment took Krishna by surprise. Her room wasn't bad, but next to his, it must've felt like a downgrade.

She seemed genuinely concerned, as if this minor inconvenience would last a lifetime.

"Krishna smiled softly, unsure how to comfort her. "Come on, Nati. It's just for one night. We won't even be here long enough to notice," he said, hoping to reassure her."

Just as Nati was about to let it go, Emilia entered Krishna's room, uninvited but entirely at ease. She had only seen the kitchen and living area so far, but that was enough for her to realize Krishna's room was far superior to her own. She breathed a sigh of relief when she spotted the fold-out sofa in the living room, as if that one detail made her feel a bit better about her own accommodations.

Emilia, in her usual animated way, began talking non-stop about how wonderful her room is, glossing over its shortcomings and making it seem as though she was staying in a palace. Her overly enthusiastic description only served to make Nati feel worse. Nati's earlier disappointment transformed into restlessness, her mood shifting visibly.

Krishna, watching the scene unfold, realized. No matter how close two women might be, there would inevitably be moments of comparison and jealousy, even if unspoken.

Nati wasn't genuinely upset about her room; she was upset because Emilia, her friend, had a room that was better—or at least perceived to be better. Meanwhile, Emilia wasn't thrilled just because her room was nice; she was secretly pleased that Nati's wasn't as impressive.

Krishna couldn't help but reflect that this wasn't something he encountered with his male friends. There was a certain complexity to the rivalry between these two women, even when it was masked behind friendly smiles and laughter.

As Krishna stood by, observing the dynamics between Nati and Emilia, his earlier realization began to crystallize even further. Emilia had grown visibly closer to him, but it wasn't hard to see why—Nati had already formed a bond with him. There was an undercurrent of competition, subtly brewing between the two friends.

"You're lucky, Emilia. You got a luxurious apartment," Krishna said, casually walking toward the door he initially thought led to the restroom. But as he turned the handle, a pleasant surprise awaited him. It wasn't a restroom at all but a lavish, spacious bedroom with an en-suite bathroom. The room was elegantly furnished, with high ceilings and beautiful décor that took the experience to another level.

"Well, would you look at that!" Krishna grinned, gesturing for the two women to see for themselves. "You know, Nati, Emilia might be lucky, but I think we're fortunate." He pointed toward the far end of the room and opened the enormous curtains. Behind them was a full-length glass wall with a sliding door, leading out to a balcony that took their breath away. The balcony wasn't just a simple space; it was adorned with red roses and vibrant flowers swaying gently in the breeze, offering a magnificent view.

Nati's face lit up with excitement. "Oh my God! What a luxurious bedroom this is!" she exclaimed, practically bouncing with joy.

Eager to compare, she dashed off to check her own room, leaving Emilia and Krishna behind. Emilia, who had been so confident earlier about the grandeur of her room, now stood awkwardly silent. Her earlier enthusiasm dimmed as she saw how much better Krishna and Nati's rooms were. Krishna could sense her discomfort but chose to remain quiet.

"Krishna, my room is amazing! It's just as good as yours!" Nati said, she didn't even try to hide her glee. She was brimming with excitement. It wasn't just that her room was lovely—it was that her room outshined Emilia's, and she was enjoying the reversal in their fortunes. The dynamic had flipped entirely. Emilia, who had been subtly teasing Nati about her superior accommodations, now found herself on the other side.

Without acknowledging Emilia's presence, Nati chatted excitedly with Krishna about the luxurious bed, the stunning view, and the grand balcony. She wasn't just talking about her room—she was rubbing it in, indirectly mocking Emilia's earlier smugness. Emilia's face, once glowing with happiness, now bore the unmistakable traces of jealousy. Her brief triumph had been shattered in mere minutes.

Krishna observed Emilia's discomfort with quiet amusement. She had been so eager to claim superiority, and now that the tables had turned, her emotions betrayed her. He couldn't help but reflect on the fleeting and relative nature of happiness. Watching Emilia go from smug satisfaction to quiet envy reinforced a deeper truth for him.

In that moment, Krishna realized: happiness is rarely absolute. It exists in comparison to others, fluctuating with circumstances, and often depends on who we're surrounded by. Emilia's earlier joy wasn't about having a wonderful room; it was about having a better room than her friend's. Now, that happiness had evaporated the moment she saw Nati's room was superior.

Krishna thought to himself, True happiness isn't found in comparisons—it's found when we don't need to measure our joy against anyone else's. He pondered how much of life's contentment is shaped by relativity. So many people, like Emilia and Nati in that moment, unknowingly hinged their joy on others' perceived inferiority. But real happiness, Krishna realized, is when you find contentment within yourself—without needing to prove anything to anyone, or to feel superior in comparison.

Happiness is not about what we have, it's about how we perceive what we have—free from comparison, expectation, or envy. In that realization, a quiet smile crept onto his face. It was a lesson he was glad to learn.

The group gathered around the large dining table for their afternoon lunch. The atmosphere was lively, with chatter filling the air as everyone enjoyed each other's company. It was a rare moment where they could all sit together, and despite a few hiccups—like Emilia's disappointment about her room—it seemed like everyone was trying to make the most of it.

Krishna's choices were slim. Traveling as a vegetarian wasn't easy, and today's lunch was no exception—a plain cheese sandwich. He didn't complain; he was used to it. Alex, ever observant, didn't let it slide.

"Look at Krishna, our saint! Vegetarian and non-alcoholic, too. How do you even survive?" Alex's voice boomed across the table, making sure everyone caught the joke. The group laughed, not maliciously, but with the kind of camaraderie that comes from shared travel.

Krishna offered a practiced smile. He'd been through these routine countless times. But Alex wasn't finished. He had a knack for holding the group's attention and was always the loudest voice at the table; today was no different. He pivoted from Krishna's eating habits to his favorite topic: work.

"You know what my boss did last week? Absolute disaster," Alex said with dramatic flair, launching into a monologue about his work life. He wasn't singing praises—far from it. Instead, he relished in recounting stories of how inept his manager was, how he had outsmarted him, how he always knew better. It was classic Alex.

Emilia chimed in with her own anecdotes, finding a rhythm with Alex as they traded complaints about their bosses. They seemed proud of how they had "proven" their superiors wrong. It wasn't a serious conversation, but more of a venting session, filled with jokes and sarcastic remarks about the incompetence of their managers.

Krishna listened, chewing quietly, but his attention drifted. Across the table, Nati was unusually silent. She wasn't contributing to the conversation; Krishna noticed her subtle gestures—raised eyebrows, the slight shake of her head. She was clearly bored, if not a little exasperated by the conversation. Krishna caught her eye. Without saying a word, they shared an unspoken understanding: this was the usual banter, and neither of them was really invested in it.

Emilia, still nursing her earlier disappointment, masked it with exaggerated enthusiasm. She was as talkative as ever, but her topics had a recurring theme: her beauty. Every story she told somehow circled back to how many men had flirted with her or how she received extra tips because of her looks. It was almost comical how consistently she redirected the conversation to herself.

"Did I ever tell you how the customers just can't keep their eyes off me?" Emilia said, casually brushing a strand of hair behind her ear, as if on cue.

Nati's eyes flicked over to Krishna, her expression unreadable except for a faint glint of amusement. It was clear she had heard Emilia's stories many times before. This is her usual script, Nati's raised eyebrows seemed to say. Krishna suppressed a smile, finding humor in Nati's silent commentary. Emilia continued, oblivious to the fact that no one was really hanging on to her every word.

Alex, on the other hand, was in full swing, holding court as he expounded on how people could improve themselves. He spoke with such an authority, as though he were an expert on all things—from personal development to how others should be living their lives. His confidence was undeniable, but Krishna noticed Nati was growing more and more disengaged, her eyes wandering around the room.

Krishna was intrigued by this dynamic. While Alex and Emilia were leading the conversation, it was evident that Nati and Krishna were mentally elsewhere.

He could see that Nati, though polite, wasn't impressed by Alex's self-proclaimed expertise. She smiled here and there, but it was clear she found the conversation tiring. Krishna, too, was passively listening, nodding at the appropriate times but not really absorbing much of what was being said.

Alex, oblivious to the disinterest around him, kept going. "You know what's wrong with people? They don't listen. They stay stuck in their old ways. But not me. I grow, I adapt. That's what I keep telling my boss, but does he listen? Never!"

Krishna resisted the urge to roll his eyes while Nati shifted uncomfortably in her seat. Alex's relentless need for approval and acknowledgment was becoming more transparent by the minute, and Krishna couldn't help but feel a bit sorry for him. It was as though Alex needed validation from everyone at the table—especially from Nati and himself—but neither of them was giving him what he wanted.

Nati finally glanced at Krishna with a look that said it all—Can we escape this somehow? Krishna smiled softly in return, signaling that he understood. This lunch, while amusing in its own way, was wearing thin. They both felt like outsiders to the conversation, as though they were observers rather than participants.

As the lunch carried on, Krishna thought back to his earlier reflection about happiness. He realized this was another example of how relative everything was. Alex and Emilia were so wrapped up in their own narratives, so caught in comparing their lives to others, that they couldn't see beyond it. Nati, on the other hand, seemed to find her happiness elsewhere—in the quiet moments, in shared glances, in something more internal.

Krishna felt a connection with her in that sense, as though they were both on the same wavelength, detached from the need to prove anything to anyone. For them, happiness wasn't found in boasting or one-upping each other; it was in the simplicity of being present, enjoying the moment, and finding humor in the small things. In that realization, Krishna felt a sense of peace.

As the group finished their dessert, Emilia launched into a story, her voice filled with pride. Everyone at the table leaned in as she began to recount a night at the casino, one that had clearly left a mark on her.

Last Thursday, Nati and I were on shift," Emilia started, her eyes lighting up as she spoke. "It was late, and the bets were still coming in, especially from this rich bull from Brazil. I mean, he was loaded, betting in multiples of $100 like it was nothing. Alex was the dealer.

Alex, seated across from Emilia, gave a small, self-deprecating shrug, but Emilia didn't miss a beat, diving into the details.

"Alex gave me a look, you know, the kind that says, "Focus on me." Why wouldn't I? The whole table was a show, with every bet pouring in hundreds, and Alex—" she gestured toward him—"was keeping up the pace. It was insane. He was giving just enough wins to keep people excited but holding back so the casino still earned big. The whole room was watching. The wine was flowing, the music was pumping—it was like a movie."

Emilia's voice dropped a little, taking on a more intimate tone. "Since I was in charge, I know how to mesmerize people." She smiled as she recounted how quickly the Brazilian had taken notice of her. "He looked back, eyes full of lust—no subtlety there. He was drunk, sure, but still rich enough to call for attention.

"Could you bring me a drink, darling?" He asked, eyes all over me.

"He kept calling me over—for drinks, for snacks, for anything. It was clear he was more interested in me than the game. But I had a job to do, and I did it well. I kept my composure, even when he got a bit too handsy."

Krishna noticed Nati's subtle shift at that. He could tell she wasn't thrilled about the details Emilia was sharing, but she stayed quiet. He caught her eye for a brief second, their unspoken understanding continuing from earlier.

"I gave him the best—a strong Chivas, 15 years aged. The kind we don't usually give out unless someone's really throwing money at the table. He took a sip, and boom, won blackjack! Right after I handed him the drink."

The table was hooked on Emilia's storytelling now. Alex, despite being mentioned, didn't say much, letting Emilia take center stage.

"He was winning left and right, no matter how the dealers changed, or the stakes shifted. He just couldn't lose. By the end of the night, he was dancing on the floor with every win—literally! People were talking more about him than the concert!"

Alex, the dealer, was sweating bullets. Every card landed in the Brazilian's favor, like the guy had a magic touch. The crowd roared with every win, feeding off the thrill.

And then, just when we thought it couldn't get any crazier, the Brazilian decided to go all in. He pushed all his chips to the center of the table. The crowd went silent. You could feel the tension in the air."

Alex dealt the cards. The Brazilian had a 10 and a 6. He asked for another card. Alex hesitated, but he had no choice. He dealt a 5. The Brazilian had 21. Blackjack. The crowd erupted. It was pandemonium." Proud whistled, "Unbelievable."

"The Brazilian stood up, raised his arms in victory, then did something unexpected. He took a handful of chips and threw them into the crowd. People were scrambling to catch them. It was chaos."

"The celebration was wild," she continued, her eyes were gleaming. "You know how it goes. When a high roller wins big, the energy in the casino changes. Everyone was cheering."

Nati smiled faintly, nodding at points, but Krishna could tell she wasn't as impressed by the Brazilian or the luck streak as Emilia was. For Nati, this was just another night at the casino—nothing special.

"And then," Emilia added dramatically, "he grabbed me, hugged me, and kissed me on the cheek—right in front of everyone!" Her tone held a mix of amusement and disbelief. "He handed me a $100 tip, called me his lucky charm."

The table erupted in laughter. "It was the craziest day of my career! Absolutely. The guy walked out with thousands. And the casino? Well, it was a rough night for them." She shrugged, "But for me, it was the biggest tip I've ever received from one person."

"And the deep kiss too!" Alex said and everyone erupted in laughter.

As Emilia wrapped up her story, everyone applauded lightly, thoroughly entertained. Even those who had been at the casino that night seemed to enjoy hearing it from Emilia's perspective, with all the added flair and drama. Krishna found it interesting how everyone's retelling of the same event could shift depending on who was narrating.

Krishna glanced over at Nati. She raised her eyebrows slightly, as if to say, "There goes Emilia again." But even Nati couldn't fully deny the strange allure of the story, the way Emilia seemed to pull everyone into her world of glamorous nights and lucky streaks. Yet, Krishna knew—beneath the story, beneath the pride in her voice—there was a sense of unease.

And as the group moved on to lighter conversations, Krishna reflected on the night Emilia described. Luck, success, beauty—they were all so fleeting. Like happiness, they were relative. That Brazilian had walked out a winner, but how long before his luck ran out? And Emilia—her pride in that story wasn't about the money or the win, but about the attention, about being seen.

Krishna realized that everyone was chasing something different, sometimes, what they were chasing wasn't always what they truly wanted. The casino was a place where fortunes could turn in a moment, but outside of those walls, life was far more complex.

Krishna had stayed quiet for most of the conversation. But now, as he spoke, the table fell silent, drawn in by his measured tone.

He wasn't one to dive into the loud banter or boastful storytelling like the others, but when he did speak, it was always with careful consideration.

"I remember that night vividly," Krishna began with steady voice. "Fortunately—or unfortunately—I was there too. I remember standing there with the others, feeling the sting of defeat. I saw the game unfold. It was quite a spectacle, I admit. That Brazilian man, full of swagger and luck, seemingly untouchable by any logic or pattern we'd normally expect. It was one of those rare moments when the game turned against us—against the house. But the truth is, moments like that are part of a dealer's life. We live through terrifying, unexpected twists like those. That's the nature of our work."

Everyone listened intently, their focus shifting completely to Krishna now. Even Emilia, who had just been the center of attention, was silent as he continued.

We all were disappointed by the loss. But Gabriel steals the show that night.

"Whatever happened," he told us, "It will happen again. Maybe not tomorrow, maybe not next week, but someday. What makes us a dealer, what defines us, isn't how many times we win. It's not even how many times we lose. It's our ability to stand up again, smile on your face, and keep playing the game with grace, patience, and maturity."

"We rob them all year round," Krishna added with a slight smile, though it wasn't one of arrogance. "The odds are always in the house's favor. Ninety percent of the time, it's the customers who leave with their pockets empty, not us. So, when a player has a night like that—when luck defies the rules we live by—we can't take it personally. It's all part of the game."

Emilia shifted in her seat slightly, unsure how to respond. Krishna's words carried a sense of wisdom that was hard to challenge. He wasn't diminishing what had happened that night, but instead putting it in perspective. He didn't see it as a loss but rather as an anomaly in the larger picture of their lives as dealers.

"It doesn't define us," Krishna continued, glancing briefly at Emilia. "What happens on any given night, in any game, doesn't define who we are. What defines us is how we deal with it. We're the ones who pull the money 90% of the time. Nothing personal to "Mrs. Beautiful"—the Brazilian man—but luck like his doesn't last. And, as for you,

Emilia..." His gaze softened as he looked at her. "Yes, your presence that night might've driven him a bit crazy, sent him soaring to new heights with all that winning. But it could just as easily have driven him into the ground if things had gone the other way."

There was a pause, a moment of reflection, before Krishna shifted the focus of the conversation. "What impressed me more than anything that night wasn't the Brazilian's win, though. It was the speech Gabriel gave afterward. He handled it like a true leader. He made us feel that it wasn't just about losing a pile of money—it was about resilience. The real strength, he said, lies in the ability to maintain your composure, to trust your hands, your skills. To welcome those moments where the game gets the better of you and still rise the next day, ready to deal again."

"He stood there," Krishna recalled, he told us, "This is a game of numbers, a game of patterns. But every now and then, the numbers break. The pattern shifts, and you must let it. Because in those moments, it's not about the money or the cards—it's about how you handle the break."

Krishna's voice took on a more thoughtful tone as he repeated Gabriel's words. "When you face a night like this, you have two choices: you can let it shake you, make you doubt the system, or you can recognize it for what it is—a rare moment when the game plays you. But remember, it's just that—a moment. Tomorrow, you're back in control."

"That's what stayed with me," Krishna concluded. "Not the Brazilian's luck or the chaos of the night, but Gabriel's calm reminder that moments like that don't last. They test us, but they don't define us. We return the next day, back at the table, back in control."

Alex, who had been involved in the game as a dealer that night, nodded, remembering the moment too.

For a moment, no one spoke. The silence pressed in, thick and unbroken, before someone finally shifted in their seat.

Then, slowly, the conversation began to pick back up, but it was softer now, less charged. The rhythm of the group had shifted, even Emilia, who had previously dominated the conversation, seemed more subdued.

She glanced at Krishna from time to time, perhaps realizing that her version of events had only told part of the story—one that highlighted her role but missed the larger, more significant truth about what that night had meant.

Krishna's words had left their mark. Everyone carried a bit of that perspective with them—a reminder that in life, just like in the casino, it's not the wins or losses that matter most, but how you handle the game.

Emilia, for her part, seemed to absorb Krishna's words. Her earlier pride softened. Though she didn't say anything, there was a look of understanding in her eyes. Krishna had subtly reminded her that even on nights when luck felt like it was spinning out of control, they were the ones who would always have the advantage in the long run.

Alex, usually quick with a sharp comment, sat back instead. His usual smirk wavered, his silence speaking louder than any critique.

It was clear that Krishna's words had left an impact on him too. He had always been quick to critique, particularly when it came to their manager, Gabriel. But now, he seemed to be re-evaluating his stance. Perhaps, for the first time, he saw the wisdom behind Gabriel's leadership and the deeper meaning in what Krishna had shared.

Nati, on the other hand, appeared deep in thought. Her eyes sparkled slightly as she observed the conversation, seemingly impressed by Krishna's insight.

She had kept a safe distance from most of the group that night, especially Emilia, but now her posture had changed. There was a quiet trust growing toward Krishna, a sense of openness in her body language as though she was finally seeing him for who he was—a man of quiet strength, wisdom, and perspective.

The meal slowly wound down, dessert plates emptied, and the conversations lightened again, but the mood was different.

The group, once loud with tales of ego and pride, fell into a quieter rhythm, the weight of the night's lesson settling over them.

Krishna had pulled them back from the surface level of wins and losses, reminding them of something far more important: the strength to endure, the wisdom to rise, and the grace to keep playing, no matter the cards dealt.

Krishna was flipping through the local TV channels when the hotel landline rang. It was Nati, calling from the room next door. He answered the call, and they chatted away. Before they knew it, 45 minutes had flown by when they finally hung up.

A smile still lingering on his face as he lay back on the bed. The gentle hum of the TV played in the background, but his mind was elsewhere, replaying the conversation with Nati.

It wasn't their first talk, but there was something different about this one—something that made his heart feel lighter, as if he was floating on air. He could still hear her soft voice, teasing him about "The Fault in Our Stars," her playful tone hiding a deeper connection that neither of them had fully acknowledged yet.

He stared at the ceiling, lost in thought. Nati's innocence, her hesitation, her reluctance to join the others without the right dress—all of it spoke of a girl who valued her dignity, someone who didn't easily step out of her comfort zone. And yet, here she was, sharing her worries with him, trusting him to find a solution, knowing he wouldn't let her down. It was in these small moments that Krishna realized just how much she had come to mean to him.

He thought about her hesitation to borrow a swimsuit from Emilia. Of course, Nati would say no. Emilia's boldness, her carefree attitude, was worlds apart from Nati's reserved nature.

It was never just about the swimsuit—it was about identity, about what she was willing to reveal.

Nati wasn't like Emilia. She wouldn't put herself out there in that way; Krishna respected her for it. He liked that about her—the way she held in, the way she wasn't willing to compromise who she was for anyone.

Krishna couldn't help but feel a growing sense of protectiveness toward her. The way she asked, "What would I do here with you all?"—it wasn't just about the next day's plans; it was about her place in his world. She didn't want to feel left out, and yet, she didn't want to be forced into something that wasn't her. He admired her vulnerability, the way she could express her uncertainty without fear of judgment, at least not from him.

He thought about how he had handled the situation, offering to talk to Emilia, knowing full well Nati would never agree. He had done it to make her laugh, to ease her worries, and it worked. Her big "No way!" had come as no surprise; and yet, it was that moment of playfulness that brought them closer. She was letting him in, little by little, Krishna was grateful for it.

And then there was the promise he made—to stay by her side if she didn't feel comfortable going into the water. It wasn't a grand gesture, but it was enough. He knew Nati wasn't one for big displays of affection; it was the small, quiet promises that mattered to her. He could tell from the way she softened after he said it, the way her tone shifted from worry to relief. She trusted him—and that was everything.

As he lay there, he couldn't help but think about how different things felt with Nati. With Emilia, everything was fast and fiery, a whirlwind of excitement and unpredictability. But with Nati, it was the opposite. It was slow, steady, and comforting. He found himself wanting to protect her, to be the one she could rely on. It was new for him, this feeling. It wasn't about the thrill of the game or the chase—it was something deeper, something real.

Even after the call ended, its warmth lingered, stretching time beyond the forty-five minutes they had spent talking.

Krishna realized just how much he enjoyed talking to her, how her innocence and genuine nature drew him in more than he ever expected. There was something pure about Nati, something that made him want to be a better version of himself.

He smiled to himself as he thought about how she had worried over the next day's plans, how her innocent questions only made him want to reassure her more. And the way she ended the call, with that reluctant goodbye—it was like neither of them wanted the conversation to end, like they could have talked for hours more.

Krishna closed his eyes, his lips curled in a lingering smile, as an unfamiliar calm settled over him.

It was peace—steady, quiet—the kind he hadn't known in years. It wasn't the thrill of a big win or the rush of a flawless night at the casino. This was different—something deeper, something that lingered long after the call had ended.

He drifted into sleep, her voice still threading through his thoughts—her laughter, her questions, her quiet wonder.

For the first time in years, Krishna felt at ease—like everything had fallen into place. Even in sleep, his smile remained.

The phone rang twice before Krishna picked it up.

"Krishna, where are you?" Alex's voice came from the reception.

"We're all waiting for you."

"Yeah, Alex, sorry. No idea how I dozed off. Give me five minutes—I'll be there," Krishna said, ending the call.

It was already 4:30 p.m. they had planned to leave at 4 p.m. He hurriedly got ready, but just as he was about to lock the door, the phone rang again.

"Coming, I'm just about to lock the door," Krishna said, picking up the call.

"Wait," Emilia said. "Natalia's not answering. Go wake her up"

"I'll come with her." Krishna hung up and went to Nati's door. After two rings, she opened it, her eyes still sleepy.

"Nati, you're still sleepy? Don't you know what time we were supposed to leave?"

"Oh, I don't even know when I dozed off. Gimme ten minutes and I'm ready," she said, splashing cold water on her face.

"Ten minutes more and they'll kill us," Krishna muttered.

"Then make something up," she said, pulling on her clothes.

Before Krishna could call the reception, the phone rang again. Alex was on the other side.

"Krishna, there's not enough space in one cab. The receptionist is getting another one to drop you at the beach. We'll meet there. Cool?"

Alex finished in one go. It wasn't a question; it was more of a directive. In a way, it was good for the duo.

"OK, see you there," Krishna agreed, not wanting to keep the whole group waiting.

It took half an hour for Nati to get ready.

"Good thing Alex and the others left. If they'd waited, their whole plan would've gone down the drain," Krishna teased.

"I knew they left—that's why I took my time. Otherwise, I'd have been ready in ten," she shot back with her reason for being late.

When they arrived, Alex and the others were already enjoying swimming.

The air was cool, but the beach buzzed with life—some people lounged with beers, others played volleyball, and the rest savored the food.

It was a nice, clean, and calm place. The long beach, white sand, and blue water made it one of the best beaches in the country.

Alex and everyone were playing ball by the water. Krishna and Nati walked on the sand. The clean seawater touched their feet as the small tides receded.

The beach was pristine, and the warm water lured anyone in, tempting them to ride the tide.

Alex saw Krishna and invited them to join. Krishna wanted to go in the water, but Nati was with him. He knew she wouldn't come. She could have, if Krishna had convinced her, but he knew she had no clothes to change into if she got wet.

"You guys continue; I'll accompany Nati," Krishna said to Alex, enjoying the walk with her.

"Alright, you two carry on," Alex smirked with light harmless sarcasm.

Emilia's expression was unreadable, but her swimsuit wasn't.

She didn't say anything, but her silence and facial expressions spoke more than words.

Krishna glanced at Nati—she stood just shy of the waterline, hesitant.

Krishna scooped water in his palm and threw it on Nati.

"No, Krishna, please. You know I don't have a dress to change into. Don't do that, or I'll go back to the hotel," she pleaded.

Krishna stayed quiet, stepping back. Her voice carried a soft innocence that made her even more captivating.

"Don't worry, I won't splash water on you. Come here, take your sandals in hand, and let your legs feel the movement of the sand," Krishna urged, wanting her to feel the water against her skin.

Krishna rolled up his jeans to his knees, while Nati, already in shorts, let the warm water brush against her skin.

"It's really nice," Nati said, touching the warm blue water with her legs.

They strolled along the bay, lost in conversation about life back home, childhood memories, and everything in between.

"What's your routine like back home?" Krishna asked, circling back to their taxi conversation that morning.

Krishna's interest in her only deepened when she spoke about her profession.

Why wouldn't it be? After all, in India, it's rare—a girl chasing her dreams, exploring the world with barely anything in her bank account." Nati's fearless approach to life left Krishna both surprised and impressed.

Nati looked at Krishna, her eyes bright with enthusiasm. "Well, I'm a psychology student. I live in Lima with my friend for my studies," she began, sharing her story.

Krishna listened intently as she continued, "My parents live in Cusco. My father is an ex-army officer and currently runs a small restaurant there."

"My mother helps him with the restaurant. They are my role models," she added with a smile. The names Peru, Lima, and Cusco were all new to Krishna, he found himself intrigued.

"Oh, and my brother—he lives in Amsterdam. He never liked Cusco and wants to settle there for good. He's happier that way," Nati said, half amused, half resigned.

Krishna was amazed by the diversity in her family.

"What a dramatic family you have! Your brother doesn't want to live in his own country, your parents are in one place, and you're chasing your dreams elsewhere."

He nodded, though the names—Lima, Cusco—felt distant, almost unreal.

They carried the weight of places he had never imagined.

"Where is Peru? Where is Cusco? This is my first time hearing those names," Krishna admitted, feeling a bit embarrassed.

Nati's eyes sparkled with pride. "Peru is one of the most ancient countries in the world. Haven't you heard about it?" She asked, her voice filled with excitement.

Krishna shook his head. "No, I haven't. Tell me more about it."

Nati's enthusiasm grew as she began to explain. "Peru is in South America. It's known for its rich history and diverse culture. Cusco, where my parents live, was once the capital of the Inca Empire. It's a beautiful city with a lot of historical sites."

Pride lit up her eyes as she spoke. "My country holds one of the most ancient traces of human civilization," she said, her voice filled with enthusiasm. Krishna couldn't help but notice the passion in her eyes as she talked about Peru's rich cultural heritage.

"I always thought India had the oldest civilization," Krishna murmured, intrigued.

"Yes, I've heard there are some similarities between India and my country," Nati replied, agreeing with Krishna's observation.

Krishna listened, fascinated by her passion. "That sounds amazing. And Lima?"

"Lima is the capital of Peru," Nati explained. "It's a bustling city with a mix of modern and colonial architecture. It's also known for its food. Peruvian cuisine is considered one of the best in the world."

Krishna smiled. "I would love to try it someday."

"You should," Nati said, her excitement contagious. "And Amsterdam, where my brother lives, is a completely different world. It's known for its canals, museums, and liberal culture. He loves it there, but I miss having him around." Krishna nodded, recognizing how families could be scattered yet still connected.

"It must be hard having your family spread out like that."

"It is," Nati admitted. "But we stay connected. And I love living in Lima. It's given me so many opportunities to learn and grow."

Krishna admired her positive outlook. "You have a very interesting life, Nati. I'm glad we met."

Nati smiled warmly. "Me too, Krishna. It's nice to share my story with someone who appreciates it."

They continued to walk along the beach, their sandals and shoes in hand, occasionally kicking water at each other playfully.

By then, they had completed a full round—about two kilometers—and returned to their starting point.

Nati was visibly tired. Krishna noticed and turned to her. They were enjoying every step of their walk together. "I am tired, Krishna. I cannot walk anymore. Let's sit here for a while," she said innocently, standing still.

Krishna found it impossible to refuse—her innocence and charm left him defenseless.

"OK, Nati, why don't we sit on the sand?" He suggested.

"Yes, that's a nice idea!" She agreed enthusiastically.

"Give me a moment, I'll be right back," Nati said to Krishna with a quick smile before walking off toward the small beachfront shop.

Krishna stayed where he was, watching the scene unfold around him. Alex, Emilia, and the others were still deep in their game, throwing water at each other, their laughter rising above the sound of the waves. They dashed in and out of the ocean, chasing the receding tides until the water was almost shoulder-deep, only to sprint back to shore when the waves rolled back toward them. Some managed to outrun the tide, while others stumbled, caught by the water, laughing even harder as the sea claimed victory.

On Krishna's right, two children were attempting to build a sandcastle. They packed sand tightly, determined to create something grand, only for each wave to sweep it away. Their mother swam nearby, a picture of quiet joy as she floated effortlessly in the water, seeming to savor every second.

Krishna couldn't help but be mesmerized by the children's persistence. They knew the ocean would eventually steal their castle, yet they rebuilt it over and over, laughing at the futility of it all. There was something profound in their simple game, a lesson in resilience, in creating even when you know it won't last.

Just then, Nati returned with cold beers and a coke for Krishna, pulling him from his thoughts.

"Where were you lost?" she asked, handing him a Coke with a playful smile.

His eyes still lingering on the children. "Just watching those kids build their castle," he said, nodding toward them. "They know it's going to wash away, but they keep building it anyway."

Nati followed his gaze, then looked back at him with a soft chuckle. "That's life, isn't it? We build things, knowing they won't last forever. But we build them anyway."

Krishna smiled at her words, feeling the weight of their truth. They sat quietly for a moment, sipping their drinks, as the waves continued their dance with the shore. After a long time, I feel like being myself. Thanks to you," Nati said, popping open the can with a soft hiss and continued.

She took a sip, enjoying the coolness of the beer, then added, "You know, it's kind of liberating. Drinking without worrying, going past your usual limits because you trust that someone is there to bring you back safely."

She sat down beside Krishna, her eyes drifting toward the ocean as she finished her thought. Krishna raised an eyebrow, a hint of playfulness in his voice. "Well, in that case, it seems like you don't trust me."

" What's the logic?" Nati laughed softly, turning to face him. "Hadn't I trusted you, I wouldn't have drunk alongside you," she teased.

"But it's just a beer. It's not exactly pushing your limits, is it?" Krishna quipped sarcastically.

Nati shook her head, amused. "You're provoking me. Quite the twist from someone who doesn't drink."

He grinned at her playful curiosity. "I'm not trying to provoke you, and I'm not one to judge people by their habits. I just try to avoid getting too used to anything."

"Nati laughed. "Mr. Philosopher, where did you come from? You make everything sound so mystical."

For a moment, they both fell into a comfortable silence. Nati took another sip, the conversation hanging in the air. Before Krishna could respond, she suddenly said, "Hey, you know, I've realized something about you."

Intrigued, Krishna looked over. "Oh? And what's that?"

"You're such an introverted person. I mean, you know everything about me—and here I am, not knowing much about you."

Krishna chuckled. "Well, it's not about being an introvert. Most of my friends say that about me, but I think it's not true with you because you haven't asked about me. It's been me asking and being inquisitive about you."

Nati raised an eyebrow, smiling. "Well then, better late than never."

Tell me about yourself. I want to listen to you," She insisted.

Who are you? Where are you from, and how did you end up here?"

Krishna looked at her, appreciating her genuine interest.

"Well, about me? I'm Krishna. I'm from a small town back in India," he began, looking out at the sea.

"I was born and brought up in a very small village in the Maharashtra province. We are two brothers. Shiva is my twin brother, my life.

His eyes sparkled with pride as he spoke. "We're all proud of him."

Shiva and I are like two sides of the same coin.

"I'm unorthodox, unpredictable, and a rebel—never caring much about what others think. Sometimes, I feel directionless, just drifting with the wind."

Nati listened intently as Krishna continued, "I spent my childhood in my village along with my siblings. It's a wonderful place, nestled in the lap of nature. I remember the best times of my life—grazing our buffaloes, swimming in the river, climbing trees. Shiva and I would sell watermelons in the small streets of our village and collect mahua flowers to earn a bit of money. Those were the best days of my life!"

Krishna's voice grew quieter, more reflective. "Looking back, all I can say is thank you, God, for blessing me with such wonderful memories." He took a sip of his coke, for a moment, there was a heavy silence between them.

"But nothing stays forever—neither good times nor bad," he continued. "Life must go on. With passing time, I learned to follow my instincts." He glanced out at the sea, his expression thoughtful. "And here I am, far from my country, looking at the unfathomable sea with the most beautiful girl in the world."

Nati laughed, the sound bright and genuine. "Very funny," she said, finishing the last sip of her beer. "By the way, it was nice drinking a beer with you. I wish I had another one," she said, glancing at the empty bottle.

Krishna nodded, a wistful smile on his face. Krishna remembered a line from a friend back in Pune: "If a person can drink with you and share their insights, they become the best friends for life." Though Krishna hadn't drunk beer, it felt like he had shared a slice of himself with someone after a long time. He realized that when we open up to someone without fear of losing our privacy or secrets, our hearts become lighter—and those people become the best friends for the rest of our lives.

Their discussion meandered from personal reflections to broader topics about their countries and surroundings. The hours slipped away unnoticed, and before they knew it, the clock showed 7:30 p.m.

"Hey, look at those kids," Nati said, pointing. "They've been doing the same thing for so long."

"Crazy," Krishna replied with a chuckle. "But See how happy they are!"

Nati nodded, her gaze still fixed on the children. "If they worried about their castle being washed away by the tide, they wouldn't be able to enjoy it as much."

"Exactly," Krishna agreed. "We all have limited time here. If we're constantly worried about our destination, how can we enjoy the journey and every moment that comes with it? It's the moments like these that last with us forever."

Nati smiled, appreciating his insight.

As the evening deepened, Krishna and Nati found themselves lost in conversation.

The children beside them were still playing with sandcastles trying to build their little castle against the relentless tide.

As they walked back to the group, Krishna turned to her with a mischievous grin.

"One thing I must confess... your friend is smoking hot."

Nati laughed.

"No wonder she gets so much attention. Her curves definitely turn heads."

she said, playfully pointing out Alex and Emilia, who were still playing in the water.

As the sun began to set, casting a golden hue over the horizon, everyone come out of the water, exhausted but happy. They had spent hours playing and would have stayed longer if they had the energy.

The beach was a tableau of laughter and contentment. The time spent there was like a cherished memory in the making.

every moment a memory that would stay with them forever. Despite it being only their second day together after work, Krishna and Nati's bond had grown as if they had known each other for ages.

They joined their friends, who were now seated in the sand near the yacht, their tired faces illuminated by the fading light. The seawater touched their feet with each higher tide, a gentle reminder of the day's end.

Nati loved taking pictures, and she had found someone equally crazy about snapping photos. She met someone just as enthusiastic about clicking pictures as she was. Their solo photos turned into selfies, laughing, splashing water on each other, and even trying to touch their tongues to their noses. They captured every possible moment together.

Krishna was amazed at how effortlessly girls struck pose after pose, never losing enthusiasm.

He was enjoying every bit of it; Each moment felt entirely new to him.

Everyone sat on the sand near the yacht, the seawater barely a foot away, touching them with each higher tide. They were too stunned by the sunset to speak.

After the sunset, everyone was so tired that they went directly to a nearby local seafood restaurant.

The restaurant buzzed with energy as they ordered their favorite dishes, but the mood was different from their lively lunch.

Everyone was too tired to initiate any conversation or respond to any talk.

Their conversations dwindled to brief, closed-ended replies—mostly just "Yes" or "No".

Everyone just wanted to get back to the hotel and throw themselves on the bed.

After dinner, they piled into a large taxi, with Krishna and Nati sharing the same one as before.

Nati was sleepy, and the dinner afterward made her feel uneasy.

"Krishna, I feel like vomiting. Would you mind if I put my head on your shoulder?" She asked gently.

"Of course, you can," his voice soft and reassuring. He adjusted his position to make her more comfortable, allowing her to rest as they made their way to the hotel.

They didn't say anything for the next 20 minutes until they reached the hotel.

Krishna let her rest, careful not to disturb her. When they arrived at the hotel, he gently helped Nati to her room, tucking her in before heading to his own.

As Krishna lay in bed, he reflected on the day. It had been a whirlwind of new experiences, from the first meeting at the coffee shop to the shared laughter and deep conversations. The day's events, especially his time with Nati, had been extraordinary. He could still feel the smile lingering on his lips, a testament to how special the day had been.

"Such a beautiful day," Krishna thought as he closed his eyes, replaying the moments in his mind. The day had been unlike any other, and he felt a deep sense of contentment as he drifted off to sleep.

The gentle sound of the waves crashing in the distance echoed faintly in his dreams. But then, the doorbell rang, jarring him from the comfort of sleep. He ignored it at first, hoping it would stop, but after the third or fourth ring, he reluctantly dragged himself out of bed.

Half-awake, Krishna opened the door to find Emilia standing there, looking disheveled, wearing what appeared to be her nightwear. Her eyes were glazed. It was clear she had been drinking.

"Hey, what happened? Everything alright?" Krishna asked, concern lining his voice.

Without answering, Emilia staggered inside and dropped onto the sofa. Krishna followed her, grabbing a glass of water. He handed it to her, trying to gauge the situation, but she brushed it off with a sly smile.

"I wish you would have come up with a hug rather than a glass of water," she said, her words slurring slightly. "But anyway, thank you."

Krishna smiled awkwardly and sat across from her, not sure how to respond. They talked for a while—about the beach, about why Krishna didn't join them in the water. He lied, saying he didn't know how to swim, hoping to cut the conversation short. He was exhausted, but Emilia kept talking, her words becoming slower as sleep began to overtake her.

"I'm freezing," she mumbled, barely keeping her eyes open. "The heater's broken, and they won't fix it. My room's like an icebox. I don't want to go back."

Krishna shifted uncomfortably in his seat, sensing where the conversation was going.

"If you don't mind, can I sleep here on the sofa?" She asked, her voice sounding more vulnerable now, though still slightly drunk.

Krishna stiffened, an uneasy weight settling in his chest.

"Uh... I only have one blanket, and how can you sleep on the sofa? You won't be comfortable," he said, hesitating.

Emilia waved her hand dismissively. "I'll be fine here. You don't need to worry."

Krishna's mind raced. He didn't know how to handle the situation. Should he call Nati? Would that make things worse? What would she think if she found out Emilia was here? His unease grew, but Emilia was already dozing off, her breathing slow and heavy.

"I won't make you uncomfortable, Krishna," she mumbled in her sleep. "Just let me stay here on the sofa. You can go to bed."

Without giving him another chance to respond, Emilia drifted into a deep sleep.

Krishna sat there, paralyzed by the situation. He couldn't just ask her to leave—especially in her state—but he was terrified of how Nati might react if she found out. His moral compass was spinning, his sense of responsibility clashing with his fear of misinterpretation. He didn't lock the door; afraid Emilia might wake up and wonder why he had done so. His mind pulled him in a dozen directions at once.

He realized two things that night: he thought too much and had a hard time saying no to people. His mind wouldn't let him rest. His sense of propriety, the need to do the "right" thing, weighed heavily on him. Emilia slept soundly, but Krishna lay awake, staring at the ceiling.

The next morning, Krishna was startled awake by the ringing of his phone. He picked up groggily, only to be greeted by Nati's sweet voice on the other end.

"Hola, buenos días," she chirped, her words carrying the melody of morning.

"Are you still in bed?" She asked.

"Yes, I am," Krishna murmured, his voice heavy with sleep.

"Same here," Nati replied, equally drowsy. "Where are we going today?"

Krishna smirked. "Look who's asking, the ever-curious Ms. Hazel."

She laughed softly and then, with a little hesitation, confessed, "Krishna, let me tell you something, —yesterday was the best time I've ever had on this cruise."

"It was the best day I've spent in a long time too," Krishna replied earnestly, feeling the warmth of her words.

"Maybe today we can explore the city and have lunch. We need to leave for the cruise at 3:00 p.m. So we'll have a short plan today. What about breakfast?" Nati suggested. "Wait, I'm getting a call from Mumma. Come to my room in 30 minutes," she added, hanging up before Krishna could respond.

He freshened up, got ready, and walked over to Nati's room. When he rang the bell, Nati was already in the kitchen, preparing coffee while on a video call with her parents. Her phone was propped up near the stove, and she spoke animatedly, recounting their day to her mother.

He freshened up, got ready, and walked over to Nati's room. When he rang the bell, Nati was already in the kitchen, preparing coffee while on a video call with her parents. Her phone was propped up near the stove, she was speaking animatedly, recounting their day to her mother.

Krishna quietly entered, unsure of whether to interrupt, and took a seat on the sofa. He felt slightly awkward, as Nati was on a call with her parents. Being in a girl's room while her parents were on a call felt... improper, but Nati carried on, oblivious to his hesitation.

"You know, Mumma, we were running up the escalator like crazy," Nati said excitedly, reliving their fun day. She was recounting every little detail to her mother, laughing as she spoke.

Krishna sat back, listening to the warmth in her voice, enjoying her energy. Suddenly, Nati called out, "Krishna, can you grab two cups? I made coffee."

He got up and handed her the cups, but before he could sit back down, Nati surprised him.

"Mumma, do you want to talk to Krishna? Here, talk to him!" She said, shoving the phone in Krishna's direction without waiting for a response from either her mother or Krishna.

Krishna froze for a second, then smiled, taking the phone.

"Hello, Aunty," Krishna greeted her mother, waving at the phone's camera.

"Hola, chico! How are you?" Nati's mother responded warmly, her voice filled with care. "Nati has told us about you."

"I'm good, Aunty, thank you," Krishna replied, smiling. Despite it being their first conversation, he immediately felt at ease. Her voice was soft and affectionate, though her English was not fluent, it didn't matter. The affection behind her words was clear.

They talked for a bit, mostly about Nati, exchanging pleasantries until Nati's father took the phone. A broad-shouldered man with a thick mustache, greeted Krishna with a smile.

"You know, son, after a long time, we're not worried about Nati. Knowing you're there by her side, it gives us peace. She seems very happy in your company."

The words settled over Krishna, heavy yet comforting, like a responsibility he didn't mind carrying.

He reassured them, "Don't worry, Uncle. She is a strong girl.

They chatted briefly, before Nati's mother took the phone back.

"I'm grateful to God," she said softly. "She's a strong girl, but she hasn't found someone to match her spirit yet. Don't feel bad if she says something harsh. She doesn't mean it."

Krishna smiled. "Don't worry, Aunty, I understand."

Nati, overhearing this, jumped in, "Enough, Mumma, you're making it sound like I'm difficult."

Her mother laughed. "I know you don't want to talk to me."

Nati grinned, snatching the phone back. "Take care of Papa," she teased. "He seems weak."

Her father, clearly in on the playful banter, replied, "See? Your mother barely looks after me. She naps more than a cat!"

Nati laughed, and soon both she and her father began teasing her mother, poking fun at her. The three of them joked around until, with one last wave, Nati hung up the call.

As the phone call ended, Krishna smiled to himself, realizing that in just a few days, he had come to be a part of Nati's world, a world filled with warmth, humor, and love.

"These pictures are incredible—pure chaos in every frame."

Krishna smiled, scrolling through the gallery on Nati's phone. But then, with a mischievous grin, he called out, "Nati!"

She turned, coffee cup in hand.

"All the pictures got erased by mistake," Krishna said, feigning concern.

Nati's eyes widened, her face going blank with shock. "Oh, ghastly..."

"Swear to God!" she whispered; her face still frozen in disbelief.

Krishna watched her, fighting to keep his composure, but before Nati could check her phone, he couldn't hold it in any longer and burst out laughing.

"Sorry! I was kidding," he said through his laughter.

Nati hit him playfully on the arm, fuming.

"Krishna, you devil! You nearly gave me a heart attack. These pictures mean everything to me. Don't ever joke like that again!"

"Sorry, sorry," Krishna apologized, though still chuckling. But her innocent, alarmed expression would be something he'd carry with him forever.

"Now take your coffee before it gets cold," she said with mock sternness, but the smile returned to her lips.

Krishna took a sip, feeling the warmth from both the cup and the moment.

"Your dad must be a strict man," Krishna mused, intrigued.

Nati shook her head, sitting beside him. "Not really. He was in the army, so people expect him to be strict, but he's never been that way at home. He's always been caring, responsible—and a gentle father and husband. My mom, though—she was the stricter one when we were kids. She knew what was best for us, and she took charge."

Krishna nodded, listening intently. Nati's voice softened as she continued. "I still remember how hard it was for us to leave Cusco for our education.

She had to be firm with us. Her strength was what carried us through. Now, sometimes she jokes that she regrets sending us away, wishing we'd stayed closer to home. But I know she's proud of us."

Her voice lingered on that last thought, as if she was reconciling the distance between past and present.

Krishna smiled. "What does 'chico' mean? Your mom called me that."

"Oh, it means child," Nati explained with a grin.

"She doesn't speak much English. In Peru, especially outside of Lima, people rarely speak English. But since my dad was stationed in Lima for a while, she picked up some."

"So, your parents moved back to Cusco after your dad retired?"

"Yes, they run a small restaurant there now. It's a quiet life, but they love it," she said, pride filling her voice.

Krishna leaned back, sipping his coffee as Nati continued. "You know, my mother tongue is Spanish. It's such a beautiful language to speak. You'd love it."

Krishna laughed inwardly.

"What a talkative girl, Krishna thought. She seemed so composed at first, but once she got going, stopping her was impossible—and he loved it."

"Wait, let me show you my country," Nati said suddenly, pulling out her phone and opening up a map. She pointed at the screen excitedly.

"This is Peru! We're in South America, sharing borders with Chile, Ecuador, Brazil, Bolivia and, of course, the vast Pacific Ocean."

Krishna studied the map, following her finger as it traced the country's borders. "If you're so far from Spain, how did Spanish become your mother tongue?"

"Well, there's a long history behind that. The story goes back to the 1500s when the Spanish came and invaded Peru in a great conquest. Before that, Peru was the center of power in South America. The Inca people were one of the most advanced civilizations on earth. They had incredible knowledge of farming, science, and culture, and they ruled vast territories. Their society was deeply connected to nature, especially the mighty Amazon."

She paused for a moment, her face growing more serious.

"But when the Spanish arrived, they didn't just conquer—they set out to erase the Incas' great heritage."

They tore down temples, massacred entire communities, wiped out so much of our history."

Krishna could see the passion and pain in her eyes as she spoke. "It wasn't just about the land. The Spanish erased the cultural memory of the Incas from the people. Over generations, their language, culture, and ways of life replaced what we once had.

We took back our land, but the scars remained. Even today, our education, our names, our systems—they're all remnants of that time."

Krishna listened in silence, the weight of her words settling over him.

"There are two Perus," Nati said softly. "The one before the Spanish, and the one after. The Peru I'm proud of—the Peru I carry in my heart—is the one that existed before the Spanish came. The Incas' legacy is still in our land, our mountains, and our people, but..."

She looked out the window, her voice becoming thoughtful. "We've moved on, though. We can't live in the past. We should remember history and be proud of it, but we can't let it trap us. Life is too short to dwell on what once was. We must cherish the present, live it fully."

Krishna nodded, deeply moved by her words.

Her deep-rooted pride and her wisdom about embracing the present struck a chord in him.

In that moment, he realized how much he admired her—her strength, her sense of self, her ability to weave together the past and the present.

Nati smiled, turning back to him. "Enough with this history. Let's finish this coffee before it goes cold."

"In many ways, your story mirrors my country's," Krishna said, his voice thoughtful as he swirled the last of his coffee."

"The British invaded us too, with their divide-and-rule strategy. They didn't just take control; they looted India's greatest treasures, its wealth, its culture, and in some ways, its spirit."

He paused; the memories of stories passed down through generations flooding his mind. "We, too, were stuck for a long time, left to heal our wounds. But slowly, we're filling those gaps. The process of recovery came with its own losses, though. Our land was divided, and what was once one country became three.

Nati watched him closely, sensing the deep connection he felt with his country's history. Krishna's gaze shifted to the distant horizon, his thoughts lingering on the centuries of struggle. "But the only way forward is to move on, to learn from the past without letting it define our future. The mistakes that cost us dearly—we must ensure they never happen again."

He smiled softly, meeting Nati's eyes. "India is on that journey now, rising again. Just like Peru, whose fate shifted in the 1500s, India's turning point came in the 1900s. We've both faced foreign rule and both had to rebuild. And though our stories are separated by oceans, they are bound by the same human spirit—the desire to reclaim what was lost, to progress, to thrive.

Krishna took the last sip of his coffee, his voice warm but contemplative.

"History—our past—it's something we could talk about for hours, right?"

Nati smiled in agreement, her gaze softening. "Yes, we could. It's a part of who we are, but like you said, we can't live in it forever."

They sat in silence, their shared histories hanging between them. Yet, the present—this fleeting moment—felt even more precious.

The world outside was vast and filled with stories, but for now, it was just the two of them, sharing a piece of themselves, connected by something deeper than words.

He exhaled slowly, realizing he couldn't hide it from Nati any longer.

He started recounting what happened with Emilia the night before, leaving out no detail.

Nati listened quietly, but Krishna could sense her tension rising beneath her calm exterior. When he finished, her voice was sharp, though she tried to contain her frustration.

"She's such a ****," Nati muttered, her eyes narrowing in anger.

Krishna gave a hesitant nod, words failing him.

"I know... She's jealous, you know. Seeing us together."

Nati continued, "Yesterday, when I showed her the pictures we took, I could see it in her eyes. She was jealous. She's always trying to make a move, trying to cause some drama."

A flash of regret hit Krishna. For a moment, he wondered if telling her had been a mistake.

But deep down, he knew that hiding the truth would have only made it worse.

Now, there was a sense of relief, a weight lifted off his chest.

"I'm glad you told me, Krishna," Nati said, her voice softening, but still laced with a bit of anger.

"You know, last night… I woke up at midnight. I couldn't sleep.

As I walked down the hallway, talking to my mom, I noticed your door was open.

"I peeked in, assuming you'd left it open by accident."

Krishna's heart raced as Nati spoke.

"At first, I thought it was you. "But then, I spotted a figure curled up on the sofa. When I saw the bedroom door was closed, I didn't push. I knew I'd get the story sooner or later."

Krishna was stunned. Nati had seen everything, yet she waited for him to explain.

"If you hadn't told me, I might have started questioning things," Nati added, her voice softening. "But the fact that you told me, —It means a lot."

A wave of relief washed over Krishna. Despite her obvious irritation with Emilia, Nati seemed at peace knowing he had been honest. Trust still held between them—and Krishna was glad he hadn't let anything break it.

Chapter 06

A Game of Chance, A Game of Habit

Life is a game of chance, but it is also a game of habit. The choices we make, the risks we take, and the habits we form shape our destiny. It is in daring to follow our hearts that we find the greatest rewards.

It was already 11:00 AM. They decided to grab lunch outside before heading back to the cruise. At 3:30 p.m., they checked out of their hotel, packed their luggage, and strolled through the city one last time. The magic of the city lingered behind them, even as they left it behind.

As they approached the cruise ship, the mighty vessel loomed large, ready to take them on the next leg of their journey.

The excursion manager greeted them with the usual routine, ensuring all employees boarded first to prepare for their duties.

"I wish we had another day here," Nati said wistfully, her gaze lingering on the city as they ascended the escalator toward the grand reception of the cruise.

"Yeah," Krishna agreed, shaking his head with a smile. "It's been one of those days that really counts."

Before they parted, Nati pulled him into a hug. Krishna paused—then laid a hand on her shoulder, still trying to catch up to the moment.

"See you at the casino," she said with a playful smile as they bid farewell.

Exhilaration trailed him like an echo—each moment from the day playing back like a melody he couldn't shake.

That evening, the crew trickled into the casino later than usual. Mr. Gabriel, ever the enthusiastic leader, held a meeting with the team, acknowledging their hard work and getting them geared up for the night ahead. This casual discussion routine kept the crew grounded and connected.

Finally, at around 9:00 p.m., The cruise began to move. The casino remained closed due to regulations about opening near the bay, there was still plenty of time. The ship pulled away from the bay, carving a path toward whatever waited next.

During breaks, Nati found him—unbothered by the quiet buzz of speculation around them.

"Krishna, let's go for a break," she would say with her usual carefree attitude. She was the kind of girl who didn't worry much about appearances or what Krishna's colleagues might be saying behind their backs.

People noticed how often Nati was with Krishna, but she didn't care. Neither did he.

Later that day, Krishna joined Mr. Gabriel in the break-out area. "You didn't come out yesterday," Krishna remarked.

Gabriel smiled, looking up from his book. "Yea, well, I was having some "me time"—chatting with a friend, reading, just unwinding. This is part of the job, you know. It's my sixth world tour; I've been to most of these places so many times that they don't excite me anymore." He paused, giving Krishna a knowing look. "What about you? I heard you convinced Nati to join you yesterday. It's become the gossip of the casino," he teased.

Krishna chuckled nervously.

"Yeah, I saw her alone and figured I'd invite her. It was nice."

Before Gabriel could answer, Emilia stepped in. Something about her had shifted—polite, almost measured, as if she'd reconsidered her stance on Krishna. It was clear the incident back in the city had left its mark; maybe, she had reflected on it.

Soon, Alex and Juan joined as well, their conversation shifted to a hot topic on the cruise—the Brazilian guy who had won big at the casino the other night.

"That guy," Mr. Gabriel started, shaking his head with a small grin. "That was beginner's luck. If he was a smart man, he wouldn't come back. But he's a gambler. His habit will bring him back here, and when he does, well… we'll be ready to give him a warm welcome."

"You sound so confident, Gabriel," Krishna said, intrigued. "How can you be so sure he'll come back?"

Gabriel's grin widened. "Because, Krishna, I've seen it before. A casino isn't just a place of luck. Want to know the biggest trick of a casino?"

Krishna nodded, listening intently.

"It's designed to create a habit. People think it's a game of chance, a fair play where luck might be on their side. But the truth is, the dealer always has the upper hand—a 52% probability of winning compared to the client's 48%. That small 2% difference? That's what makes a casino a money-making machine. That's where the house always wins."

Krishna sank into his chair, the weight of Gabriel's words settling in. Gabriel's words carried a quiet certainty—seasoned, precise, and just unsettling enough to linger. The world of gambling, much like everything else in life, seemed to have its own hidden rules, and Gabriel knew them all too well.

"Have you ever heard how the biggest hotel chain, Holiday Inn, makes most of its money?" Gabriel asked, his voice taking on a knowing tone. Krishna shook his head.

" Nearly all of Holiday Inn's profit—98%—comes from just two casinos in Las Vegas. The rest of their hotels? They barely scrape together the remaining 2%" Gabriel explained. "You know, casinos conducted a survey of their clients to find out where their revenue really comes from. The result? 90% of their revenue comes from regular customers. The regulars know the odds aren't in their favor, but they keep chasing the high."

Krishna was quiet, digesting the information. Gabriel leaned in slightly, emphasizing his point. "That's the beauty of human psychology. It's not about the winnings; it's about the craving. Once people get a taste, they chase that feeling, thinking that the next time might be their lucky break. But it rarely is."

Gabriel spoke with the certainty of a man who had studied human nature and mastered its patterns. As a casino manager, his insight into human psychology was what gave him an edge. "Human nature follows patterns," Gabriel continued. "Anything that happens once may happen again. But if it happens twice, you can bet it will happen a third time and more."

He paused, allowing the words to sink in before adding, "That's why we track regulars. We don't just let them go. We give them special treatment—discounts, free drinks, even premium wine. We make sure they feel important. Big spenders are like gold mines. We keep them coming back."

As they sat in the smoking area, the conversation shifted. Juan, curious, asked, "How did you feel the other day when that Brazilian guy won big and caught us all off guard?"

Gabriel, ever the cool-headed manager, chuckled. "It was a dramatic loss, no doubt. But I don't see him as a threat like most do. Everyone fears him coming back, but I welcome it. He's an opportunity."

Krishna raised an eyebrow, impressed. "That's what makes you different, Gabriel. You don't see defeat as the end—you see the bigger picture," he remarked.

Gabriel nodded. "As a manager, I can't afford to be shaken by one loss. If I falter, how can I lead my team? It's about consistency. I teach my team to see things from different perspectives. The dealer isn't just a dealer. He's also a strategist, a part of a larger system. We can't just look at the game—we must understand the players and their psychology."

He paused, eyes scanning the group. "That Brazilian guy? He'll be back. Not because of the money he won, but because of the craving for more. He's already hooked. And trust me, it wasn't just the winnings that got him—it was that feeling of excitement, the thrill of the game. And maybe," Gabriel added mischievously, "the sexy lady with the tattoo that caught his eye."

The group erupted into laughter. Gabriel always found a way to spin a lesson, slipping insight into even the lightest moments.

"That craving," Gabriel said as the laughter died down, "it's stronger than most people realize. And that's why I'm so confident. He'll be back. He won't be able to stay away."

The contrast between Emilia and Nati was something Krishna had quietly observed over time. He had spent countless hours in the casino, watching the ebb and flow of the people, the games, and the stories unfolding at each table. But more than anything, he noticed the two women who, despite their shared profession, embodied entirely different energies.

Emilia—bold, vivacious, and exuberant—wore her uniform like a second skin, exuding confidence in every step she took. Her curves were accentuated by the tight fabric, and she knew exactly how to use that to her advantage. There was no hesitation in her movements. No second-guessing her presence. She radiated a playful, almost dangerous allure, inviting those around her to partake in the thrill of the moment. There was something intoxicating about the way she held herself, like she was the main event in a show designed to captivate, and she did so effortlessly.

Nati, on the other hand, was Emilia's opposite. In the same uniform, she managed to convey an entirely different aura. Her beauty was undeniable, but it was of a different nature—subtle, restrained, and elusive. She didn't seek attention in the way Emilia did, and yet, for those who took the time to notice her, there was something captivating in her quiet reserve.

Emilia welcomed the world with open arms whereas Nati held it at a measured distance, choosing her company with quiet deliberation.

Krishna found this contrast fascinating. It wasn't just the clothes they wore; it was the energy they put into them. Emilia's openness was a performance, a deliberate invitation for others to look, to admire, to desire. Nati's closed-off demeanor, on the other hand, suggested something deeper—a protection of her own world, where only those she trusted could enter. The dress may have been the same, but it was the women wearing it who defined its power.

An invisible force kept them close, yet always at a distance, unable to fully connect. They complemented each other, but their balance was fragile—too close, and they would clash; too far, and they might drift apart.

And then there was Krishna, caught between them, neither fully belonging nor entirely apart.

He was the catalyst between these two magnetic forces, not by choice but by circumstance. In the quiet moments, when the casino was still and the music had faded, he found himself in the middle of their dynamic—observing, understanding, and occasionally caught in the crossfire of their contrasting personalities.

The night of the Brazilian gambler had been a perfect illustration of this. Emilia had thrived in the chaos, basking in the attention, reveling in her ability to mesmerize the rich bull from Brazil. She had played her part flawlessly, knowing exactly how to tease and tantalize, pushing just enough without breaking the unwritten rules of the casino. She was in control, or at least she appeared to be.

Nati, however, had watched from a distance, cautious and reserved.

She poured drinks, offered polite smiles, yet stayed anchored, unaffected by the storm Emilia had summoned.

There was a quiet strength in Nati's presence, a sense that she wouldn't be swept up in the same way Emilia had been. She valued her boundaries, and in a world where everyone seemed to be chasing something, Nati was content to let things come to her on her own terms.

Krishna admired how she navigated life—deliberate, selective, never rushing to let someone in.

Emilia, for all her boldness, was fleeting. She enjoyed the thrill of the moment but rarely stayed long enough to invest in anything deeper. Nati, on the other hand, was someone who, once she let you in, would be there for the long haul. She didn't make friends easily, but those she did have were for life.

It was this difference that intrigued Krishna the most. He knew that in the world of the casino, where everything was about instant gratification, Emilia fit perfectly. She was made for that world of high stakes and fast games, where nothing lasted beyond the night. Nati, however, was a puzzle—someone who seemed almost out of place in a world that demanded constant exposure. She was like a secret, kept under lock and key, only revealed to those who earned it.

Krishna, the silent spectator, felt the pull of both women—each stirring something different within him. Emilia was exciting, full of life and energy, a woman who made the night come alive. But Nati—Nati was the mystery he couldn't quite solve, the one who made him curious in a way he hadn't been in a long time.

And now, as the three of them sat together in this strange, unspoken triangle, Krishna realized something profound. They were all playing their own games, each with different stakes and different rules. Emilia was playing to win the attention, the admiration, and perhaps even the affection of those around her. Nati was playing to protect herself, to maintain the integrity of her small, trusted circle. And Krishna—well, he wasn't sure what game he was playing yet. Perhaps he was simply a spectator, watching as these two forces moved through their lives, occasionally intersecting with his own.

With each passing day, Krishna and Nati became inseparable, like two sides of the same coin. Their routines began to mirror each other, and their week-off plans aligned effortlessly. Every morning started with a phone call, either from Nati or Krishna. It had become an unspoken ritual between them. Even when they weren't together on the cruise, they stayed connected by their phones, filling the gaps between their work schedules with endless conversations.

Even apart, their voices bridged the distance, soft conversations stretching through the night. They'd adjusted their sleeping arrangements, both moving their beds closer to the charging socket so they could answer the phone without getting up.

Over time, they developed the ability to speak so softly that even their roommates Emilia and Alex wouldn't notice the late-night whispers.

Over time, they mastered the art of whispering, their voices blending into the quiet hum of the night, unnoticed by their roommates.

It was a skill many couples learned—the secret language of lovers, whispered beneath the hum of daily life.

More than once, they drifted off mid-conversation, their phones resting beside them, only to wake hours later and continue as if no time had passed.

Their week-off schedules synced effortlessly. At first, Krishna found the questions about his time off annoying—until he realized he'd started looking forward to it. They deliberately planned for those shared moments, whether it was breakfast in the cafeteria or lunch and dinner.

Their days settled into an unspoken rhythm. They would wake up, talk on the phone, get ready and meet for lunch. Afterwards, they'd either walk around the cruise or stop by a coffee shop for a moment, sipping on coffee while listening to music. They'd discuss everything from love to life, from psychology to philosophy. Their topics of conversation seemed endless. Each conversation flowed into the next, an endless river of thoughts and ideas. There was no subject they hadn't explored, no corner of each other's minds they hadn't wandered into.

Krishna marveled at how easily they had found a rhythm together. "It takes some couples a lifetime to adjust to each other," he thought. "And here we are, completely different, yet perfectly aligned."

He dealt cards, she studied minds. One driven by career goals, the other content with letting life unfold as it may. Their differences were striking, from language to culture, from ambitions to outlooks on life. And yet, it all worked. Despite the odds, they complemented each other in ways neither of them had expected.

Krishna smiled, realizing that sometimes, the strangest pieces form the perfect puzzle. With Nati, everything fell into place. Their connection had grown naturally, their routines falling into place without either of them needing to try too hard. They were different in every way that mattered—and that was exactly why it worked.

On Thursday, Krishna and Nati synced their schedules for a shared day off. Nati had promised Krishna that they would explore the cruise together, as they had done so many times before. Usually, they would start their adventures around 2 or 3 p.m. But today, Nati called Krishna at 11:30 AM. It was an unusually early call, Krishna, still half-asleep, groggily answered the phone.

"Get ready, we're leaving at noon," Nati said firmly before hanging up. She was clearly excited. Krishna, still disoriented, scrambled to get dressed.

At noon, Nati knocked on Krishna's door. He answered, fully dressed, while Alex slept soundly, oblivious to their plans.

"Where are we going?" Krishna asked as they walked through the passage, the cruise bustling around them.

"Did I ask where we were going in the city last time? That was your plan. I followed it. Now, it's my plan. Just follow me," Nati responded with a teasing smile.

"Okay, today's your day," Krishna said, surrendering to her lead.

They picked up sandwiches and shared a signature antipasti platter, a spread of cured meats and crisp vegetables. Krishna marveled—despite the lavish breakfast, Nati brimmed with energy. They enjoyed their coffee, but Krishna couldn't resist asking, "At least give me a hint about what we're doing today."

Nati grinned. "You haven't seen the best of this adventure yet. Exploring it with your best friend makes it magical. Today, you'll discover a side of the cruise you never knew existed."

She guided him to an entertainment deck where trampolines and virtual reality merged for a gravity-defying experience.

Krishna was surprised at the sight of the high-tech setups that let guests defy gravity in ways he never imagined. Nati was practically glowing with excitement. "You've never seen the capsules suspended over the deck for unobstructed views of the sea, have you?" Krishna shook his head, curiosity and anticipation swirling within him.

They moved quickly toward the ship's open-air swimming pool. The terrace pool, with its transparent glass walls, blurred the line between water and the endless ocean. The view was breathtaking, stopping Krishna in his tracks as he took in the sheer scale of it all.

"Are we going to swim?" Krishna asked, still slightly unsure.

"Of course," Nati replied confidently. "Remember, the other day you wanted to swim, but we didn't have time. Today, we're going to dive right in."

"We didn't bring swimsuits," Krishna reminded her."

Nati laughed, always one step ahead. She knew the cruise pool had rental swimwear. Within minutes, they were both suited up and ready to dive into the cool waters.

He couldn't help but tease her, "I thought only Emilia could turn heads on this cruise. Thank God no one has seen you yet."

Nati shot him a playful look. "Are you going to swim or just keep staring?"

They spent a long time in the water, laughing and enjoying themselves. Afterward, they rested on a pair of lounge chairs by the poolside, basking in the warmth of the sun and the relaxing rhythm of the waves.

"This was amazing. You really nailed it," Krishna remarked, still catching his breath.

After lunch, they wandered deeper into the ship. Krishna still couldn't grasp its sheer scale—maps pointed toward Central Park, the promenade, the entertainment quarter.

It felt like a whole city floating on the water.

From the top deck, the view split in two—on one side, endless ocean; on the other, Central Park, a lush oasis floating above the waves. It was an adults-only pool area, complete with hot tubs, a bar, plenty of seating.

"This feels like something out of a movie," Krishna said, captivated by the scene.

They wandered further, eventually coming across a pool with a retractable glass roof. The clarity of the glass made it hard to tell where the pool ended and the sea began. A group of people was playing water games, led by the pool coordinator, who ensured everyone was having a good time.

After a couple of hours of exploring and lounging, they returned to the lounge chairs under the glass roof. Nati stretched out with satisfied smile on her face. "I wish I had a book to read."

A movie was playing on a poolside screen, casting a familiar rap song into the warm afternoon air. Nati's eyes lit up as she scrolled through the film schedule. "They're going to screen The Fault in Our Stars! later this week! You must promise me we'll come back here and watch."

Krishna chuckled. "Of course, Nati. I promise we'll come to both."

The day's adventures had left them tired but fulfilled. As evening approached, they wandered toward the poolside restaurant, where Nati insisted on treating Krishna to dinner. The menu was extravagant, far pricier than what Krishna was used to.

"Nati, why don't we go back to our usual café? This place is way too expensive," Krishna suggested, feeling uneasy about the cost.

Nati shook her head. "Don't worry about it; Today's my treat."

Krishna hesitated, but gave in, the restaurant still feeling like too much.

The food, however, was exceptional—novel dishes crafted from local ingredients, followed by a stunning dessert that left them both in awe.

"This place feels unreal," he murmured.

Nati smiled. "It is a dream, Krishna. And we're living it."

They walked on, their fingers intertwined, as if the rest of the world had faded away.

Their next adventure took them to Central Park, a lush oasis tucked inside the colossal cruise ship. Krishna shook off his fatigue, determined to keep up with Nati's boundless energy. They walked toward the sports arena. It was crowded with adults basking in the sun and laughing as they participated in water games.

But the real thrill lay ahead—a four-story high Blackhole slide that wound its way down in a terrifying spiral.

A long queue of people waited to take the plunge. As Krishna and Nati stepped inside, their hearts began to race.

They approached the glass platform with steady breaths, bracing for the adrenaline-fueled drop ahead. The glass floor threw off their balance, revealing a dizzying drop to the sea below. Nati's heart was pounding as they stood at the edge, ready to leap into the unknown. The lights around them changed, cycling from green to red to yellow, signaling the impending rush. But this was no ordinary slide. Its heart-pounding drop tested the courage of anyone who dared to take the plunge.

Nati, as confident as she had been all day, began to falter when they reached the top of the slide. Standing on the glass platform, looking down into the abyss, she suddenly seemed unsure.

"Krishna, let's go back. Or you go—I'm not doing this," she said, her voice betraying her nerves.

Krishna gave her a gentle smile. "Nati, it's your day, your plan. If you don't want to do it, I won't either. But if you're up for it, I'd love to go. I want to face this fear."

He waited patiently, watching the internal struggle play out on her face. Nati sighed dramatically, playfully accusing him, "You're blackmailing me, Krishna."

Krishna shrugged. "No, if you're out, I'm out too. Let's head back."

Nati stalled, teeth grazing her lip. "Wait... Okay, I see what you're doing. Fine, let's do this! But you go first—I'll follow."

They closed their eyes, gripping the edges of the platform, and with the whistleblower's scream they pushed off. The ride wasn't long—fifteen seconds at most—but it was enough. It felt like they were weightless, suspended in midair, as though gravity had abandoned them. The sheer intensity of the drop, the speed, and the feeling of the world rushing past them stripped away any hesitation they'd felt. In that moment, they weren't just on a ride; they were facing their fears head-on, together.

After the initial shock wore off, they found themselves sliding through the dark, twisting tunnel. The slide's momentum picked up, sending them through a full 360-degree loop. They screamed, but this time, it wasn't out of fear—it was pure exhilaration. The thrill of the ride overtook every other feeling.

When they finally splashed into the pool at the bottom, they felt an overwhelming sense of freedom. Nati clung tightly to Krishna, her arms wrapped around him as they floated in the water, hearts still racing.

"Life is so amazing when we face our fears," Nati mused as they walked away from the ride, their bodies soaked, their hearts still racing from the excitement. It was the kind of moment that made you feel invincible, as if no challenge was too big, no fear too insurmountable.

"Krishna! I did it!" She exclaimed, her face lighting up with pride. "I never thought I'd go through with it. If anyone had told me this morning that I'd do something like this, I wouldn't have believed them."

She leaned back just enough to meet his eyes, her eyes wide with excitement and gratitude.

"Thank you, Krishna."

Krishna smiled at her, still catching his breath. "You were amazing. You faced your fear head-on."

Nati was practically bouncing with excitement now, her earlier hesitation replaced by pure joy. "I can't believe we did that! Let's go again!" She urged, laughing as she tugged him back toward the water.

Krishna couldn't help but laugh with her, feeling lighter than he had in a long time. They splashed around in the pool, diving back into the water and reliving the thrill of their slide. Nati was alive with the sense of accomplishment, having faced her fear and emerged victorious. She wrapped her arms around him in a burst of joy, and together they waded to the edge, ready to take on whatever the day would bring. Krishna froze for a moment, For a moment, everything else faded, leaving only the warmth of her embrace. It was a strange feeling—an inexplicable familiarity that washed over him. He had felt it the first time he laid eyes on her, again when she had bid him farewell after their first day in the city.

By evening, as they wandered into Central Park, the energy of the day faded into a slow, steady rhythm. The lush greenery and towering tropical trees were a stark contrast to the wildness of the day. The park spiraled around two large ponds, creating the illusion that they were no longer at sea but rather in the heart of nature itself. The sounds of water and rustling leaves calmed them. For a moment, it was easy to forget they were on a massive vessel floating on the ocean.

Central Park, located at the center of the ship, was home to specialty restaurants, each casting a warm, inviting glow. The illumination of the park created a spellbinding atmosphere, one that seemed to draw everyone in. People gravitated toward the space, walking hand in hand, jogging, reading, or simply sitting back and enjoying the view. The beer shops were crowded, with the hum of conversation filling the air. Each step through the park felt like a stroll through the memories of the day. These weren't memories from a distant past, but from the immediate present, still vivid and fresh in their minds. In those hushed moments, life was stripped down to its simplest, most beautiful form.

Beyond the adrenaline and adventure, it was about them—being raw, unfiltered, and entirely themselves. They didn't need to put on any masks or play any roles. They could be crazy, vulnerable, innocent, and adventurous all at once. In moments like these, amazing things didn't happen by chance—they happened because they found every reason to be together. Together, they could take on anything. Life was amazing for Krishna and Nati, simply because they were together. The most important part wasn't just the thrill of their adventures or the beauty of the places they explored—it was that they could be unapologetically themselves around each other. No masks, no pretenses. They were raw, real, and completely comfortable in their own skin. There was something pure and refreshing about their connection, the way they embraced each other's crazy, innocent selves.

But those incredible moments of connection didn't come without effort. They weren't handed out for free. These moments were born from a shared wish—a wish to find every reason to be together, no matter what. Over time, that wish deepened into a desire, a pull to create opportunities to see each other, to carve out spaces in their lives where they could exist side by side. With that desire came a sense of possessiveness—not the kind that smothered, but the kind that made them both fiercely protective of the time they had together. It wasn't about control or jealousy, but about the need to hold onto something precious, to ensure that the bond they had created was nurtured and valued. Each laugh, each stolen glance, each quiet moment was proof of the invisible thread pulling them closer.

They didn't need grand gestures to prove it—their love was in the little things. It was in the way Nati would smile when Krishna said something unexpected, or the way Krishna's eyes would light up when Nati shared a small, vulnerable truth about herself. It was the way they constantly found new ways to be close, even in the busiest of times. Every choice they made, consciously or not, brought them closer, deepened their bond, making them realize that what they had was something truly special.

Their shared wish—to be together—had turned into a shared life, one where they didn't just find each other, but found themselves, too.

I Wish to Be with You

I wish to see you, speak your name,
Feel your laughter, touch your flame.
On winding paths where soft winds sigh,
I wish to walk with you—just you and me.

My thoughts are filled with dreams of you,
A simple wish, that's grown so true.

What once was fleeting, faint, and small,
Has grown into my every call.

This wish has bloomed—a fire untamed,
A whisper turned to love unchained.
A longing fierce, yet soft as light,
That pulls me closer, day and night.

No longer just a wish I keep,
But love that runs so wild and deep.
I feel it hum beneath my skin,
A melody that sings within.

I know now what it means to yearn,
To watch the stars, to wait, to burn.
To find your breath in morning's hue,
To taste the night and think of you.

You linger in my quiet sighs,
A love that never fades nor dies.
From dawn's embrace to midnight's gleam,
You are the pulse within my dream.

I feel it now, I know it's true,
This love that wakes and walks with you.
With every heartbeat, every breath,
I'm yours in life, in love, in death.

Seated together on Krishna's cozy sofa, the gentle hum of music filling the room, he couldn't ignore the question nagging at him. He stole a glance at Nati—her face calm, lost in the moment—before finally speaking up.

"Nati, can I ask you something?" Krishna's voice broke the quiet. They had grown so comfortable with each other over time, their shared moments blending into a rhythm of companionship. It wasn't uncommon for Nati to stay with

Krishna when Alex was away, just as Krishna often stayed at her place when Emilia wasn't around.

Nati turned her head, looking at him with curiosity. "Yes, tell me", she said, smiling slightly.

Krishna hesitated for a moment, unsure if he should ask, but he couldn't hold it in any longer. He took a breath and blurted out, "Do you have a boyfriend?"

Her expression softened as she stayed quiet for a beat, locking eyes with Krishna. A charged silence settled between them, thick with unspoken words.

"Well, what do you think?" Nati asked, her lips curving into a playful smile.

Krishna was caught off guard by her counter-question. "I mean... I don't mind; I was just asking. You know, casually. Whether you have one or not, it doesn't really make a difference," he added, his words rushing out a little too quickly.

"Really?" She asked, raising an eyebrow.

Krishna, trying to recover, felt a flicker of desperation inside him, though his mind tried to convince him otherwise. What difference does it make? he told himself, yet deep down, he wanted to know, even hoped she didn't have anyone else.

Nati decided to end the suspense. "Actually, yes," she said with a pause. Krishna's heart momentarily sank. But before his thoughts could spiral, she continued. "Well... he's not exactly my boyfriend. His name is Joshua. We grew up together and went to school together. He's like my other side."

Krishna felt a slight pang but listened closely.

Nati spoke of Joshua with warmth, describing him as the one who understood her in ways she couldn't always explain.

"He's too caring, always there. He has all these amazing qualities," she continued. Krishna realized the depth of their bond. He could see how Joshua was important to her, but the way she spoke made it clear that there was no romantic commitment. A wave of relief washed over him.

They spent the next few hours in that easy, flowing conversation that had become natural to them. Sharing stories, likes, and dislikes, talking about their lives and people they knew—it all felt so effortless. They soon fell into a new routine, spending almost every moment together, whether it was walking through Central Park, lounging by the pool, or simply listening to music.

Their connection was growing stronger by the day. They had become inseparable, so much so that when Alex and Emilia weren't around, it was just the two of them, sharing each other's world.

One evening, after another casual conversation about life and work, they found themselves back at Nati's place, playing cards and laughing over small wins and losses. The conversation shifted, as it often did, to playful banter.

"You've become quite the blackjack player," Krishna teased. "But you still owe me one."

Nati looked confused. "What do you mean?"

"You promised to teach me how to persuade girls," Krishna said with a mischievous grin.

She burst out laughing. "Right, but I haven't seen anyone around here who's good enough for you to practice on."

Krishna leaned back with teasing glint in his eye. "Well, I do see someone impressive sitting right here. Maybe you should start with her?"

Nati rolled her eyes but smiled, unable to hold his gaze for long. "Don't even try applying psychological tricks on a psychology student," she quipped. "You'd have better luck with Emilia."

They both laughed, but there was something unspoken in the air now. Krishna's words had stirred something, a recognition of what they both felt but hadn't voiced yet.

Krishna fell silent for a moment before murmuring, "I wish we had crossed paths in my homeland."

Nati's gaze softened, a shadow of sadness flickering across her face. "Krishna, I wish we had found each other sooner too," she said, voice barely above a whisper.

Then, with a sigh, she stood up. "I need a beer," she said, grabbing one from the fridge.

Krishna watched her, thinking about the fleetingness of time. "You know, the world is smaller than it seems. We'll find each other again, even if we part ways for now."

Nati gave him a small smile. "That's a nice thought. But unless one of us moves across the world, I'm not so sure."

"Well," Krishna added thoughtfully, "even if we don't, these moments will stay with us. They're the kind of memories that never fade."

She looked at him, their connection deepening in the quiet.

After a beat, Krishna stood up and offered his hand. "I want to make this moment count," he said gently. "I want to dance with you."

The soft melody of "My Heart Will Go On" was still playing in the background. Without a word, Nati took his hand and they began to move to the rhythm, swaying softly, lost in each other's presence. Time seemed to slow as they danced, their bodies moving in sync, every small step perfectly aligned.

Krishna's hand moved to her neck and their eyes locked. They were close now—closer than ever. As he leaned in, Nati closed her eyes, breath quickening. His lips brushed her forehead in a tender kiss.

Nati opened her eyes and smiled.

Krishna felt a wave of calm wash over him as she rose slowly, stretching with a quiet readiness for the day ahead. As Krishna held her, a fleeting thought crossed his mind. Why should your girlfriend be just up to your shoulder? The question echoed softly; a mental reflection that made him smile inwardly. He didn't know where the thought had come from—perhaps from an old belief or an expectation ingrained somewhere deep inside him. But in this moment, as Nati rested against him, none of that mattered. Her presence felt perfect—familiar, yet new. This wasn't about height or expectations; this was about feeling connected, as if her very heartbeat had aligned with his.

He brushed a stray lock of hair from her face, careful not to disturb the tranquility of the moment. The faint scent of her perfume lingered in the air, blending with the soft glow of the lights spilling through the window. For the first time in a long while, Krishna didn't feel out of place. He wasn't thinking about the place, the crowd, or even his hesitations. All he could focus on was the quiet warmth they shared.

Her heart swelled with trust, knowing that in Krishna, she had found someone she could truly lean on. She wrapped her arms around him and held on, not wanting to let go, as the world outside their embrace seemed to melt away. Time is a trickster. When you're living our dream, it vanishes like tidewater in the sand—swift, silent, and always too soon.

For Krishna and Nati, their time together felt like a dream racing by, flying like a bullet as the ship sailed closer to Miami. Each moment brought them nearer to the inevitable. Though neither Krishna nor Nati had spoken the words aloud, love hummed between them—in their lingering proximity, the weight of their gazes, and the quiet spaces that needed no filling.

Their hearts chased and craved each other, seeking comfort in every moment together. They found ways to spend time in each other's presence, as if proximity alone could hold off the inevitable separation.

They moved beyond just listening to music. The songs—from The Carpenters to Katy Perry—became the soundtrack of their time together. Now, the real melody was in their connection, the way their hearts synchronized with each beat, each lyric. It was more than just sound; it was a shared pulse, an unspoken rhythm between them.

Beneath the shimmering glass roof of the cruise's pool, they found one of their favorite escapes—a place where sky and sea seemed to merge. The crystalline ceiling created an illusion of floating between sea and sky, blurring the lines between water and horizon. The pool's coordinator ensured everyone had a good time, with teams competing in various games, but Nati and Krishna found their own enjoyment—simply being together, laughing at the poolside antics.

As the destination approached, Nati grew more anxious. The closer they got, the harder it became to ignore the ticking clock. She worried about saying goodbye, the weight pressing on her more each day. Krishna shared her unease, though he tried to bury it beneath their routine of shared music and conversations.

The cruise was closing in on Miami. The countdown had begun. Still, they made plans—small dreams wrapped in denial, spoken as if Miami weren't creeping closer with every breath.

But in their hearts, they both felt the pressure of it, ticking away with each moment that passed.

Chapter 07

When Forever Had a Deadline

Time is fleeting, and love must be cherished in every moment. When forever has a deadline, we learn to appreciate the present and make the most of the time we have with those we love.

"Seven days, Krishna," Nati said, her eyes searching his. "That's all we have before the end."

"I wish I could stretch these seven days into forever," Krishna murmured, drawing her close. "I want to live every moment with you. I want to take a bag full of memories with me, something to carry beyond this time."

Nati's faint smile faded into something more distant, her gaze turning wistful. "Why didn't we meet earlier, Krishna? Life would've been different…" she said, her voice trailing off innocently.

Her phone buzzed again, cutting through the moment. It had been buzzing with WhatsApp calls from home, which she had been avoiding. Krishna noticed and nudged her gently.

"Why don't you pick up? Aunty must be waiting for you," he said, glancing at the phone. But Nati didn't reach for it.

"You know, Krishna…" Nati paused, her brow furrowing. Something was clearly weighing on her mind. "Let it be. This isn't Mumma calling—it's Josh, Joshua."

Krishna raised an eyebrow. "Joshua?"

"He probably wants to check whether I'm with you or alone," Nati said, her voice filled with frustration.

"He doesn't want me to be happy."

Over the past few days, Krishna had picked up on Nati's unease—her hesitation, the way she tensed up at certain moments. He knew Joshua wasn't just a friend. There was more to the story, more beneath the surface. Joshua might have been in love with Nati—that would explain a lot. Yet Krishna couldn't shake the feeling that there was more to it.

Nati sighed deeply, her eyes reflecting a conflict within. "It was all perfect until I came here alone," she began. "Joshua and I…we were always together, you know? He was the one I felt most comfortable talking to. He made me believe the world was a cruel place—that people stayed only when it suited them. I believed it, Krishna—until I met you."

Krishna stayed silent, absorbing her words.

He could see how much Nati had been influenced by Joshua, how deeply rooted her friendship—or perhaps more—had been with him. But there was something changing in her now, something that Krishna had unknowingly sparked.

"I wasn't ready to open up before," Nati admitted. "But you... you help me be myself. No pressure, no expectations. You just... let me live. And now, I'm starting to feel free again. But Joshua—he can't accept that. He can't handle the fact that I'm happy without him. He thinks I should only be happy with him."

Krishna nodded, letting her words settle in.

"Maybe he's just protective of you," he said, though a part of him was conflicted.

Who tries to dictate someone else's happiness? If he's so concerned, why didn't he come along?

But Krishna held back those thoughts, trying instead to see things from Joshua's perspective. He didn't want to criticize Joshua outright. "He must be caring for you, Nati. That's why he doesn't want you roaming around late at night or alone with strangers."

To his surprise, his sympathetic response seemed to help Nati open up even more.

If he'd been harsh, Nati might have defended Joshua. But his understanding disarmed her.

"Why can't he be like you, Krishna?" Nati asked, her voice filled with frustration. "We were supposed to explore the world together—it wasn't just my plan; it was our plan. But he backed out at the last minute, leaving me to go alone. I broke down in front of him, pleading for him to stick to the plan, but he was convinced I couldn't survive without him. He wanted me to crumble, to be alone. But now that I've learned to stand on my own, he's the one unsettled—calling nonstop, looking for a fight."

Her voice carried a raw edge, the kind that comes from old wounds reopening.

He wondered how many times she had replayed the moments that left her so vulnerable, and he found himself wanting to shield her from further pain, even if only through the comfort of his presence.

"Do you love him, Nati?" He asked, his tone gentle but probing. "I mean, he's a good-looking guy, looks out for you, protects you. Your parents even like him…"

Nati hesitated, her eyes downcast. "He did propose to me," she admitted. "We were just friends, but we got so used to each other. It was only later that he told me he had feelings for me. But I didn't respond."

"What could be better than turning your best friend into your life partner?" Krishna asked, curious to understand her feelings.

"Nothing, actually," Nati agreed.

"I thought about it too. We know each other so well, and I like him. I know he loves me. But…"

Krishna smiled slightly. He had always found it fascinating how the word but could negate everything said before it. "What's your 'but'?" He asked softly.

"He's not serious about life," Nati confessed. "He loved me, yes, but he's not committed to anything beyond that. We started college together, studying psychology, he was a topper for three years. But then he lost interest. He dropped out to manage his father's business, but even that didn't last long. He doesn't follow through with anything. I made it clear—if he wants to marry me, he needs to be settled. My parents would never agree otherwise."

When a girl falls in love, she gives everything. She'll turn over every stone to follow her heart. But before she lets herself fall; she'll analyze every angle. It's the pragmatism of love, trying to find out if someone could really be the right partner.

It clicked for Krishna. Nati was looking for stability, for someone who had the same dedication to life that she did. She had tried to support Joshua, but in the end, his lack of direction was driving them apart.

"What about you, Krishna? Do you have a girlfriend?" Nati asked inquisitively.

"No," Krishna replied simply.

Nati's eyes widened. "What! How is that possible? You're telling me you've never had a girlfriend? Or you just had a breakup?"

Krishna smiled gently. "No one broke up, Nati. I'm from a place where people fight for survival. We spend most of our time building a platform to live life. The idea of having a girlfriend just… never fit in. By the time I realized it was something I might want, too much time had passed."

Nati listened closely. For the first time, she was learning about Krishna's personal journey. "It's so ironic," she said, almost laughing at the contrast. "Here you are, career-oriented, and on the other side, Joshua came into my life because he was so relaxed and carefree. Now I'm drifting away from him for the same reason."

"That's life, after all," Krishna said softly. They both smiled at the irony.

It was already 11:30, Nati had just finished her third bottle of beer. The quiet clink of glass bottles littering the table signaled the end of another long day.

Krishna checked the time, expecting Emilia to appear any moment.

He and Nati always made sure not to cross paths with her. Emilia was as unpredictable as she was observant, and the last thing either of them wanted was to be caught together, especially after such an intense night. Nati and Krishna had drawn closer over the past few weeks, but something about tonight felt different.

There was an unspoken tension between them, one that had been building for days as their time aboard the cruise ship neared its end. They had explored nearly every nook and cranny of the ship, even stumbling across an old, unused detention area—something like a small prison intended for maintaining law and order on the ship.

Ironic, wasn't it? The vast sea symbolized freedom, yet even here, a cell awaited anyone who dared to step out of line.

With each passing day, the excitement among the passengers grew as the cruise's countdown began. But not for Krishna and Nati. They felt no joy at the thought of leaving. Every step closer to the destination weighed heavier on them.

After the day's shift, as they walked back to their hotel room, the silence between them was deafening. Not once during these unforgettable days had they shared time without talking—yet now, not a single word found its way between them.

Gabriel's words from earlier still lingered, pressing into the silence.

"These are the final five days, fellow cruisers. Next week, we'll be kicking back on Miami Beach. So, make the most of these last moments—go all in, connect with people, and who knows? Our paths might cross again!"

His words left a lasting impression, but they had also made Nati and Krishna nervous. They had shared so much together, yet suddenly the future seemed uncertain. Nati broke the silence first, her voice soft, almost trembling.

"Will we meet again?" She asked, her eyes moist, reflecting the same fear Krishna felt.

Krishna's throat tightened. For the first time, he struggled to find the right words. The weight of Nati's question—of their impending separation—hit him harder than he expected.

"I don't know, Nati," he finally replied, his voice thick with emotion. "I don't know if we'll meet again. But I hope we do. For the first time, I'm scared. I'm scared because I don't know how to meet you again. I've always believed that if I knew what I wanted, the 'how' would follow. But now... now I'm unsure."

Nati didn't respond. They both felt the same sorrow, the ache of an imminent goodbye neither was ready for. Their time on the cruise had been a dream—an escape from reality—now fading, slipping through their fingers.

Every waking moment of Krishna's days had been filled with Nati. But in these final days, the air between them was heavy with the sorrow of separation. Meanwhile, their friends, Alex and Emilia, had moved on. They had even started referring to each other as a couple, leaving Krishna and Nati to navigate their own complex emotions. Alex, ever the optimist, had found his own path, spending more time with Emilia than Krishna.

Occasionally, Alex would cheekily warn Krishna not to come home early. "Amigo don't ruin the mood tonight! My sweetheart's coming over," he would say, a grin plastered across his face.

With each passing moment, the casino grew quieter, the crowds thinned, and the time to say goodbye approached fast. Everyone around them was caught up in the frenzy of exchanging contact information, making promises to stay in touch, and talking about plans. They had all pushed themselves beyond their limits on this journey, finding friendships they never thought possible, learning things about themselves they hadn't known before.

Some were making plans for future travels, grand promises that may or may not come to fruition. But none of that mattered right now. What mattered was the present, the joy they had shared in this brief but magical window of time.

This journey had taught Krishna a truth he hadn't grasped before.

The most courageous thing anyone could do was to throw themselves into the unknown—into new people, new places, new experiences. The dreamiest journeys weren't always the ones with grand, permanent plans. Sometimes, the temporary, fleeting moments are the ones that left the deepest marks on our hearts.

The next morning, a crisp voice crackled over the intercom, echoing through the ship's halls: "Welcome to Miami."

Cheers and applause filled the halls as passengers embraced, savoring the final moments of their month's journey.

The cruise staff, once again back on duty, made sure the departure went smoothly.

There were no frantic goodbyes, no last-minute chaos—just a quiet, bittersweet farewell to the sea and to each other.

The final farewell party, organized by the cruise for the staff, was a different kind of gathering. No uniforms, no responsibilities—just people who had worked together, laughing, dancing, and savoring their last moments as a team. Krishna danced with Nati, their movements slower than the music's beat, but the laughter between them was real, even if it was tinged with sadness.

At the end of the night, the cruise manager delivered a heartfelt speech, thanking everyone for making the journey such a success. Every single person had contributed in their own way, and now they had six days of cool-off time before heading back to work at the Miami casino headquarters.

But for Nati, this was only a pause. She would soon board another cruise, this time bound for home, stepping into a new chapter of her life.

Krishna, meanwhile, was relieved that Gabriel and Alex would be joining him at the Miami casino. The business there was huge—far bigger than Krishna had initially thought. He had learned that the cruise ship casino was just a service provider, a small piece of a much larger industry.

As the final farewells were made and the passengers began to disembark, Krishna and Nati found themselves standing alone on the deck, the Miami skyline looming in the distance.

"This is it," Nati whispered, her voice barely audible over the gentle breeze.

Krishna nodded with heavy heart. "Yeah... this is it."

They stood frozen, clinging to the moment, uncertain if their paths would ever cross again.

Chapter 08

Love Finds a Way—Or It Doesn't

Chasing your heart might seem insane—but sometimes, madness is what keeps us truly alive.

As their days together ran out, Nati stuffed her bags, preparing for what came next.

Krishna, however, stayed behind, the weight of their impending goodbye pressing down on him. His own path would take him to the Miami club headquarters for three months before embarking on the next world tour back to India. With each passing day, Nati's departure became an unavoidable ache neither could escape.

They walked across the bridge, night air cool and salted by the nearby ocean. Below, waves murmured in the dark, offering little comfort. Nati broke the silence, her voice a mix of hope and hesitation.

"When will you come to see me, Krishna?" she asked softly, the ache behind the question impossible to miss.

Krishna looked at her, unsure of how to respond. After the farewell party, they had skipped sleep and gone straight to work, hoping to savor every moment together. "I wish I could come, Nati. Really, I do. I'd love to meet your family, especially your parents. Your mom always insists I talk to her whenever she calls, I can tell they're special people." He paused, looking out at the horizon. "I don't know when, but I want to come one day."

Nati's eyes sparkled. "You should! I'll show you my country, Krishna. Cusco, Machu Picchu... it's heaven on earth."

He smiled faintly. Her pride was unmistakable—and honestly, he'd follow her anywhere. Each passing day made it clearer to Krishna—Nati meant more to him than he had ever admitted.

Even as they strolled through the sun-soaked streets of Miami, sharing meals at seaside restaurants, the city's charm paled in comparison to the time he spent with her.

Fate had one last surprise—Nati's departure was delayed by three days. To them, it was fate's final mercy, a stolen gift of borrowed time. A blessing, yet it only deepened Nati's desperation.

"Krishna, why don't you just come with me?" Nati asked, her voice more serious this time.

Krishna hesitated. He nudged his food aimlessly, his eyes locked on the table. He could feel the weight of her question, but he wasn't ready to answer. Deep down, he didn't believe he could just follow her to Peru. His future felt too set in stone, too practical.

Nati refused to let the conversation die so easily. "We've made it this far together, Krishna. Why not Peru? What's stopping you?"

Each mention of their looming goodbye pulled the tension between them tighter, like a stretched wire ready to snap.

Nati's voice grew sharper, laced with the hurt she had been trying to keep at bay.

"Let it be. Why would you come with me, anyway? Who am I to you? No one, apparently. You don't want to be with me anymore," Nati snapped, her voice breaking. "If you wanted to be with me, you would have come by now."

Her eyes glistened with unshed tears; Krishna froze. He had never seen her this raw, this shattered. A single tear slid down her cheek, in that moment, Krishna felt his heart break in a way he had never imagined.

Nati's tears unraveled something deep inside him. He always prided himself on being strong, pragmatic, and unaffected by emotions. He had always told himself that he was pragmatic and that emotions didn't have the power to sway him. But now, standing before Nati—her innocent eyes filled with love and pain made Krishna realize how wrong he had been.

Strength wasn't about suppressing emotions; it was about feeling them fully, letting them wash over you. And for the first time, Krishna understood that true strength came from allowing ourselves to be vulnerable.

They stood in silence, tears slipping down their faces. She couldn't bear the thought of letting him go, and Krishna, seeing her in pain, felt it more than he could handle. Without saying a word, he gently pulled her into a hug, holding her close. It was all he could do—there were no words left to comfort her.

After they finished dinner, walking slowly back to the hotel, Nati handed Krishna a small gift box. Her eyes were still wet from tears, but there was a determined look on her face. "This is for you," she said softly. "I know you won't come, but I want to be close to you. This will help me feel connected to you, no matter where we are."

Inside lay a sleek silver apple 8 smartphone. An undeniable upgrade from his old, worn-out device. The weight of the gift—and what it symbolized—hit him like a wave.

"Nati... why did you buy this?" he asked, his voice quiet, unsure of how to react. He knew Nati didn't earn much on the cruise ship. This was a huge expense, probably something she had been saving for a long time. "You didn't have to do this."

Nati smiled faintly, though the sadness still lingered in her eyes. "I wanted to. I've saved up for this. It's important to me, Krishna."

Her gesture made his heart ache even more. She had given him a piece of herself, a way to stay connected even when they were miles apart. And in doing so, she had made the thought of leaving her even harder.

"Nati, you're making it impossible for me to say goodbye," Krishna whispered, his voice thick with emotion. "Thank you... I don't know what else to say. I'm going to miss you for the rest of my life."

They both stood in the hallway of the hotel, holding each other in a long, silent embrace, knowing that in just a few days, their paths would diverge. Yet, in that quiet moment, with Nati's tears staining Krishna's shirt and the silver phone glinting in his hand, they both knew that no matter how far apart they were, they would always carry a piece of each other with them.

The day slipped away unnoticed as Krishna and Nati savored their last hours on the beach. They didn't even realize it was 8:00 p.m. until the cool evening air began to nip at their skin, reminding them of how far they still were from their hotel.

They had planned to dine at a famous Miami Beach restaurant, celebrated for its seafood and vegetarian dishes.

When they finally arrived at the restaurant, they found it closed. The host kindly informed them that they could either wait at the reception or take another walk while the staff prepared for the evening. Instead of waiting, they stepped outside. The dampness from the beach clung to them, the night air sharp against their skin.

As they strolled along the sidewalk, Nati started shivering from the chill. She had spent the entire day in the water, and her wet clothes clung to her in the increasingly cold weather, yet she pressed on, determined to spend every remaining moment with Krishna before their inevitable goodbye. Krishna saw her shivering, but Nati pressed on, unwilling to let discomfort steal these final moments.

The dinner at Miami Beach was their final night together before Nati would board the cruise. Nati wrapped her arms around herself for warmth, while Krishna remained deep in thought. He wanted to tell her something, but every time he tried, the words stuck in his throat.

"Nati, can I tell you something?" He asked as they stood at the reception, waiting for the restaurant to open.

She turned toward him; her eyes full of curiosity. "Of course," she said, eager to hear what was on his mind.

Krishna took a deep breath, trying to muster the courage to say what he'd been feeling since the day they met. He remembered seeing her that first day at the café, sitting with her book, completely absorbed. She had captivated him from the start, but he had never found the right moment to tell her. He wanted to admit that it wasn't just her who had grown attached. He, too, had felt a deep connection from the very beginning.

"I... I've wanted to tell you this for a long time," Krishna began, his voice soft and careful. "It wasn't just you who came close to me. It's been mutual, Nati. From the very first day, I was amazed by you."

Nati's eyes brightened with excitement. She waited, anticipating more, her gaze fixed on him. For a moment, Krishna met her eyes, and all the words he had prepared melted away. He felt exposed, vulnerable. Before he could speak again, a hostess appeared beside them.

"Sir, your table is ready," she said with a polite smile.

Krishna latched onto the distraction, letting the moment slip away. They were led to their table, where the warmth of the restaurant provided relief from the cold. The moment was gone, swept away by the noise of the crowded dining room.

Nati, however, wasn't ready to let their intimate conversation slip away entirely. As they settled into their seats, Krishna broke the silence.

"What's the first thing you're going to do when you get home?" He asked, hoping to steer the conversation in a lighter direction.

"First? I'll call you, of course—gotta let you know I made it back in one piece." She laughed, but her voice softened as she continued, "And then I'll probably tell all my friends about this amazing trip and the wonderful person I met. I'll tell them about our walks on the beach, the music we listened to... and, of course, I'll miss you. I'll wish to see you again as soon as I can."

Krishna smiled, feeling a twinge of sadness in her words. "You seem different now, Nati. I don't see the same girl who was upset about being ignored by her best friend."

Nati rolled her eyes playfully. "That's because I'm not that girl anymore. I feel like things are going to be different now. Maybe... maybe he'll realize what he's lost, but honestly, I don't care anymore."

Krishna leaned forward; his expression serious. "Mark my words, Nati. The guy you were circling around. He's going to come back. This time, he'll be the one chasing after you."

"Don't joke, Krishna," Nati said, shaking her head. "It's not going to happen. But... I can tell you one thing: it won't bother me anymore. Whether he listens or not... I don't care."

Before Krishna could respond, a waiter interrupted them. "How can I help you, sir?"

Nati jumped in before Krishna could answer. "Two vodkas, please," she ordered confidently.

Krishna hesitated, staring at the glass in his hand, unsure of what to do. His fingers curled around the glass—cold, unfamiliar, heavier than it looked. The promise echoed louder than the guilt. For Nati, he lifted it, not to drink, but to honor the space they'd chosen to share. He had promised to accompany her tonight in everything.

A flood of memories crashed into him—his grandfather's stern warnings, his parents' unshaken beliefs, the weight of tradition pressing against his chest. He could almost feel their disapproving eyes on him as he held the glass.

Nati, sensing his hesitation, smiled gently. "Krishna, it's not the drinking that's bad. It's losing yourself in front of the drink that's dangerous."

Encouraged by her words, Krishna took a small sip. The vodka burned, briny with an unexpected bite of spice. He wasn't sure what to make of it, but he finished half the glass quickly, pretending it didn't affect him. But it did. His mind started to loosen, and soon enough, both he and Nati were laughing, talking, and sharing more deeply than ever before.

As they continued drinking, Krishna began to open up. Nati learned about his humble beginnings, his family, his love for the stock market, and the losses that had driven him to leave Pune. She discovered his self-respect, as well as his unwillingness to stay where he felt unappreciated.

For Krishna, the night was equally revealing. He learned more about Nati that evening than he ever thought possible. Through her laughter, her stories, and her confessions, she opened up about her past love for Joshua—a relationship she had tried to leave behind, but one that clearly still lingered in her heart. She held deep respect for Joshua, and whether he loved her or not, something real had existed between them. Nati had walked away, torn between her feelings and the reality of Joshua's lack of financial stability and seriousness about life.

As Nati shared her inner turmoil, Krishna found himself contemplating the complexities of her emotions. A woman's heart is like an ocean—deep, mysterious, often hiding more beneath the surface than what is visible. Nati's decision to leave Joshua was one that seemed logical, but beneath it lay an ocean of doubt and second-guessing.

She wondered if her leaving Joshua had been a mistake. What if he became more successful after she stepped out of his life? What would people think of her decision? Was she justified in leaving him simply because he didn't fit into the future, she envisioned for herself? Nati had carried these questions with her, unable to share them with anyone because she believed no one would truly understand her.

Krishna stayed quiet, letting her words settle, letting his own thoughts churn beneath the surface. He found it fascinating how a girl who longed for a carefree, playful boyfriend would change her expectations when it came to marriage. Nati had wanted Joshua to be lighthearted and fun, but when the idea of a future together became real, her hopes shifted toward a man who was settled, responsible—someone forward-thinking.

"Do you think I did the right thing?" Nati asked, her voice barely above a whisper.

It was a tricky question, and Krishna knew there was no easy way out of it. He had never been one to sugarcoat his opinions, but this was delicate. Nati wasn't just asking for advice—she was seeking validation, clarity, maybe even some peace for her conflicted heart.

He chose his words carefully.

"Nati, I don't know what love feels like, not in the way you've experienced it. I've never fallen in love, so I don't know how it feels. but if you love someone truly, if you love them from the bottom of your heart, then everything else becomes secondary. Love can find a way through any obstacle. But if he couldn't accept you for who you are, or if you couldn't accept him as he is, then maybe it's better you parted ways. Love shouldn't force us to change who we are."

Nati watched him closely, her eyes searching his for answers, for truth.

"If Joshua truly loves you," Krishna said, "he would have met you halfway. Love finds a way, or it wasn't strong enough to begin with."

But love also means accepting someone for who they are, without trying to change them. What kind of love forces you to reshape yourself? You can't be happy pretending to be someone else."

He paused, letting the weight of his words sink in.

"If you couldn't accept him for who he is, and if he couldn't accept you as you are, then maybe it's better you parted ways. It's hard, but sometimes, love is not enough to keep two people together. That doesn't mean it wasn't real. It just means that it wasn't meant to last forever."

Nati nodded slowly, taking in everything Krishna had said. He saw the uncertainty in her eyes shift, just slightly, into understanding.

"Keep the love and the memories alive," Krishna added softly. "But don't be bitter if it didn't work out. Be yourself, and love someone without expecting anything in return. If you judge the success of love by whether you marry, then maybe it's time to change how you think about love."

Nati was quiet for a moment, her gaze drifting down to her drink before she looked up at Krishna again. A small, sad smile played on her lips.

"Why he is not like you?" She asked, her voice almost a whisper.

Krishna held her gaze, a faint chuckle slipping through. "And why am I not him?" he said, the humor in his voice barely veiling the ache beneath.

Nati let out a soft laugh, tilting her head as if brushing away the weight of the moment.

"Seems like the vodka's working its magic," she said, the laughter lightening her tone.

They both laughed, knowing they had revealed more about themselves in one night than they ever had before. their hearts would remain hidden beneath the surface. The night had revealed much, but not everything. Some truths, it seemed, would take a little longer to come out. The soft strains of classical melodies wrapped themselves around the crowd, setting the perfect mood. The air shimmered with elegance—wine swirling in crystal, golden light pooling in corners, and soft voices folding into the music. Couples moved gracefully on the dance floor, their bodies swaying in unison. Time unraveled at their feet, each step dissolving their worries into the rhythm of the night.

Nati and Krishna, too, found themselves lost in the moment. They danced in perfect harmony, their steps effortlessly synchronized as if they had been dancing together for years. Under the dim glow, Nati seemed ethereal—like the night itself had shaped her in its image. Krishna stared, captivated—like she was someone new, yet utterly familiar. Love songs had always been melodies—until now, when every note seemed to echo his own heartbeat. Every note seemed to be written for them, every lyric resonating in his chest. This night, with her by his side, felt like a dream—perfect music, perfect company.

Long past midnight, they drifted out of the restaurant, leaning into each other, laughter still dancing on their lips. He was cautious, though. His mind flickered with concern, wondering if things might go wrong. Yet, they were so happy, too swept up in the moment, to care about anything else.

When they finally reached their hotel, the night was far from over. They continued dancing, laughing, and spinning, carried by the momentum of their joy. Vodka hummed in Krishna's veins, softening the edges of restraint—Nati swayed beside him, just as untethered.

They danced slowly to Henrique's "I Found a Girl," a song that seemed to narrate their very story.

As the music played, Krishna's body grew heavier, and soon he found himself resting against Nati's shoulder, the alcohol lulling him into a hazy stupor.

The night wrapped around Nati like silk steeped in wine—heavy, heady, and slow. She guided him to the bedroom, gently laying him down and pulling a blanket over him. She was about to leave for her own room when Krishna, half-asleep, hold her hand.

"Nati, I want to tell you something..." His voice was soft, slurred by sleep but filled with the sincerity of a confession long held back. "I couldn't gather the courage to say it..."

Nati paused, her heart skipping a beat.

Krishna's subconscious had taken over, speaking words that his waking self-had been too afraid to voice.

"My life has changed since I met you," Krishna mumbled, his eyes half-closed. "I'm imprinting on you, Nati... Maybe you don't know, but I feel alive when you're around me. The moments I spend with you... they're worth a lifetime."

Nati stood frozen, watching him, her breath catching in her throat.

"I don't know what love is, but when I'm with you... it feels like time stops. I think... I think I'm in love with you, Nati. I love you."

The words hung in the air, tender and fragile. He had finally said it, though he was barely conscious. Nati didn't respond, knowing he wouldn't hear her.

She bent over him, pressing a kiss to his hand, then his cheek—a silent answer to words he wouldn't remember.

In that moment, Krishna had expressed something deep within his heart—something so profound that not even wine had been able to coax it out until now.

When Krishna woke up the next morning, Nati was curled up beside him, sleeping peacefully in his arms. She lay there, innocence etched across her face, fragile in a way that undid him. Krishna's heart swelled as he felt the warmth of her breath. He stayed frozen, suspended in a moment he didn't dare disturb. Fragments of the night flickered through his mind, scattered like puzzle pieces he couldn't quite fit, but all he could remember was falling asleep on Nati's shoulder in the cab. He ran his fingers through her hair, letting its softness linger in his hands. When Nati stirred and opened her eyes, she smiled shyly for a moment, but the awkwardness quickly faded.

The night had changed everything. In that instant, Krishna wasn't just close—he belonged beside her.

"Is this a dream?" Krishna asked, still holding her close.

"No," Nati replied, her voice playful as she pinched him lightly. "This is very real."

A rush of heat surged through him, his pulse hammering beneath the weight of the moment.

There was no escaping it now—love had taken root, undeniable and deep.

"Nati," he began, his voice hesitant, "I... I'm sorry if I said anything last night that might have hurt you. I was drunk; I don't really remember everything... If I said something wrong, please forgive me."

Nati's eyes sparkled with mischief, her lips curving into a knowing smile.

"Does that mean you didn't mean what you said last night?"

Krishna froze, unsure of how to respond.

"I... no, I mean... yes. I mean, no, I didn't mean—"

"Oh," Her grin widened. "What if that's exactly what I wanted to hear?"

Krishna groaned, running a hand over his face. She was enjoying this way too much.

"Nati, don't tease me," he said, laughing nervously.

"Yesterday," Nati continued, her tone softening, "someone told me how much he loves me... and held me so tightly, like I was the most precious thing in the world. I haven't slept so deeply, so peacefully since I left Peru."

Krishna couldn't recall the details, but he could feel it— he could feel the peace that had settled in his heart.

Even though the memory was hazy, something deep within him remembered. He pulled Nati closer, kissed her forehead, and closed his eyes, content to simply listen to the sound of her heartbeat.

Time unraveled around them, the world beyond these walls slipping away.

Hours passed, but it felt like mere moments. It was 12:30 when Krishna reluctantly got out of bed, preparing for his meeting with Gabriel.

The clock had continued its steady march, but in that room, with Nati, it was as if they had stepped outside of time itself.

Chapter 09

When Dreams Say Yes

It all begins with a decision to jump, even if we don't see the wings that will carry us. Our dreams become reality when we dare to pursue them.

"Aah, a 12-year-old Chivas," Gabriel said with a gleam in his eyes, inspecting the bottle Krishna handed him. "I'm so pleased to get this gift. Thank you, Krishna." Gabriel said, welcoming him with a firm handshake.

Dressed and ready, Gabriel stood in an apartment that echoed his nature—tidy, methodical, pulsing with quiet precision. Every item sat with intention, like the room had been drawn from a meticulous blueprint.

It was no surprise to Krishna; Gabriel was the type of man who was always on top of things, no matter where he was.

Gabriel had already helped himself to a drink. He swirled the liquid, grinning. "So, Krishna, what's next? Enjoyed the journey?"

"Yes," Krishna replied, pulling a Coke from the fridge. "Unforgettable. I wish I had another month—it's the kind of journey that will stay with me forever."

He refused Gabriel's offer of a drink, reminding him gently that he didn't drink.

"Never?" Alex's eyebrows shot up. A memory flickered—sharing a drink with Nati, a moment sealed between them, untouched by anyone else.

Gabriel knew Krishna didn't drink; Krishna had let a small lie protect that memory.

Gabriel gave him a knowing look. "If it was so wonderful, why don't you live it all over again?"

Krishna chuckled, shaking his head. "I wish I could, but that door's closed now."

"Why would anyone leave a journey when someone as beautiful as Nati is alongside them?" Gabriel teased, his eyes twinkling mischievously.

Krishna laughed, but Gabriel's words sparked something deeper within him. "What do you think, Krishna? Is life a choice or a chance?" Gabriel asked, leaning back with his glass in hand.

"For me, life's always been about chance," Krishna said, weighing his words.

"Everything that's happened to me—it's all been a matter of chance.

Helping Shiva, dropping out, picking poker over stocks, boarding a cruise —all of it, pure chances.

I'm grateful for the opportunity's life has given me, even though it's all been outside my control."

Gabriel listened carefully, then leaned forward slightly. "Was it chance, or was it your choice?"

"Chance is something we don't control. It's something that happens to us." Gabriel continued,

"What you're describing is not chance—it's reactive living. Letting changes dictate your path without you actively choosing them makes it feel like chance. But think about it— didn't you decide to drop out of school to help Shiva? You decided to learn how to gamble in Goa. And then later, didn't you only decide to work on the cruise ship?"

Krishna stared at Gabriel.

"Life is a series of choices. Every one of them shapes who we are—and who we become."

The difference is whether you live by choice or let life's uncertainties push you around. Every choice has a consequence—what you need to ask yourself is whether those consequences are regrets or align with your passion."

Krishna fell silent, reflecting on his past. Was his life one of regret, or one of passion? He thought of the adventures he'd had, the changes he'd embraced, and the risks he'd taken. It wasn't a life of regret; it was a life he had crafted— shaped by the choices he'd made with conviction and pride.

Gabriel's words stirred something in him. "You're right," Krishna admitted. "I've crafted my own path. It wasn't just chance; it was choice."

Gabriel smiled. "Exactly. We always have a choice. Even when we feel like we don't."

A strange mix of clarity and courage settled over him.

"You know, I've got three months before my next cruise sets sail. I was thinking… maybe I could explore Latin

America in the meantime. Any chance I could get on board for a tour there?"

Gabriel and Krishna looked at each other. For a moment, the room fell silent.

Gabriel smirked, breaking the silence. "Latin America? Or a Latin girl?"

Krishna chuckled nervously. "Well, yes, I'd like to see her again."

Gabriel's eyes twinkled. "I mean, closing your eyes doesn't mean the world stops watching."

Krishna's laughter turned sheepish, but he admitted, "I want to walk with her again, Gabriel. I don't know if I'll ever meet her again, but I need to try."

For the first time, Krishna gave his feelings a voice, something inside him felt lighter.

Speaking his truth, he felt lighter, as if shedding a weight. "I know it's not practical. I might not make any money, but I'd be happy if I could just be with her."

"Well, Krishna, if you'd told me earlier, I might've arranged something. But now... it's a bit last-minute," Gabriel said with a hint of sympathy. "I'll talk to the crew manager, though. Let's hope for the best."

Krishna's heart sank for a moment, his hope wavering. But he smiled, grateful for Gabriel's willingness to try. "Thank you, Gabriel." They talked for hours—casual on the surface, but each word carried weight.

As Krishna prepared to leave, he felt lighter. He wasn't sure what the future held—whether he'd get to see Nati again or not—but he was proud that he'd finally taken a step forward.

"Excuse me, sir, you have a call from Mr. Gabriel," the receptionist said as Krishna and Nati returned from dinner. It was almost 10:30 p.m. Gabriel had called three times since the afternoon, leaving messages for Krishna to meet him as soon as possible. Krishna sensed urgency in Gabriel's call but had no clue what was behind them.

They both turned toward Gabriel's hotel room, which was on the third floor of the same building.

"Krishna, finally! I've been waiting all afternoon. Where were you?" Gabriel called out, ushering them in.

Nati smiled, stepping into the room as well. "Nice to see you, Gabriel."

Gabriel leaned forward, his voice taking on a serious tone. "Well, at this time, you should be packing your own bags too."

"What?" Krishna was confused. "I still haven't received my new assignment."

Nati looked between the two, clearly lost. Gabriel ignored her confusion, locking eyes with Krishna.

"You can wait for the casino to plan your schedule, or… you can follow your heart. But if you choose the latter, you better start packing."

Suddenly, it clicked for Krishna—the conversation they'd had the other day. The memory flooded back, along with a rush of hope, though he still feared it might be too good to be true.

"Gabriel, you've got to be kidding," Krishna let out a breathless laugh, barely hiding the thrill in his voice.

Nati, completely in the dark, raised her hands in exasperation. "Can someone please tell me what's going on?"

Gabriel, ever the cool-headed manager who pulled strings behind the scenes. "Krishna, it's done. You're going to Latin America."

Krishna's pulse quickened. Gabriel had made the impossible happen in record time. He was going to Latin America—with Nati. The thought hit like a wave. He grabbed Gabriel in a grateful hug, too stunned for words.

Nati was still figuring things out. "Krishna, will you please tell me, or should I leave?" She said, half-joking, but truly puzzled.

Krishna turned to her with bright smile lighting up his face. "Nati, my darling, we're going on another journey together!"

"What?" Nati asked, her voice full of disbelief.

"I'm following my heart. I'm going with you," Krishna said, his excitement bubbling over. He grabbed her and pulled her into a joyful hug, spinning her around in a circle.

Nati's eyes widened, her disbelief turning into a mix of joy and shock. "Wait… what? Are you serious?" She could barely contain herself now.

"Yes!" Krishna was practically shouting with excitement. "This is real, Nati. We're going to live our dreams! Peru, Cusco, Machu Picchu, everything you promised to show me... we're doing it, together!"

Nati burst into laughter, swept up in Krishna's excitement. The craziness of the situation hit her, and suddenly, all their shared dreams—walking through the ancient ruins, exploring the cities, living the adventure—seemed within reach. She hugged Gabriel with overwhelming gratitude. "Thank you, Gabriel. I don't even know how to say it—thank you. It's like my prayers have been answered!"

Gabriel leaned back, watching them with a knowing smile. He let them celebrate before he gently cut in. "Krishna, hold on. I need you to hear the terms before you jump in."

Krishna paused, looking at Gabriel, still floating on cloud nine.

"The best I could negotiate is fifty bucks a day until your next cruise. It's not a lot; there's no fixed salary during the time you're off the cruise," Gabriel explained. "You'll be on your own for most of it."

Nati and Gabriel both turned their eyes to Krishna, waiting to see his reaction. The offer wasn't ideal, but Krishna didn't even blink. "Gabriel, I'd do it for free. Time with Nati. That's priceless."

Gabriel let out a sigh of relief. He'd expected Krishna's enthusiastic response but was glad it was now official.

The conversation wound down, after discussing a few more details, Krishna and Nati finally left Gabriel's room around 2 AM, their thoughts still buzzing with possibility. They were giddy with excitement, unable to sleep as they thought about the journey ahead. It felt like their wildest dreams were coming true, as if the universe had conspired to give them this opportunity.

Chapter 10

Santiago: Where the Dream Begins

In the next two days, Krishna completed all the formalities. With a U.S. visa already in hand, he faced no major obstacles. After a whirlwind of planning, everything was finally falling into place. Krishna dialed Shiva's number, his fingers trembling with excitement.

"Shiva! How are you, brother?" Krishna said, his voice brimming with excitement. Though time had passed, Shiva's voice felt like a wave of homecoming washing over him.

"Krishna! It's you. What a surprise! How are you? It's been ages since we last heard from you. You didn't call back. We've been worried! What's going on? You were supposed to check in. How could you forget about us?" Shiva fired off his questions, his voice bouncing between relief and frustration. He wasn't going to let Krishna off the hook easily.

Nati listened in from across the room, amused by the brothers' dynamic. For a moment, she wondered how Krishna could go so long without contacting his family. He's so carefree, she mused, shaking her head in disbelief.

"I'm perfectly fine, Shiva. Don't worry," Krishna reassured him. "How are Mumma and Papa? How's everything back home? I've reached Miami safely."

The brothers quickly fell into a conversation about their family, catching up on the small details of home. Shiva mentioned how their mother had been pressuring him to get married, which made Krishna laugh. Some things never changed—not even oceans away.

Krishna laughed, picturing his mother's relentless matchmaking attempts. As they spoke, Shiva wove a colorful tale of her latest efforts, making Krishna shake his head in amusement.

"What about you?" Shiva finally asked. "When are you coming back? Do you have friends over there?"

Krishna hesitated for a moment, glancing at Nati, who was occupied with something in the room.

"I'll be back in about three months. My cruise returns then."

"What happens after three months? You told us you were coming back." Shiva's voice grew a little more concerned.

"I will. But before that, I'll be heading to Latin America for another cruise."

"But you said you were going to Miami…" Shiva's confusion deepened. "I'm not following."

Krishna let out an easy laugh, hoping to settle his brother's worries. "Trust me Brother. I'm having the best time of my life right now. Take care of Mumma and Papa and try to arrange a call with them soon."

Shiva let out a sigh. "Alright, I will. But before you go… what about the beautiful girl with you? Who is she? A friend? Or something more?"

A sharp jolt ran through Krishna as his eyes flicked to Nati. Of course, Shiva had seen the pictures. Nati had shared some with him—now there was no escaping the conversation.

"Shiva..." Krishna started, trying to deflect, but his brother wasn't letting go.

"Who is she? Is she working with you? A traveler? Come on, Krishna, don't keep me in the dark!"

Krishna sighed, resigned to the inevitable. Switching to Marathi, he muttered, "Tiche naav Natalia aahe. Nati. She's from Peru. Aani mi Peru la tichya sobatach chalalo aahe."

Nati, unaware of the language switch but sensing the subject, raised her eyebrows, amused yet intrigued. Krishna smiled sheepishly, knowing that she'd figure it out soon enough.

"Oh, my brother!" Shiva laughed heartily on the other end. "I'm so happy for you! I want to talk to her!"

Trapped with no way out, Krishna sighed and passed the phone to Nati. "Shiva's eager to talk to you," he admitted with a lopsided smile.

Nati took the phone with a teasing smile. "Hola Shiva. How are you?"

Shiva's voice came through with excitement. "Hello, Natalia! It's so nice to talk to you. We were all so worried about Krishna. He doesn't doesn't mingle with people easily, but now that we see you with him, we're feeling much better. Thank you for being with him."

Nati smiled, touched by Shiva's warm words. "It's my pleasure. He's been wonderful."

They chatted for a few minutes, mostly about Krishna—his family, the stories Shiva told about him, and, of course, Nati's family in Peru. When they finally said their goodbyes, Shiva promised to connect them with Krishna's parents soon.

As Nati handed the phone back, Krishna's curiosity was evident. "What did you two talk about?" he asked, leaning in.

Nati gave him a sly grin. "That's between me and Shiva. You don't need to know everything."

Krishna chuckled. "My family's falling for you already."

"They're lovely. And your brother is so kind and straightforward. You're lucky, Krishna," Nati murmured, a soft curve playing on her lips.

Krishna shot her a teasing look. "Oh, look at you, Miss Philosopher. You've got everything figured out."

In just two days, everything was set. Krishna and Nati stood on the edge of a new adventure—one not driven by duty or money, but by love.

Had someone in Goa predicted he'd cross an ocean for love, Krishna would've laughed it off. But now, standing on the brink of a dream with Nati by his side, it felt surreal.

Their 30-day journey from Miami, through the Panama Canal, to San Antonio in Chile was about to begin. Krishna didn't know what the future held, but with Nati beside him, he knew one thing for certain—he was exactly where he needed to be. Every step felt like the start of a new adventure. He was with her, and that made all the difference.

This was his dream, a journey of love, happiness, and being truly alive. Now, it was real!

Santiago marked the start of a new chapter. Krishna and Nati started their cruise from Miami, USA, sailing through Santa Lucia, Gustavia, and finally arriving at their final port in San Antonio, Chile. Nati and Krishna were now free to explore the city without any deadlines or constraints.

Each moment was a dream brought to life—a journey where they turned fantasies into reality.

At the ship's bow, they stretched their arms wide, reenacting the iconic Titanic pose. They strolled through Central Park hand in hand, dove into the pool, and even gave surfing a shot.

They wandered through Brazil's vibrant streets, strolled barefoot on sun-warmed beaches, and let the scenery sink into their souls. Every moment carried a spark of magic. They embraced it all, holding nothing back.

For this journey, they were not just travelers—they were together, inseparable.

Emilia had joined them for part of the trip and still hovered nearby. She tried inching closer to Krishna and Nati, but Krishna kept his distance. He knew Nati wouldn't be at ease with Emilia hovering too often. This was their journey, their time together. San Antonio, Chile—the final stop of their cruise—signaled the end of one chapter and the dawn of another.

Upon arriving in Santiago, they checked into their hotel.

The cruise had ended, marking the beginning of their time on land. Krishna still had two months before flying back to India from Miami.

They had yet to book their flights from Chile to Peru, but Nati had a different plan—she wanted to explore more of Chile before heading home.

They had saved enough to afford a week-long tour of Chile.

Until now, they had shared their journey with the crew, but with the cruise over, everyone had scattered in different directions.

Now, it was only Krishna, Nati, and Emilia. But as Krishna and Nati grew closer, Emilia seemed more like an outsider. Engrossed in each other and making plans for two, Krishna and Nati left Emilia feeling like an outsider.

Finally, Emilia decided to leave. "I think I'll book my ticket back to Peru," she said. "I'm feeling a bit homesick. You guys carry on with your plans. I'll meet you back there."

Nati, who had made no real effort to include Emilia in their plans, didn't object. This was her time with Krishna; she wasn't planning on sharing it.

Krishna sensed the shift and stayed quiet. Emilia had no place in what was becoming their journey.

The next morning, they said their goodbyes to Emilia. By 10 AM, they had checked out of their hotel, as the cruise liner's stay covered only two days. Nati took charge of the situation, booking just one hotel room for them—after all, they didn't need two. Since Miami, the second room had only served as extra storage.

Santiago de Chile is an incredible city. Krishna marveled at its cleanliness and organization. Nati, who had never been to Chile before either, explained how Chile had earned its place as one of the most developed countries in Latin America.

"Over a century ago, Peru and Bolivia fought Chile over land disputes," Nati said as they strolled through the city.

"Chile's military was strong; they won the war, but the loss still stings for many Peruvians. Ever since then, there's been no major conflict, but that defeat still lingers in the hearts of many Peruvians. People here respect Chile's economic success, but many Peruvians don't vacation here. It's a generational grudge."

"That's similar to India and China," Krishna added, drawing a parallel.

Santiago, with its breathtaking beauty, was one of the most vibrant places Krishna had ever seen. The smooth roads, lined with gardens and framed by the majestic Andes Mountains, left him in awe. He remembered reading about the Andes in his tenth-grade geography book but seeing them in person was a different experience altogether.

The sunrises and sunsets reflecting off the snow-capped peaks were among the most stunning views Krishna had ever seen. The mountains, blanketed in ice, seemed to glow under the changing light. He quickly understood why Santiago was so admired—it stood among the most beautiful cities in Latin America.

The people were open-minded and active, with parks full of people walking, cycling, and exercising from morning until evening. The vibrant energy of the city was infectious, and both Krishna and Nati were completely taken by it.

This was a journey unlike any other—a journey of love, discovery, and being fully alive. The cruise may have ended, but their adventure was just beginning.

"Are you sure you want to stay here for a week?" Krishna asked as they walked down one of Santiago's charming streets, lined with cafés and boutique stores.

"Absolutely," Nati replied, her eyes shining with excitement. "There's so much to explore. We might not come back to Chile for a long time, so why not enjoy every bit of it?"

Krishna couldn't help but smile. Nati's infectious energy always drew him in, he loved how she wanted to make the most of everything. Her plan to explore Chile felt spontaneous yet perfect.

They stopped at a street vendor selling fresh empanadas. As they sat on a nearby bench, biting into the flaky, savory pastries, Nati brought up something she had been pondering.

"You know, it's funny how we've talked so much about our cultures—Peru and India—and yet here we are, in Chile, learning new things about each other," Nati said, tilting her head like she was still unraveling the thought.

Krishna nodded, glancing up at the imposing Andes. "It's like we're not just learning about a new country, but about each other too. I think traveling does that. It breaks down walls."

Nati smiled, leaning her head on his shoulder for a moment. "I couldn't agree more. This trip… it's changing us. I sense it."

Krishna felt the weight of her words sink in. The bond between them had indeed grown stronger during their journey. From the beaches of Brazil to the lively streets of Santiago, every moment felt like a new layer being added to their relationship.

They continued their tour around the city. The open-roof bus ride they took later in the day provided a panoramic view of Santiago's iconic landmarks—the Plaza de Armas, the towering Gran Torre Santiago, and the bustling Bellavista neighborhood. As the sun began to set, the Andes were bathed in a golden glow, making the view surreal.

As the bus passed by the bustling streets filled with locals and tourists alike, Krishna was struck by the vibrant energy of the city. "You're right about the people here," Krishna said, breaking the comfortable silence between them. "That warmth you mentioned about the people of Santiago. They're so full of life."

Nati laughed softly, "I guess Latin American warmth is universal."

When they returned to their hotel room at night, both exhausted yet exhilarated, Krishna realized how much had changed since they left on their journey. It wasn't just about seeing new places or checking items off a list. It was about sharing those experiences with someone special.

As they sat on the balcony of their room, sipping hot tea and looking out at the illuminated city, Nati turned to Krishna with a mischievous grin. "So, do you regret extending the trip with me?"

Krishna raised an eyebrow, pretending to think about it. "Hmm, let's see. Endless adventure, beautiful company, and amazing food. Nope, no regrets."

Nati laughed, playfully nudging him. "Good answer."

They stayed up late into the night, talking about everything and nothing, their laughter echoing softly into the night air. Santiago had given them the space and time to connect on a deeper level. The city, with its colorful streets, stunning mountain views, and vibrant culture, became the backdrop to a chapter of their lives.

Their journey through Chile was just beginning, but they both knew that it wasn't just about the places they would visit—it was about the memories they would make together.

Krishna was captivated by Santiago's vibrant culture, but the open displays of affection in public were something he was still adjusting to. Couples kissing and embraced openly in parks, at bus stations, and on metro platforms. This kind of public intimacy was not something he was accustomed to back in India. He glanced at Nati, wondering if it made her feel the same discomfort, but she seemed completely at ease, enjoying the freedom that came with traveling through such an open-minded country. It was a different world, with such public displays of affection being normalized. He even noticed the high number of lesbian couples, confident and unafraid to express their love openly. Chile's openness to all kinds of love made Krishna realize how different this society is from what he had grown up with. He began to understand why people say, "The West is the West."

Santiago's metro ran like clockwork, and even with countless cars on the road, gridlock never seemed to take hold. Nati mentioned weekly car-free days dedicated to cycling, reflecting the city's well-organized nature.

Santiago's beauty was mesmerizing, Krishna couldn't get over the vibrant energy of the city.

From morning until evening, the roadside gardens brimmed with people walking, cycling, and exercising. The city's smart urban design made this possible—open gyms lined the parks, and cycling ranked as one of the nation's most popular hobbies, second only to the Netherlands. The Chilean people were not only active but also appeared strong and healthy. Chile's beauty was unlike anything he had seen. Lush greenery, stunning mountains, and a vibrant city pulsing with life.

"Chilean people are so warm," Nati said, noticing Krishna's reflective mood. "They don't hold back. It's part of their charm, don't you think?"

Krishna smiled, acknowledging her observation. "Yeah, it's different from what I'm used to, but it's also refreshing. People here seem so… free. They live in the moment. You can feel it in everything they do."

Nati nodded, her eyes sparkling as she looked out at the bustling streets. "Exactly. It's like they don't carry the weight of judgment. They, just live."

Groups of boys and girls filled the streets—dancing, making music, diving into all kinds of fun. College students cycled, worked out, strummed guitars or harmoniums. The energy was infectious.

"Latin people take so much pride in their language," Nati said as they cycled through the city.

Unlike in India, where people are more inclined toward English, here they hold Spanish in high regard. It's not about whether you speak English fluently or not. Their cycling tour through Santiago felt like an embodiment of that spirit. During their cycling they met with group of young tourists from the U.S., Nati and Krishna quickly found themselves part of a lively pack, pedaling through the city's streets, laughing and sharing stories. The group was diverse—two boys and three girls, all enthusiastic and curious, just like Krishna and Nati.

"Hey, can you tell us the cycling route to Cristobal Hill?" One of the boys asked Nati, mistaking her for a local.

She grinned, shaking her head. "We're tourists too, but I can help with the map!"

Krishna couldn't help but admire how effortlessly Nati interacted with strangers. Her openness made it easy for people to approach her, and soon enough, their small group became a lively, collaborative team, eager to explore Santiago together.

"Do you mind if we join you guys?" One of the girls in the group asked.

"Of course, the more, the merrier," Nati said warmly.

Together, they cycled through the city, stopping at iconic spots like Plaza de Armas, Estación Central and the lush gardens of Santa Lucía Hill. Every stop was filled with laughter and conversation, the group bonded quickly as if they'd known each other for years. For Krishna, the experience was a whirlwind of sights and sounds. The city's beauty was undeniable, from the towering Andes to the vibrant streets filled with cyclists, dancers, and musicians.

By the time they reached San Cristobal Hill, the sun was beginning to set, casting a golden light over the city. Krishna paused for a moment, taking it all in—the panoramic view of Santiago.

"This city is incredible," Krishna murmured, more to himself than anyone else.

Nati turned to him, her smile soft and genuine. "I knew you'd love it."

Their cycling tour ended at the Costanera shopping complex, the tallest shopping center in Latin America, towering over the city with its 65 stories. They parked their cycles and wandered through the bustling mall, taking in the luxury stores and lively atmosphere. The group decided to part ways for a few hours to freshen up, but not before exchanging numbers and making plans for the following days.

"We're heading to Valle Nevado tomorrow for ice skiing," one of the boys said. "You guys should join us."

Nati's eyes lit up. "That sounds perfect! We've been meaning to go there."

Krishna laughed, feeling the energy of the group pulling him in. "Looks like our plans just got better."

Later that night, after dinner with their new friends, Krishna and Nati returned to their hotel room. The day had been long and exhilarating, filled with new experiences and new faces. As they sat together, winding down from the excitement, Krishna felt a sense of contentment he hadn't experienced in a long time.

"This trip," he began, his voice soft, "it's changing me. I can feel it."

Nati met his eyes, something soft flickering in her gaze. "Travel has a way of doing that. It shows you things about yourself you never knew."

Krishna nodded, leaning back against the headboard. "I'm starting to realize it."

The next few days flew by in a blur of adventure. They visited Valle Nevado, skiing through the pristine snow-capped mountains, and explored the wine region of Maipo Valley, savoring the rich flavors of Chilean wines. Their final stop was Viña del Mar, where they spent their days strolling along the golden beaches and soaking in the relaxed coastal atmosphere.

Through it all, Krishna and Nati grew even closer. Their connection deepened with each new experience, each shared laugh, and every quiet moment they spent together, whether cycling through Santiago's bustling streets or sitting side by side on a beach, watching the sun dip below the horizon.

As their time in Chile began to wind down, Krishna couldn't help but feel grateful for the journey they had shared. This trip had been more than just a vacation—it had been a transformative experience, a journey that had brought them closer in ways he hadn't anticipated.

Nati, as always, sensed his thoughts. "You ready for the next adventure?" she asked, excitement sparkling in her voice.

Krishna smiled, looking at her with a mix of affection and anticipation. "With you? Always."

Valle Nevado sprawled across hundreds of acres, a winter wonderland draped in pristine snow, its rolling hills glistening under the morning light. The fresh snowfall from the night before made the ice soft and foamy, perfect for winter sports but treacherous for the inexperienced. Krishna and the group had been having the time of their lives, playing ice games, laughing, and enjoying the stunning surroundings.

Their excitement snowballed, pushing them into bolder, more reckless antics. Nati and the girls, emboldened by the fun, decided to jump into a deeper patch of snow, about 20 feet down, a place known as the "jump point." The excitement of the leap was exhilarating at first, but the thrill quickly turned to panic as they realized the mistake they had made. The snow was too soft, their feet sinking in past their knees, making it nearly impossible to move.

Krishna had warned Nati, but like always, she ignored him. Now, her joyful laughter was turning into a desperate plea for help as she realized just how stuck they were.

"Krishna, please!" Nati's voice trembled as she called out. She was on the verge of tears, her usual confidence shaken by the sudden realization of their precarious situation.

Krishna's heart pounded. He had been watching from a distance, unaware of the danger unfolding before him. He saw the watchkeeper from the nearby post blowing his whistle in warning, but none of them had noticed until now. The girls were stuck, and panic was beginning to set in.

Without hesitating, Krishna jumped in after Nati.

The snow clamped around his legs like quicksand, dragging him down with every grueling step.

He reached her, grabbing her hand firmly and, with all his strength, pulled her close. She clung to him, relieved, as he lifted her up and cradled her in his arms.

"I've got you," he whispered, trying to calm her, even though his own heart was racing.

It wasn't easy. The snow made every step a struggle, each one heavier than the last. He half-crawled, half-stumbled back toward solid ground, his arms burning from the strain of holding Nati. But he didn't stop. All that mattered was getting her out safely.

The other girls shouted for help, but Krishna's focus tunneled in on Nati—getting her out came first.

It wasn't until he had gotten her to the edge, where the boys helped pull her out, that he realized the others were still waiting.

Taking a deep breath, he turned back, wading through the snow once again to rescue the other two girls. One by one, he pulled them out, his legs burning with the effort. Dripping wet and drained, Krishna barely stayed upright once the last girl was free.

Nati, still shaken but relieved, ran to Krishna and hugged him tightly. "Thank you," she whispered, her voice muffled against his chest.

Krishna held her, his heart pounding from both the exertion and the fear that had gripped him when he saw her struggling. They all laughed nervously, the tension melting away now that they were safe.

Luis from their group had accidently filmed the entire ordeal, from the girls' joyful leap into the snow to the chaotic rush to get them out. Later, as they rewatched the footage, laughter erupted—Krishna's single-minded rescue of Nati standing out like a scene from a dramatic movie.

"You really were in hero mode," one of the girls teased, wiping away the last of her tears from laughing so hard.

Krishna shook his head, embarrassed but laughing along. "I just reacted. Didn't even think."

Nati playfully nudged him. "Well, I'm glad you did. You saved me!"

Their laughter echoed across the snowy hills as they replayed the video, over and over, unable to believe how crazy the whole situation had been. Their fun adventure had turned into a nerve-wracking experience, but in the end, it had brought them all closer together.

Later, as they wound their way down the hilly road, Nati began to feel the toll of the day's excitement. She turned pale and soon leaned over the side of the car, vomiting from motion sickness. Krishna rubbed her back, trying to comfort her as best as he could.

"You, okay?" he asked, his voice tight with worry.

Nati nodded weakly, resting her head on his shoulder once she had calmed down. "Just dizzy," she muttered. "I'll be fine."

Nati dozed against Krishna's shoulder, her breath slow and steady, the day's chaos finally giving way to quiet. He looked out the window, his mind swirling with the day's events. From the jump into the snow to their shared laughter, everything felt like a whirlwind. Despite the challenges, there was something magical about it—about how they had faced everything together.

The next day, the group returned to Valle Nevado for some snow surfing and skating. While Nati and the others were naturals on the snowboards, gracefully gliding down the slopes, Krishna was the opposite. A first timer, he spent more time falling than standing. But each time he managed to stay upright for more than a few seconds, he felt a small victory.

"Look at you, getting better every time!" Nati cheered, with a teasing voice full of encouragement.

Krishna grinned, though his legs were shaky. "Barely staying up, but I'll take it!"

By the end of the day, despite the falls, the laughs, and the scares, Krishna couldn't have asked for a better experience. It was a day full of memories he knew he would carry with him for a long time. Nati smiled at him, her face flushed from the cold, he realized that it wasn't just the adventure—it was sharing it with her that made it all so unforgettable.

The group's last adventure took them to the Atacama Desert—one of the driest places on Earth and a setting rich with ancient history.

It was New Year's Eve, and Atacama was a prime destination for tourists, a celebration unlike any other in Latin America. Krishna and Nati had been reluctant at first, but the group were insistent—this was a once-in-a-lifetime experience, and the cost wasn't too high.

For just $100 in airfare from Santiago to Calama, followed by a three-hour drive, the trip was well worth the effort. Though the tour cost more than Nati had expected—around $500—the idea of spending New Year's Eve in the desert beneath a vast, star-lit sky made the decision easy. Krishna, of course, was ready to follow Nati wherever she led.

They booked their trip at the last minute. The desert was calling them, another adventure waiting to unfold. Their flight was scheduled for 4:30 AM, meaning they had to be at the airport by 2:30 AM. That night, exhaustion took over, Nati curled up in Krishna's lap, her face relaxing into peaceful sleep. They stayed that way for hours, alternating between light conversation, brief naps, and quiet moments of comfort.

At 8:00 AM, after a short sleep and some restless chatting, they woke up feeling refreshed. With breakfast behind them and the day stretching out ahead, they decided not to waste time. A quick suggestion from the hotel's young receptionist led them to visit Fantasilandia, one of the top recreational centers in Santiago, renowned for its thrilling roller coasters and games. Excited, they got ready in no time.

Arrangements were quickly made. Within half an hour, Nati and Krishna were on route to one of Santiago's most happening places. The receptionist, with a smile, added, "Sir, you look Asian—if you get the chance, I suggest you visit the Jewels of India restaurant. It's one of the most highly rated foreign restaurants here in Santiago."

The moment they arrived at Fantasilandia, towering roller coasters stole their breath, their tracks twisting and looping into the sky.

Nervous but eager, they took on the highest coaster first. As the ride ascended, Nati clutched Krishna's hand tightly, her heart racing. When the coaster reached the peak and paused for a moment, they both took in the breathtaking view before plummeting downward at breakneck speed. Nati's eyes squeezed shut, her heart seemingly flying free, while Krishna—initially just as terrified—opened his eyes and took in the exhilarating experience. With each ascent and heart-stopping drop, they screamed, laughed and cherished the thrill of being so close to one another. By the time they rode it a third time, Nati had conquered her fear, keeping her eyes open the entire ride. They snapped crazy pictures, rode the water rides until they were soaked, and laughed as the roller coasters dried their clothes once again. By the time they left the park, it felt like they had experienced a dream—a day full of fun, laughter, and pure joy.

Later that evening, they headed to the Jewels of India restaurant. The moment they stepped inside, India enveloped them—warm spices in the air, soft sitar music humming in the background. The entrance featured a large copper vessel filled with water and floating red roses, centered around a blooming lotus flower. The waitstaff, dressed in traditional sarees and dhotis, greeted them with a respectful "Namaste," their hands folded in a welcoming gesture.

Nati's eyes swept over the walls, where towering depictions of the Taj Mahal and Mumbai's skyline transported her deeper into the heart of India. The lighting was soft and warm, creating a cozy, inviting atmosphere. As they were led to their table, an Indian couple performed a traditional welcome ceremony, marking Krishna and Nati's foreheads with kumkum tilaks. The gesture surprised Nati, who found herself fascinated by the depth of Indian customs.

As their plates emptied, Mr. Singh—a man with a booming laugh and kind eyes—appeared, cradling a bowl of glistening Gulab jamun. He introduced himself warmly and struck up a conversation with Krishna in Hindi, an unexpected delight for Krishna after being away from his homeland for so long. Mr. Singh shared the story of how he had come to Chile on a cycling tour, only to find love and establish one of the finest Indian restaurants in Latin America. His words, "It's all because of love, my friend," echoed in Krishna's mind, sparking a quiet reflection on the power of love and destiny.

Intrigued by Mr. Singh's tale, Nati asked to meet the woman who had inspired his journey. Moments later, a graceful woman emerged, greeting them with a gentle smile. The couple spent time with Krishna and Nati, talking about life, love, and the strength of following one's heart. They talked for a while, exchanging stories and enjoying each other's company. By the time they left, it was close to 11:30 p.m., the restaurant had closed its doors to new patrons.

The night felt magical, full of warmth, connections, and heartfelt stories. Mr. Singh arranged a taxi for them, and as they left the restaurant, both Krishna and Nati were lost in thought. Mr. Singh's incredible journey for love lingered in their minds, a testament to the power of destiny. For Krishna, a practical man, it was a revelation—love could indeed inspire the most unbelievable of adventures.

Back at the hotel, past midnight, they knew sleep was a lost cause. Instead, they stayed up, listening to music, curled up together. Without realizing it, they drifted off to sleep.

At 3:30 AM, they were jolted from their deep sleep by loud knocking on their door. The alarm had been ringing, the phone buzzing, and the receptionist had been trying to reach them, but nothing had woken them up. Nati sprang out of bed, realizing with a start, "Krishna! We missed the flight!"

Panic set in as they hurriedly packed their bags, tossing clothes and passports into suitcases without much thought. They rushed to the taxi, apologizing profusely to their friends and the receptionist, who had been knocking from at least half an hour. Luis, one of the group members, stood outside, fuming but relieved. They sped to the airport, unsure if they would make it. The streets were eerily empty, but time felt like it was slipping away.

The check-in dragged unbearably. As the final boarding call rang out, they tore through the terminal, barely making it. Against all odds, they stumbled onto the plane, breathless, their laughter tangled with exhaustion and relief. As they settled into their seats, Krishna pulled Nati close. "We almost missed the flight today," he said with a grin.

"We got lucky," she replied, still catching her breath, "but it's part of the adventure, isn't it?"

As the plane lifted into the sky, the two finally relaxed, ready for their next adventure in the surreal and breathtaking Atacama Desert. Krishna stared at the parched earth, its cracks running like veins across a lifeless expanse stretching beyond sight.

It is the world's driest desert—the Atacama.

The ground stretched out in a pale, cracked expanse, baking under the relentless sun. It was his first glimpse of what the world's driest desert could look like—a place where life seemed absent. In the distance, giant solar panels gleamed under the relentless sun, covering the open space as far as the eyes could see.

The driver, a local with a sun-weathered face, enthusiastically shared stories about the Atacama Desert and its unique treasure—solar energy. This region, he explained, is one of the largest producers of solar power in the world, thanks to its constant, blazing sunshine. The desolate beauty of the desert was unlike anything Krishna had ever seen.

When they finally reached San Pedro de Atacama, it felt like stepping into another world. The village—San Pedro, a tiny oasis nestled between towering sand mountains, shimmered under the desert sun.

Despite its small size, San Pedro was bustling with tourists, all drawn for the famous New Year celebrations.

The narrow streets were crowded with travelers from around the globe; every hostel and restaurant were packed.

Krishna's group had booked their stay at Hostel Perita, a cozy spot conveniently located near the town's main attractions like the historic St. Pedro Church, the ancient ruins of Pukara de Quitor, and the central square. As they walked through the streets, the heat was oppressive; however, the energy of the place kept them moving. The village had its own unique charm—simple but vibrant, with small pizzerias and cafés lining the streets. San Pedro thrived on Chilean flavors, untouched by the global sprawl of global fast-food chains like Domino's or McDonald's.

The group managed to negotiate a three-day tour package with a local travel agency, thanks to Krishna's persistence. He had stepped in to handle the haggling, much to the relief of the others, who weren't keen on the back-and-forth bargaining. In the end, his efforts paid off, securing them a fair deal for the adventure ahead.

Day One:

After an early breakfast at the hostel, the group piled into a van for the first full day of their tour. Their destination: the famous Atacama salt flats and the breathtaking Antiplanic Lagoons. As the van made its way through the barren desert landscape, the group marveled at the scenery.

The salt flats were a vast, shimmering expanse of white, stretching out like a sea of snow under the bright sun. Krishna marveled at the vast, unbroken stretch of white, a landscape so alien it felt like stepping onto the surface of the moon.

The tour continued as the van climbed higher into the Andes, winding through dramatic landscapes that seemed to change with every turn. Soon, they arrived at the Miscanti and Miñiques Lagoons, nestled in the shadows of towering volcanoes. At over 13,800 feet above sea level, the lagoons were a sight to behold—deep blue waters surrounded by rugged, volcanic terrain.

The moment they had been waiting for arrived—the chance to swim in the lagoons. It was a surreal experience—like floating in the Dead Sea. The salt-rich water kept them afloat with ease, their bodies refusing to dip beneath the surface. Krishna and Nati, along with the others, laughed and splashed around, playing water games and racing each other in teams. It was a joyful, carefree moment amid the harsh desert.

After their swim, they headed to the small village of Socaire for a traditional lunch. The food was simple yet flavorful, showcasing the local cuisine—freshly made bread, hearty stews, and delicious roasted meats. Satiated and pleasantly worn out, they leaned back in their chairs, letting the warmth of the meal settle.

On the way back to the hostel, they made a brief stop at the Toconao village, where they visited the famous bell tower and the San Lucas Church. The quiet beauty of these historic sites contrasted sharply with the wild, adventurous energy of the day. When they stumbled back to Hostel Perita, sleep was the only thing on their minds. They barely managed to grab a quick dinner before collapsing into bed, too tired to do anything but fall into a deep sleep.

As they parted ways with the driver, he offered a piece of advice with a knowing smile: "Make sure to bring your sweatshirts tomorrow. It gets cold up in the mountains."

Day Two

"Good morning, everyone! Today, we're going to witness one of the most incredible geothermal fields," the tour guide announced with enthusiasm. His cheerful voice clashed against a chorus of half-hearted grumbles and muffled yawns.

It was 5:30 AM. The group was barely awake, adjusting to the early morning chill of the desert. Everyone's eyes gave away their exhaustion from the day before. The first stop of the day was the Tatio Geyser field, one of the highest geothermal fields in the world, sitting more than 4,000 meters above sea level. The air was thin and cold, yet breathtakingly crisp. The rising steam from the earth greeted them as they stepped out into the geothermal wonder.

Despite the near-freezing air, the steaming thermal pools beckoned, their warmth curling like whispers of relief against the cold. The contrast was exhilarating—icy air met with the warmth of the spring, nature's perfect fusion.

As they soaked in the hot springs, the group marveled at the beauty of their surroundings. Hot springs gurgled, sending streams of boiling water cascading down rocks before cooling rapidly into icy rivers only a few meters away. Around them, vibrant wildflowers bloomed, brightening the rocky landscape, while wisps of fumaroles rose into the clear blue sky.

Afterward, they took the road back toward San Pedro de Atacama, pausing to appreciate the desert's surreal beauty. Native flora and fauna dotted the landscape, their guide continued narrating the history and significance of the region. Their next stop was the tiny village of Machuka, an ancient settlement once home to llama shepherds.

Machuka's adobe and cactus homes stood like relics of a bygone era, each wall a silent witness to generations of Andean life. The village specialized in local products like llama meat, empanadas, and handwoven crafts, each item telling a story of the region's rich cultural heritage.

As the day drew to a close, the group passed through the Valley of the Moon, an otherworldly landscape nestled in the heart of the desert.

The Valley of the Moon felt unearthly, its dunes rising like frozen waves, its jagged rocks chiseled by centuries of desert wind. The sunset painted the sky in violent streaks of crimson and gold, as if the desert itself had caught fire.

As the sun dipped below the horizon, a full moon rose in the east, casting a silvery glow over the landscape. It was a scene so perfect that it felt surreal, a quiet moment of fulfillment as the desert cooled and the stars began to appear.

Day Three

On the third day, they slept in—finally. It was a leisurely morning, waking up at 9:00 AM after two days of non-stop exploration. Their itinerary for the day was simple: a relaxed day of cycling around San Pedro de Atacama and exploring the village's charms. They rented bicycles and spent the day riding through the narrow, dusty streets of the desert town, stopping to enjoy local cuisine and take in the mesmerizing scenery.

By late afternoon, San Pedro buzzed with restless anticipation. New Year's Eve had arrived, and the energy in the air crackled like a live wire. As the group cycled back to their hostel, they noticed preparations for the town's New Year's celebrations in full swing. Moon Valley called them back, this time bathed in moonlight. The desert morphed into an alien dreamscape—sand domes loomed like sleeping giants, and salt caves shimmered under the silver glow.

When they returned to San Pedro, the town had come alive. Funky dummies were being strapped to chairs, symbols of the year's hardships and sorrows, ready to be burned in ritualistic fires at midnight. By the time the clock struck 7:00 p.m., the streets were aflame with anticipation. The traditional fires were lit, and with them, the town burst into a frenzy of music, dancing, and celebration. The streets pulsed with bodies, music, and the smoky scent of burning wood. Locals readied effigies—manifestations of the year's struggles—preparing to send them up in flames. As the sun set, the celebrations kicked into full gear. Krishna and Nati found themselves swept up in the madness, dancing with strangers around the bonfires. The air was thick with the smell of burning wood, and fireworks lit up the sky. People shouted, laughed, and sang, their joy was infectious.

At the stroke of midnight, fireworks ignited the sky.

"Happy New Year, Nati," Krishna whispered, pulling her close.

"Feliz Año Nuevo, Krishna," she replied softly, her voice carrying a warmth that cut through the cold desert night.

Krishna glanced at Nati—her face aglow in bursts of red and gold, her eyes reflecting the fire above. Without thinking he pulled her close and their lips met in a kiss that felt both inevitable and electric. The world around them seemed to fade away, leaving only the two of them standing together.

The freezing night held them in its grip, their breath curling together like smoke in the cold. It was a moment of pure, unfiltered connection. The desert, the fire, the madness of the crowd—they all faded away as Krishna and Nati shared their first kiss, lost in the moment. The night continued in a blur of dancing and celebration, the crowd growing wilder as the hours passed. By the time they stumbled back to the hostel, it was well past 2:30 a.m., the alcohol still coursing through their veins. Exhausted—but happy.

The receptionist later told them that a kind local had found them wandering aimlessly and brought them back to the hostel, using the visiting card Krishna had kept in his pocket.

Chapter 11

Not My Kind of Coffee

The next morning, they woke up late, heads heavy from the night before. It was nearly 12:30 p.m. when the receptionist knocked on their door, reminding them of their 2:30 p.m. checkout time. Krishna and Nati, along with the rest of their group, barely made it out in time.

The trip to Atacama was over, but the memories would last a lifetime. By 5:30 p.m., they were in Kalama; by 8:30, they were back in Santiago. The U.S. group invited them to join the next leg of their journey to Torres del Paine National Park, but Nati was homesick by then. Peru was calling her back, and besides, the trip would have been too expensive.

They parted ways with their U.S. friends, who were heading to Torres del Paine. Krishna and Nati shared one last meal together. The group invited them to join, but Nati, feeling the pull of home, declined. Their journey had been unforgettable, but it was time to return to Peru.

When Krishna returned to the hostel around 9:30 p.m., Jackie and Bruce had another plan up their sleeves. Buzzing with excitement, they roped Krishna into their next mischief.

"Hey, Krishna, we're going to check out a club later. You should join us," Jackie said, grinning.

Nearby, Dimitri and Maria exchanged knowing glances, clearly aware of Jackie and Bruce's destination.

"Okay, we'll go together," Krishna replied, oblivious to anything unusual. What he didn't know was that these places weren't exactly welcoming to women. Jackie and Bruce had something very specific in mind.

A few minutes later, Jackie casually mentioned the destination to Nati. "We're going to Café con Piernas," she said. "We wanted Krishna to come, but he doesn't want to go without you. What do you think?"

Nati smiled knowingly. She had heard of Café con Piernas, a Chilean institution famous not just for its coffee, but for the scantily clad waitresses that served it. "You can take Krishna. I'm too tired; honestly, I'd rather rest," she said with a light chuckle. "But have fun!"

Unaware of the café's reputation, Krishna assumed they were simply going out for coffee. The name sounded harmless enough—"Coffee with Legs"—he imagined it was some quirky, lively café.

"I'll be back soon," he told Nati, as the group headed out.

The café was deep in Santiago's downtown, near Plaza de Armas. As they walked, the city was still alive with the afterglow of New Year's celebrations. Krishna felt the energy pulsing through the streets. Soon, they arrived at a small, nondescript building with a heavy door. It didn't look like any café Krishna had seen before, but he followed Jackie and Bruce inside.

As soon as they stepped in, Krishna was struck by the dim lighting, loud music, and smoky air. The café was nothing like Krishna had imagined. The walls were lined with mirrors, reflecting the dim neon lights that gave the place a strange nightclub vibe. There were no chairs, just long counters where customers stood, their eyes fixated on the waitresses. The women—tall, long-legged, dressed in incredibly revealing outfits—moved gracefully between the patrons, offering drinks with flirtatious smiles.

Krishna froze. This wasn't a café. Not in the way he had imagined. This was "Café con Piernas," literally "coffee with legs," and it was clear that the focus here was far less on the coffee and much more on the atmosphere of sensuality. He glanced around uncomfortably, noticing the older businessmen and tourists standing casually, some with loosened ties, others engaged in playful conversations with the waitresses. The waitresses were performing pole dances circling around the person. Mirrors lined the walls, doubling the presence of waitresses in short skirts and towering heels, their outfits leaving little to the imagination.

Krishna quickly realized what "Café con Piernas" truly meant: coffee served by women whose legs were as much the focus as the drinks.

Bruce and Jackie seemed completely at ease, already ordering drinks and chatting with one of the girls. Krishna, on the other hand, was in shock. The place was filled with an air of playful but suggestive energy, feeling more like a performance than a simple café experience. Every movement of the waitresses seemed designed to catch the eye, and the mirrored walls ensured that no matter where you stood, you had a view of the entire room.

The waitresses moved with ease, their practiced smiles never faltering. Every movement seemed calculated; every smile perfectly timed. Krishna couldn't help but feel out of place, his discomfort growing as he realized how normalized the whole setup was. It was not just about the coffee; it was about the experience of being served by beautiful women in a way that blurred the line between casual café culture and something more suggestive.

He watched as one of the waitresses approached their group. Her dress was so short it was practically non-existent, with her long legs on full display. She smiled as she took their order, leaning in slightly as she asked what they wanted. Jackie, clearly in his element, flirted back with ease, while Krishna remained quiet, still absorbing the scene.

"Café con piernas," Jackie said with a wink, ordering for all of them.

As Krishna stood awkwardly by the counter, Jackie leaned over and grinned. "This is it, man! Café con Piernas, Chilean style! What do you think?" Krishna gave a half-hearted smile.

By their easy rapport with the waitresses, it was clear—these men weren't first-timers. Every so often, a waitress would stop to chat, flirt, occasionally receiving a generous tip that ranged from a few hundred Chilean pesos to several thousand. Some even kissed the customers on the cheek as a form of greeting or thanks for a larger tip.

Krishna took a sip of his coffee once it arrived. It was strong, almost bitter, but good. The taste, however, was secondary to the entire experience happening around him. Men flirted, cracked jokes, and slipped tips to the waitresses, who played along with casual charm. Every now and then, one of the waitresses would lean in for a kiss on the cheek—a standard part of the interaction for those who tipped well.

The whole atmosphere was a strange blend of casual coffee culture and something more risqué. It aggressive, but it was certainly designed to push boundaries. Krishna felt a little out of place, not quite understanding how he had ended up in such a situation.

As they finished their coffees, Jackie and Bruce were already buzzing with energy, talking about the next coffee. They'd heard about another coffee menu that offered something called "Happy Minutes," and they were determined to check it out. There was even talk of heading to a strip club afterward. Krishna, however, had reached his limit. The whole experience had left him feeling uneasy, he was ready to call it a night.

He glanced at Jackie and Bruce, who were clearly on a different wavelength, fully charged from the café's strange blend of sensuality and caffeine.

"You guys go ahead," Krishna said, standing up. "I think I'm done for the night."

Jackie and Bruce tried to convince him, but Krishna shook his head. "I'll catch up with you later," he insisted, already thinking about getting back to the hotel and reuniting with Nati. As much as he enjoyed hanging out with his friends, this wasn't the kind of experience he wanted to carry with him.

Stepping out into the fresh air, Krishna felt a wave of relief. The night had been bizarre, a strange detour from the adventure he and Nati had been on together. The night had taken an unexpected turn, but in the end, it wasn't where he belonged.

Krishna's mind was still spinning from the café's intense atmosphere as he walked toward Plaza de Armas, ready to leave the smoky, mirrored walls of Café con Piernas behind. The contrast between the seductive energy of Café con Piernas and the calm of Santiago's quiet streets began to settle in. His mind raced, Nati's voice echoing. He felt a swirl of emotions—guilt, frustration, and responsibility.

Thirty minutes passed before Nati started calling Krishna, her anxiety spiraling into obsession. Krishna stood near Plaza de Armas, oblivious to Jackie and Bruce, who were lost in their own world.

When Krishna finally checked his phone, he was startled—it had 32 missed calls from Nati, all within half an hour. He immediately called her back, but Nati was furious.

"Krishna, you don't talk to me. You boys are all the same! Do you know how many times I called you? Thirty-two! Were you too busy enjoying your coffee with piernas?" She said, her voice filled with anger, anxiety and jealousy.

"I'm sorry, Nati. My phone was on silent. I just saw the missed calls," Krishna tried to explain, but her anger only intensified.

"Why did you go? You're all the same. I don't want to talk to you anymore," she snapped.

"Nati, you told me to go! I wasn't even planning to, you know that!" Krishna countered, trying to stay calm.

"Yeah, I said it, but it doesn't mean you should've gone!" Nati's voice was restless.

"Where are you now?" She demanded.

"I'm outside the café. They're still inside having coffee. I doubt they'll even need dinner after all the 'coffee and beauties' they're indulging in," Krishna added, trying to lighten the mood.

"I want you to come right now! I'm at Plaza de Armas. I couldn't stay still, so I came," Nati confessed.

"Nati, are you crazy? It's 10 p.m. we're in a foreign place! You shouldn't have come alone!" Krishna said, feeling a mix of worry and disbelief.

"Wait there, I'm coming," he added, quickly heading back into the café.

Loud music and thick smoke hit him the moment he stepped back inside. Jackie was sipping his third coffee while a scantily clad waitress performed a pole dance right in front of him, much to his delight. Krishna didn't waste time. He walked straight up to Jackie and said, "Nati is outside. I'm leaving. You guys continue." Without waiting for a response, Krishna quickly left the café.

Once outside, Krishna called Nati. "Where exactly are you?"

"I'm near the church," she replied.

"Stay there, I'll be there in five minutes."

Krishna made his way to the church, The moment Krishna spotted her, standing under the dim light by the church steps, he felt a wave of relief. Nati saw him too and ran toward him, throwing her arms around him before he could say a word. She was trembling, her breath uneven. He couldn't hold back his emotions.

"I'm so mad at you," she whispered, her voice a mix of anger and relief. "You left me alone, Krishna… you didn't answer. I thought—"

"I know. I'm sorry," he said softly, hugging her tightly. He could feel her heartbeat racing. "But I was only away for half an hour."

"It felt like forever. I… I couldn't bear it," Nati confessed, burying her face into his chest. "I almost came to drag you out of that place."

He gently placed his hand on her cheek, lifting her face to meet his gaze. "You don't ever have to worry, Nati. I'm here, always. I missed you too."

She looked at him, her wide eyes full of emotion. "You don't understand. When you didn't pick up, I was in panic. It was like a piece of me was slipping away."

Krishna gently pressed a finger to her lips, silencing her, before pulling her into a comforting embrace. He could feel the weight of her worry and guilt lifting between them. As they stood there, the seductive atmosphere of the café, with its smoky air and sensuous allure, felt like a distant memory.

What mattered now was the purity of Nati's love, her innocence shining brighter than any temptation the night had offered.

They headed toward the church together.

Inside the church at Plaza de Armas, one of the oldest and most sacred places in the city, Nati knelt to pray, her expression soft and serene. Krishna watched her in awe. In this quiet moment, he saw a side of her he hadn't seen before—calm, reflective, and at peace. There was no trace of the playful, sometimes restless energy that usually surrounded her. She was completely still, her hands clasped as if her soul was speaking in silence.

For the first time, he saw Nati in a different light—silent, composed and deeply spiritual. Her usual energy and chatter had given way to a serene calmness. Krishna couldn't bring himself to pray; instead, he found himself mesmerized by the sight of Nati, her face a picture of quiet devotion.

It was a rare moment. Nati's lips were still, her mind focused on something beyond them both. Krishna felt a wave of love and admiration wash over him. In that moment, he realized how multifaceted she was—full of life and energy, yet capable of such deep, peaceful reflection. He stood there, watching her, and understood that this quiet, praying Nati with her pure heart and innocent soul was the true essence of her beauty.

The dim light from the church's candles illuminated her face, softening her features, making her appear even more serene. It was a stark contrast to the heated argument they'd shared earlier. The anger, jealousy, and confusion that had clouded her mind seemed to dissipate in the sanctity of the church. Krishna couldn't help but admire how easily she transitioned from chaos to calm—from the fiery woman who had frantically called him 32 times in a frenzy to the peaceful figure kneeling before him now.

He took a seat beside her, letting the silence wash over him. While he had always been more of a thinker than a man of prayer, this moment felt sacred in an unfamiliar yet profound way. Perhaps it wasn't the church or the prayer, but Nati's presence—her vulnerability, her raw emotion—

that made him feel connected to something greater than himself.

As she prayed, Krishna found himself reflecting on the events of the evening. The Café con Piernas, with its mirrored walls and flirtatious waitresses, felt worlds away now. He hadn't enjoyed it the way Jackie and Bruce had, nor had he been as drawn into the seductive atmosphere. In fact, he had felt out of place, constantly thinking about Nati, wondering how she was doing and whether she'd be angry. And she was. But now, seeing her in this quiet moment, he felt a deep sense of gratitude that she had come for him, even in her anger, even when she didn't need to.

Nati eventually opened her eyes and turned to him, her face soft, no longer tense with frustration. "I prayed for us," she whispered, her voice calm but full of emotion. "I don't want to fight with you anymore, Krishna."

Krishna smiled softly, reaching for her hand. "Neither do I. I'm sorry for tonight, Nati. I should've called you sooner, or maybe... I shouldn't have gone at all."

Nati squeezed his hand gently, her eyes searching his for sincerity.

" I don't care that you went," she admitted. "I just hate the idea of losing you. When you didn't answer, it felt like you were slipping away."

Krishna frowned, pulling her closer. "You'll never lose me, Nati. I'm right here."

"I know," she replied, though a hint of uncertainty lingered in her voice. "But it's hard sometimes, you know?

I've been alone for a long time, and now that I have you, I just don't want anything to take you away."

Her vulnerability hit him deeply. He hadn't realized how much she feared losing him. Now that he understood, he wanted to reassure her in every way possible. He leaned in, placing a soft kiss on her forehead. "I'm not going anywhere."

For a moment, they sat in silence, the hum of the church around them, their hands intertwined. It was as though time had paused, leaving just the two of them in this sacred space, connected by something far greater than either of them had imagined when they first met.

Finally, Nati broke the silence, her voice light but serious. "Next time, I'm coming with you to those places. I'm not letting you go,out of my sight."

Krishna chuckled, relieved to hear the humor returning to her voice. "Deal. But I don't think I'll be going to any Café con Piernas anytime soon."

Nati smiled, her eyes twinkling with mischief. "Good. Because I'm the only one you need to have coffee with."

They both laughed softly, the tension between them fully dissolved. As they left the church together, hand in hand, Krishna couldn't help but feel that they had crossed a new threshold in their relationship. It wasn't just about attraction or companionship anymore. It was trust, understanding—a deeper connection neither of them had anticipated but both now cherished.

The bustling chaos of Santiago and the memories of the café were distant now, overshadowed by something simpler and stronger. In that peaceful space, Krishna realized that Nati wasn't just someone he cared for—she was becoming someone he couldn't imagine being without.

Nati walked close to Krishna, her arm linked through his. She rested her head lightly on his shoulder. For a while, neither of them spoke.

Descending into the Plaza de Armas metro station, Krishna marveled at the architectural beauty of Santiago's underground. It was one of the most advanced and efficient systems he had ever seen—automated gates, sleek trains, and a design that blended functionality with artistry. As they made their way down the steps and into the tunnel, melancholic strains of a violin echoed around them.

A young musician stood near the entrance; his eyes closed as he poured his soul into the instrument. The melody was unfamiliar but hauntingly beautiful. Krishna felt compelled to stop and listen. Moved by the performance, he reached into his pocket and tipped the violinist 1,000 Chilean pesos. Nati did the same, smiling warmly at the musician before they continued.

At the turnstile, Krishna swiped his metro card and passed through, turning to say something to Nati. He noticed she wasn't beside him. She was standing on the other side, a puzzled look on her face as she rummaged through her purse.

"What's wrong?" he asked.

"Krishna, my card's balance is empty. I've got no cash left," Nati said, her voice tinged with worry. She added, "I gave the last of my money to the violinist. How stupid of me!

" Here, take mine," Krishna offered, handing his card back over the barrier.

She swiped it, the turnstile flashed red. Insufficient balance." she read aloud, her shoulders slumping. "Great. And I just gave my last pesos to the violinist too."

Krishna checked his pockets, but all he could find was a few coins—not nearly enough for a ticket. They had left their cash back at the hotel for safety, carrying only small amounts of cash while exploring.

A wave of helplessness swept over Krishna.

"Nati, wait. Let me come back out—we'll figure something out," he said, but before he could think of a plan, Nati did something unexpected.

As he began to look around, Nati glanced nervously at the sparse crowd and the station officials nearby. Without warning, she took a quick step back, eyed the turnstile and in one swift motion leaped over the gate.

"Nati!" Krishna hissed, his voice urgent and filled with disbelief.

"Come on!" She urged, a mischievous grin on her face. "Before they see us!"

she had already taken off, running through the station. He heard the shrill sound of a whistle—probably a police officer who had spotted her. Without hesitation, Krishna sprinted after her, catching up in a few seconds. He grabbed her hand, and they ran together, their faces filled with terror as they glanced over their shoulders, hoping no one was chasing them.

When things go wrong, they tend to spiral. As they reached the platform, the metro doors slid shut just in front of them and the train sped away. They stood in silence, catching their breath, hiding behind one of the large pillars. Nati was shivering, both from the cold and the adrenaline. Krishna held her hand tightly, trying to offer some comfort.

Finally, the next train arrived. The station was mostly empty, but the metro itself was full—it was the end of the workday, and many were heading home. There was only one seat left, and Krishna insisted that Nati take it. He stood beside her as the metro started moving, both finally able to breathe a sigh of relief after their wild escape.

Nati's eyes sparkled. "Sometimes you have to break the rules a little," she teased.

They exchanged a look, eyes locking with a mix of disbelief and amusement. The tension began to melt into laughter. "We're insane," Nati said, her voice soft but full of affection.

"I know," Krishna agreed, grinning.

Krishna stood beside her; their fingers still entwined.

Nearby, a couple remained locked in a kiss, oblivious to everything around them. It was a common sight in Chile—people openly expressing their affection in public places, whether at metro stations, parks, or theaters. For a moment, the chaos of their situation melted away as Krishna and Nati watched the couple. An older lady sitting next to Nati looked at them and smiled kindly. "Would you like to sit next to your lady?" she asked Krishna, hinting that he should take the seat beside Nati. They both chuckled and politely declined, sharing a secret smile as they held each other's hands.

As the train passed station after station, they felt a warmth growing between them. Nati suddenly stood up, moving closer to Krishna. "Krishna, I want to make this metro ride memorable," she whispered, her voice filled with affection.

Before Krishna could respond, she leaned in, her breath warm against his skin, and kissed him tenderly. It was a soft, lingering kiss, filled with warmth and passion. For the first time, they kissed in public, surrounded by strangers, yet entirely wrapped in their own bubble of love. When their lips parted, they realized they had missed their stop, carried away by the moment. Laughing, they hurried off the train at the next station.

It was late when they finally reached the hotel after their wild metro adventure. The streets were quiet, with only the occasional passerby, and the air was crisp with a chill. Nati and Krishna, still catching their breath from their impromptu sprint and kiss, walked closely, leaning into each other with a sense of relief, excitement, and exhaustion.

As they entered the hotel lobby, it was nearly 11:45 p.m. The warmth of the building was a welcome contrast to the cold outside. Krishna looked at Nati, her cheeks flushed from the cool air and the rush of the evening. He had a sudden urge to surprise her and dashed over to a nearby shop that was just about to close.

"Wait here for a second," he said, hurrying toward the store window where he had spotted a bright yellow top on display. The shopkeeper was about to turn the lights off, but Krishna pleaded for just a moment.

The man reluctantly agreed, and Krishna quickly bought the top—a beautiful, sunny yellow with the words "You are mine" written across it. He ran back to Nati, who was waiting at the hotel entrance, her expression both curious and amused.

"What did you just do?" She asked, playfully.

"I got something for you," Krishna said, grinning as he handed her the bag. Nati opened it, her eyes lit up when she saw the top.

"Oh my God, Krishna!" She exclaimed, holding it up. "This is beautiful! You didn't have to—"

"I had to," Krishna interrupted, his smile warm. "You're mine, remember?"

Nati laughed softly, her eyes glistening. Without a word, she ran upstairs to their room to change into it. When she came out, wearing the yellow top, Krishna's breath caught. The bright color made her glow, she looked even more beautiful than he had imagined.

"Save me, Nati," Krishna said dramatically, placing a hand on his heart. "I'm falling for you all over again."

Nati giggled, coming closer to him. "You're ridiculous."

"I'm serious!" Krishna teased, wrapping her into his arms. They hugged again, tightly, as though the night's craziness had only brought them closer. The cold outside was nothing compared to the warmth they shared in that moment.

But as they held each other, Krishna suddenly pulled back with a mischievous grin. "You know what I really want right now?"

Nati raised an eyebrow. "What?"

"Chocolate," Krishna said, his eyes twinkling. "I want chocolate."

Nati blinked. "Krishna, are you mad? It's freezing outside, it's almost midnight. There's no way I'm going back out there again."

Krishna pouted, putting on his best pleading expression. "Come on, Nati. Tomorrow we're leaving, and I won't get another chance to try this famous chocolate here. Please? For me?"

Nati groaned, clearly exhausted but unable to resist the look on his face. "Ugh, fine! But you owe me, Krishna. I'm tired."

Before she could protest further, Krishna scooped her up, lifting her onto his back with a playful laugh. "Don't worry, I'll carry you to the ice cream parlor near the Tobalaba metro station!"

By the time Krishna and Nati reached the ice cream parlor, the air was crisp, their breath visible in the cold. Yet it did nothing to diminish their warmth and the shared moment. The small shop was winding down for the night, but the welcoming glow of its lights invited them in. The scent of chocolate and waffle cones filled the space as they stood at the counter, ordering their treats.

Krishna handed Nati her chocolate ice cream, his eyes sparkling as he watched her take the first bite. She shivered, both from the cold and the overwhelming sweetness of the moment. They sat on a bench outside the parlor, nestled together against the chill, laughing softly as they shared the absurdity of having ice cream in the freezing night.

"This is crazy, Krishna," Nati said, shaking her head. "It's freezing, and here we are eating ice cream."

"It's the best kind of craziness though, isn't it?"

"It's perfect. Chocolate, the cold, and you." Krishna nodded, savoring the moment.

Nati looked at him, her eyes softening as she took in the warmth of his expression and nodded. She took another bite of her ice cream, letting the cold treat melt in her mouth before speaking again. "You know... I never thought I'd be doing something like this. Running through metro gates, kissing in public, eating ice cream in the dead of night..."

Krishna smiled, reaching out to brush a strand of hair from her face. "Life's full of surprises, Nati. I'm glad I get to share them with you."

They stayed there for a while, huddled together on the bench, sharing chocolate ice cream under the starlit sky. The city was quiet, almost as if it was just for them. Despite the cold, the warmth between them made everything feel right.

She turned to him, her face lit by the streetlamp, her breath visible in the cold air. "You make me do things I wouldn't normally do," she said, her voice softer now. "Things that scare me, things that make me feel alive."

He chuckled, rubbing his hands together to keep warm. "That's because you're always overthinking. Sometimes, you just have to live in the moment."

Nati gave a small laugh, her lips curling into a smile. "I know. And you're the one teaching me that."

The two sat in silence for a few minutes, finishing their ice creams and simply enjoying the quiet of the night. Despite the cold, there was a sense of warmth between them, a comfort that neither of them wanted to break. Finally, Krishna stood up and stretched.

"Alright, enough ice cream for now. Let's head back before we freeze."

Nati laughed and stood as well, rubbing her hands together for warmth. "You're right. I don't think I can feel my fingers anymore."

Krishna gave her a playful grin and offered his hand. "Come on, let's go warm up."

They walked back to the hotel, their steps slower now, more relaxed. The streets were quiet, the city seeming to fall asleep around them. Nati leaned into Krishna, her head resting on his shoulder, and he wrapped an arm around her, pulling her closer.

When they finally reached the hotel, they were both tired but content. Nati changed into her new yellow top, the words "You are mine" shining softly under the dim hotel room light. Krishna watched her, his heart swelling with affection as she looked back at him with a playful smile.

"How do I look?" She asked, spinning slowly to show off the top.

"Like you're about to steal my heart again," Krishna teased, pulling her into a hug. "You look beautiful, Nati."

They stood there, wrapped in each other's arms, the world outside their little bubble of warmth and love. For a moment, time seemed to stand still, the only sound the soft hum of the city beyond the window.

"I think we've officially had the craziest night ever," she murmured, her eyes half-closed.

Krishna lay down beside her, pulling the blanket over them both. "And it's not over yet."

Nati peeked at him, a playful smirk on her face. "What do you mean?"

He grinned, leaning closer to her. "I mean... I think we still have some room for dessert."

Nati laughed softly, but before she could respond, she drifted off to sleep, her head resting on Krishna's shoulder. He smiled to himself, feeling an overwhelming sense of peace and happiness. The night had been chaotic, crazy, and a little terrifying at times, but it had also been filled with moments of pure joy.

As he closed his eyes, Krishna knew that this night, with its laughter, kisses, and chocolate, was one he'd never forget.

Chapter 12

The Art of Walking Away

Walking away takes courage, but it is in letting go that we find the strength to embrace new beginnings. Sometimes, the bravest thing we can do is leave behind what no longer serves us and step into the unknown.

By 9:00 AM, sunlight streamed through the window, waking them. Nati groaned, pulling the covers over her head, while Krishna stretched lazily. "Morning already?" she mumbled.

Krishna chuckled softly, leaning over to kiss her on the forehead. "Afraid so."

They had to check out by noon, but the memories of the previous night made them reluctant to leave. Nati eventually sat up, rubbing her eyes and glancing at Krishna with a sleepy smile.

"I'm never going to forget this night," she said softly, her voice filled with emotion.

Krishna smiled back at her, reaching out to take her hand. "Neither will I."

Their flight back to Peru was scheduled for noon, and with their bags packed and farewells exchanged with their

American friends, they headed to the Santiago International Airport.

As they boarded the flight, a quiet blend of excitement and nostalgia moved between them. It wasn't a long journey—just three hours from Santiago to Lima—but the experience felt profound. As the plane soared above the Andes, the captain's voice came over the intercom, giving a brief history of the majestic mountain range. He urged passengers to take in the breathtaking sight below. The snow-covered peaks stretched endlessly, and deep ravines sliced through the landscape like veins running through the earth. Krishna and Nati pressed against different windows, eager to take in every angle of the surreal view.

Their excitement was contagious—an air hostess smiled at them as if they were some of the craziest passengers she'd ever seen. For them, this might have been routine, but for Krishna and Nati, it was a once-in-a-lifetime experience.

They landed in Lima at 4:30 p.m.—the city that Nati had been homesick for. It felt like they had returned home after a whirlwind of adventure. The bustling capital of Peru greeted them, but Nati kept their arrival quiet, not telling any of her friends just yet.

They took a cab to Miraflores, one of Lima's upscale districts, settling into hotel for the night. They decided to stay in a hotel that night, giving Nati the chance to ease back into her life before meeting with friends and reconnecting with the busy rhythm of the city. By 8 AM the next day, the real frenzy began. Nati's friends, who hadn't seen her in months, bombarded her with messages and calls after she announced her return on WhatsApp.

Her popularity surged—not just for her vibrant personality, but for the travel stories she shared online. Travel reshaped Nati, shifting her perspective in unexpected ways. She was no longer the same person who had left for a world tour. It was a transformation that went beyond just travel—it was a profound shift in her perspective. The trip taught her to focus less on pleasing others and more on living fully, embracing the moment. Being back in Lima, her home, felt different now, like she was seeing it with new eyes. The city itself, with its Spanish influences and bustling streets, had always been familiar to her, but now, after all the adventures, it felt like a new world.

In Peru, people hardly speak English, but Nati navigated it effortlessly. She was excited to be back and even more excited to introduce Krishna to her world. Her friends, especially her roommate Camila and Joshua, couldn't wait to meet him.

Joshua threw a surprise party for Nati soon after she announced her return, gathering all their close friends. Krishna was the center of attention, though he wasn't used to it. Everyone greeted him with affection, adopting the Spanish custom of kissing on the cheek—a gesture that made Krishna a bit uncomfortable at first. In this land of Spanish speakers, Krishna felt like a fish out of water, but with Nati by his side, he never felt alone.

Joshua, once distant, had re-entered Nati's life, and their relationship had begun healing after some time apart. He had been unsure of Krishna initially, meeting him with casual politeness, but it didn't take long for the two to bond. Joshua was a kind-hearted person, and over the next few days, their circle of friends expanded to include Krishna, making him feel welcome in this new environment.

Days in Lima fell into a comfortable routine. They'd wake up, get ready, have lunch, then explore the city either by bicycle or by car. In Latin America, cars were the norm; Krishna hardly ever saw two-wheelers except for the occasional motorcycle delivering pizza. It was the only visible trace of India in such a distant corner of the world.

Nati's apartment had become more of a formality. She and Krishna spent nearly every moment together, whether it was exploring the city or simply enjoying each other's company. The only times they went back to her room were to grab Nati's clothes or when Camila—Nati's roommate wasn't home. Krishna sensed that Camila wanted to spend more time with them, but Nati always found a reason to keep some distance, wanting to preserve the special bond between her and Krishna.

Nati's parents, unable to visit due to family engagements, often called to check on them—especially on Krishna. They had grown fond of him, and though they couldn't meet him in person just yet, their warmth and care were always felt over the phone. Despite the challenges, Krishna never felt out of place. Being with Nati, surrounded by her friends and family's love, made even the most unfamiliar places feel like home.

One evening, while Nati was busy with her thesis at the college, Krishna roamed around the city, often spending his time in Miraflores. The district was beautiful, its name meaning 'look at the flowers,' and it lived up to that promise, filled with parks, gardens, and a vibrant mix of people—from joggers and dog walkers to tourists taking in the scenery.

Krishna came across a vibrant circle of elderly dancers swaying to upbeat music in a garden. Their laughter and carefree movements captivated him, radiating a joy that transcended age. The scene fascinated him. They were strangers who found joy in each other's company, dancing together with a carefree spirit that was inspiring. For them, age seemed irrelevant—just a number that couldn't stop them from living fully.

As Krishna wandered through Miraflores, he took in the vibrant energy of the district—the chatter of café-goers, the scent of fresh flowers, the ocean breeze rolling in from the cliffs. Camila messaged Krishna, asking if he was bored and invited him to dinner with her friends. She had always been warm toward Krishna, her easygoing nature making conversations flow effortlessly. Nati once remarked that Camila seemed eager to spend more time with their group, though she herself kept a subtle distance. Krishna agreed without much thought, later that evening, Nati joined them, slipping into the group with her usual quiet grace.

After dinner, as they strolled near a food street, Krishna's eyes fell on a large, well-lit casino just a few blocks away. The casino pulsed with energy, its neon glow and buzzing crowd pulling Krishna in like a moth to a flame. As he saw the blackjack table, something stirred in him—a rush he hadn't felt in days—drawing him toward it. Card games had always been his weakness, and the casino promised the perfect fix. His eyes sparkled with excitement, and after some convincing, the group headed inside.

The casino dripped with extravagance—marble floors gleaming under chandeliers, every detail crafted to seduce gamblers into the world of high stakes. Downstairs, rows of slot machines blinked and whirred under dim golden light, their hypnotic glow drawing in elderly patrons.

Upstairs, the stakes were higher. Five blackjack tables were arranged in a semicircle, with two roulette tables on the side and a private room reserved for high rollers. The sound of chips clinking and cards shuffling blended seamlessly with the smooth tunes of a live band playing nearby. The music added a touch of sophistication to the air, underscoring the thrill of the game.

Everything about the casino's design—from the complimentary wine and soft drinks to the elegantly dressed hostesses in high heels and sleek dresses—was crafted to entice. They moved gracefully among the players, offering service with warm smiles, adding to the seductive charm of the space. It was a world designed to invite you in, make you forget everything else, and dive deep into the games, the chase, the thrill of winning—or losing.

Krishna's eyes were on the blackjack tables. After some initial hesitation, Nati, Camila, and their friends started gambling on a small scale, playing with just 20-sol stakes. It didn't take long for the group to realize that luck wasn't on their side. One by one, they were wiped out—except for Camila, who managed to stay just above her starting money.

When Nati ran out of cash, she teasingly slipped her hands into Krishna's pockets, pulling out 100 soles and insisting that it was his turn to play. Krishna resisted for a while, knowing full well how emotionally charged the game could be. But with Nati's persistence and a sly smile, he finally caved.

"Uno... Dos... Tres... cuatro... up until Veinti-uno. The numbers might have been called differently, but the game itself was the same. It didn't matter where he was—whether in Peru or anywhere else—the thrill of blackjack remained unchanged. The mechanics of the game, the rush of the cards, it was all familiar to Krishna.

Krishna had long mastered the game—reading opponents, calculating risks, spotting traps most players never noticed.

In truth, Krishna had won against many, not through luck but through skill, patience, and an almost instinctual understanding of how the cards would play out. As the dealer called the numbers in Spanish, it didn't faze him. The language was different, but the game was the same—and for Krishna, that meant one thing: he was ready to win.

Sitting at the table, Krishna's demeanor changed. His face became stoic, his focus razor-sharp. He started small, playing two hands at a time—a strategy he knew well from his previous experiences. At first, it was just about breaking even. Soon, however, Krishna hit a winning streak. His steady, mechanical approach to the game started paying off, and before long, his stack of chips began to grow.

As the night went on, the casino floor buzzed with excitement. People gathered around Krishna's table, drawn by his calm yet commanding presence. Even the dealer seemed impressed, though trying to remain professional. Nati watched in awe as Krishna effortlessly built up his winnings, eventually turning 100 soles into over 5200.

Three straight losses drained Krishna's stack, sending a ripple of murmurs through the onlookers, their excitement dimming as they watched his streak falter. But he remained calm, his expression unshaken, as if nothing had happened. With a relaxed smile, he thanked the dealer, gracefully sliding a chip across the table as a tip.

Krishna rose from the table, every movement calm and deliberate. He'd played his hand—now it was time to walk away. The crowds at his table were buzzing with excitement. Nati and her friends, now thoroughly drunk on both wine and Krishna's success, cheered for him as if they were all victorious. It was the perfect end to a night of high stakes and fun. He wasn't in a rush to chase more wins or push his luck further. His calm composure showed he knew when it was time to walk away. Victory or loss—it made no difference to him. He played on his terms, not the casino's.

Krishna's unwavering focus held the room, even as the casino's free drinks and subtle temptations tried to pull him deeper into the game.

He thanked the dealer, tipped him generously, and left the table with a grin, despite pleas from the others to keep playing. He knew better than to push his luck—winning was as much about knowing when to quit as it was about the cards.

The casino's adrenaline-fueled rush bled into the night, sparking an evening of reckless abandon and unfiltered joy. By the time they made it to the Larcomar beach, their spirits were soaring, the alcohol still rushing through their veins. The sound of the waves crashing against the shore mixed with the laughter of their group as they sprawled out on the sand, drinks in hand, under the blanket of stars above. It was a surreal moment, as if the universe had opened its arms wide to let them be as free as they wanted to be.

Krishna sat with Nati by his side, his feet sinking into the cool sand as the tide brushed against them. The group was loud, dancing to the beat of invisible music, their inhibitions long gone. Camila and her friends were already several drinks in, swaying with the rhythm of the night, laughing like nothing in the world could touch them."

Nati leaned her head on Krishna's shoulder and let out a contented sign. "You really surprised me, tonight." she murmured, her voice slurred but full of admiration. "I didn't know you still had it in you."

A slow smile spread across Krishna's face as he pulled Nati closer, his arm tightening around her waist. "I didn't either," he admitted. "It's been a long time since I've touched cards, but once I'm in the zone…"

"You become unstoppable," she finished for him, a proud smile on her face. "I've never seen anyone play like that."

The ocean breeze brushed against them, cool and refreshing, a stark contrast to the heat of the moment they had just left behind in the casino. Krishna looked out at the water, feeling at peace, the chaos of the night settling into a calm that he hadn't realized he needed.

"Doesn't this feel like a dream?" Nati asked, her voice soft, almost wistful. The stars shimmered in her dark eyes, reflecting the night's quiet magic.

Krishna turned to meet her gaze, his own smile fading into something more thoughtful. "Sometimes," he said quietly. "But then I remind myself that it's real—that we're here, in this moment, and that's what matters."

She nodded; her eyes still locked on his. "I don't want to wake up from this. I don't want to lose what we have."

"You won't," Krishna said, his voice steady, full of reassurance. "I'm here, Nati. I'm not going anywhere."

They shared a quiet moment, the world around them fading into the background as the ocean whispered its endless song. The others were still laughing and dancing, but for Krishna and Nati, time seemed to slow down, the weight of their connection filling the space between them.

Eventually, the night grew quieter, their group too tired to continue the party. One by one, they began to gather their things, ready to head back to their hotel. The beach was now empty except for the occasional passerby, the city's lights in the distance casting a soft glow on the horizon.

As they made their way back, Krishna and Nati lagged behind, walking hand in hand, their steps unhurried. They didn't need to say much. The night had already spoken volumes.

They spent the rest of the day taking it easy, catching up with friends, and preparing for the days ahead. It was Nati's turn to show Krishna around, to introduce him to her world. As the days passed, they both realized that this wasn't just a vacation—it was the beginning of something much deeper, something that had the potential to change their lives forever.

Lima's nights settled into a rhythm—strolling the coastal cliffs, whispering secrets under starlit skies, finding peace in Miraflores' hidden gardens. And through it all,

Krishna and Nati grew closer, their bond solidifying in ways neither of them had expected.

One evening, as they walked through the streets of Lima, Nati turned to Krishna, her eyes bright with excitement. "I have a surprise for you," she said, a mischievous grin spreading across her face.

Krishna shot her a sideways glance. "What kind of surprise?"

"You'll see," she teased, taking his hand and leading him toward the heart of the city.

Whatever it was, Krishna knew it would be unforgettable—just like everything else they had experienced together so far.

Sometimes Krishna would accompany Nati to her university, and it always struck him as a place full of energy and life. It felt vastly different from Shiva's college back in India, where structure and seriousness were the norms. Here, students seemed carefree, their lives revolving around friends, passion, projects, and spontaneous fun—flirting, dancing and music.

Nati's work at the university was minimal—just submitting her progress reports and getting guidance on her thesis. Krishna would wait for her in the cafeteria, hanging out with her friends.

Though her friends understood English, they had a bit of difficulty speaking it, so Nati became his translator. Krishna quickly realized he wasn't a stranger to the group anymore, thanks to their shared moments on social media—

pictures and videos of him and Nati had circulated enough to make him a familiar face. For the first time, he understood the power of social media to shape relationships and create connections.

Nati, being one of the older students, had already finished her final year and was just waiting for her thesis to be approved, while the rest of her friends were in their third or final year. Joshua was the constant figure in her university life, helping her with her thesis. He was the classic 'rich daddy's boy—smart, privileged, and always the default sponsor for coffee and snacks. Joshua never missed a chance to boast about his family's business, his talents, or his grades, talking without pause and often criticizing others for not being as sharp as him—much to the amusement and eyerolls of the group.

Nati and Joshua had a complicated friendship. Though they were project partners, working on their final-year research about industrial behavior and the psychology behind decision-making, they often clashed. Despite their differences, they remained friends throughout their four years together. Joshua's ego and Nati's determination to prove him wrong made for an interesting dynamic, but their mutual respect for each other's intellect held them together. Krishna noticed Joshua maintained a certain distance from him, while the rest of Nati's friends embraced him wholeheartedly, making sure he never felt like an outsider.

At first, Krishna was completely unaware of Spanish. but hearing it every day slowly made it feel less foreign. He began picking up words here and there, blending into the group seamlessly, even if he couldn't always fully join the conversations. The laughter, guitar strums, and playful bets on who would sponsor the next round of coffee made every day feel like a celebration.

In the evenings, Krishna and the group had a ritual: they would hit the casino, where he had his own rules for gambling. He was disciplined—if he lost 100 sols, he would immediately stop playing. But on lucky days, when he won, the group partied hard. For them, winning money wasn't about saving—it was about funding their fun. As the losses were controlled, the winnings were celebrated extravagantly.

Once Krishna reached his gambling limit, they'd move to a bar, where dancing and drinking stretched the night even longer. The unspoken competition of who could drink more was always in play, and though Krishna tried to keep up, he quickly learned that his limit was just the starting point for Nati and her friends. The nights felt endless—full of laughter, music, and a sense of freedom he hadn't known before.

Despite the closeness of their friendship, Nati preferred to keep her roommate, Camila, at arm's length. Camila would often find reasons to join their night-outs, but Nati subtly managed to avoid her most of the time.

When Camila wasn't around, Krishna and Nati would head to her apartment to cook. Nati was a fantastic cook, often preparing empanadas—traditional Peruvian pastries made with sweet potatoes, much like samosas but less spicy. Their evenings together were simple but cozy—cooking, sharing a meal, and listening to music and savoring the quiet moments after the chaos of their social life.

For Krishna, these moments were the heart of his time in Lima—far from the casinos, the drinks and the lively nights. It was in the quiet times, with Nati, where he found something deeper: a sense of home, even in a place that wasn't his own.

"Hola, Nati! My parents are downstairs. I forgot my keys at home. Are you around?" Camila's voice came through the phone, sounding a little rushed. "If not, we'll just wait in the garden until you get here," she added.

Nati's pulse quickened. "Oh, the key…right! Hold on," she fumbled for a moment, checking for her keys. "I'll leave it in the shoe stand. You can grab it from there." She hung up quickly, turning to Krishna with a sense of urgency. "Krishna, hurry up! They'll be here any second."

She grabbed her things and bolted for the door. Krishna was still struggling to get his shoes on.

Nati impatiently pressed the lift button and, as it arrived at the second floor, grabbed Krishna's hand and pulled him toward the stairs. They had barely made it one floor down when Camila and her parents appeared at the top of the stairs, just outside their flat.

Camila called Nati again to see if she is around.

Nati froze, then quickly blurted out, "Oh, I'm not home! I'm out meeting a friend. I'll come by later, you guys go ahead," and hung up.

She glanced at Krishna and whispered, "If they caught us, we'd be stuck with them for at least two hours."

They laughed about the close call and continued their day exploring Lima together. The days seemed to fly by as Nati and Krishna explored every corner of Lima together.

They had become a pair of wandering souls, eager to soak in every experience before Krishna's return to Miami loomed closer. Their carefree adventures were about to take on a new dimension with the impending visit of Nati's parents.

Chapter 13

When the Heart Finds Home

The following weekend, Nati's parents finally arrived. Krishna, perhaps even more than Nati, was excited to meet them. Their conversations during the cruise had already sparked a bond—something that felt like family. Their flight was scheduled to land at 7:00 AM on Saturday. They weren't morning people, but Nati and Krishna stood at the airport—half-asleep but smiling—to welcome them.

When they finally saw Nati's parents coming through the arrivals gate with their luggage, Krishna's nerves spiked. He knew he was more than just Nati's "friend" in their eyes, Meeting the parents always came with a layer of quiet pressure. But any anxiety faded as he watched the couple approach. Nati's father looked disciplined and youthful, while her mother exuded modern elegance.

Nati sprinted forward and threw her arms around her father. "Papa, you took forever to meet me—I'm mad at you!" she said, her voice bubbling with affection, turning mock anger into something irresistibly sweet.

She clung to him for a moment before moving on to her mother.

Krishna stood back, feeling slightly nervous. Instinctively, he bent to touch her feet—a quiet mark of respect. Her mother looked momentarily confused but then smiled warmly, pulling him into a hug.

"Oh, Krishna! It's wonderful to finally meet you," she said. "We've heard so much about you."

Krishna repeated the gesture with Nati's father, who responded with a firm handshake and a pat on the shoulder. The ice was broken almost instantly. Soon, Nati was snapping pictures of the four of them and posting them online with her usual flair.

Fortunately, Camila had left to visit her hometown with her parents, which meant there was plenty of space for Nati's parent to stay comfortably. Nati and Krishna had an itinerary ready for their visit, starting with an evening at the famed Magic Water Circuit, a sprawling park filled with lighted fountains and music. That night, the fountains danced to the rhythm of the music, their water illuminated in a myriad of colors, creating a mesmerizing show. The park stretched across acres, feeling like a place where magic and reality intertwined. Nati and Krishna joined the rain dance, getting drenched as water sprayed around them. Her parents stood back, enjoying the spectacle and snapping countless photos.

"You've inherited the picture-taking habit from him," Krishna joked to Nati.

Her uncle chuckled. "Oh, yes! You know, when I first fell for your aunt, we were learning how to take photos together," he said, his eyes twinkling with nostalgia.

Later that evening, as they returned home, Nati and her mother prepared a traditional Peruvian dinner. The rich aroma of cumin, garlic, and aji Amarillo filled the air, teasing

Krishna's senses, making his mouth water. Krishna's conversation with her uncle shifted from proud military memories to grim truths—politics, corruption, and war. Uncle uncorked a bottle of pisco, although Krishna didn't drink, he gladly joined them with a glass of chilled soda in hand. As the pisco flowed, so did the stories—tales of life in uniform, sharp takes on politics and corruption, and even reflections on the war with Chile back in the 1880s.

The conversation meandered from memories of glorious moments in service to the harsh realities of politics, corruption and war. Nati's father spoke with a mix of pride and regret, recalling the scars of the War of the Pacific, a deep wound for the older generation. "You know, we lost a lot back then," he said with a distant look in his eyes. "Not just land, but a sense of our strength. It still echoes, even if the young don't feel it the same way." They were talking about the war between Chile and Peru.

Krishna listened intently, observing the depth of emotion and history in the proud retired soldier's words. It was a side of Peru that Nati's generation didn't seem as connected to—her friends, including herself, were more in awe of Chile's modern lifestyle and progress than held back by old resentments.

As the night wore on, Krishna found himself drawn deeper into the conversation. He was learning that being a good listener wasn't just a skill; it was a bridge to understanding another person's world. Nati's father spoke with the wisdom of a soldier who had seen and experienced more than most, Krishna could sense the underlying pain in his words. The past may have been buried deep, but it was not forgotten.

Krishna found himself growing closer to Nati's father, a disciplined yet warm man who reminded him of his own father back in India. Despite cultural differences, they shared a mutual understanding, shaped by life's battles and the silent respect for each other's experiences. By the time Nati and her mother called them to dinner, Krishna felt like he had found a new mentor in her father.

The meal was extraordinary—Nati's mother was a master in the kitchen, and Krishna could see where Nati got her culinary skills from. As they all gathered around the table, sharing stories and delicious food, it felt like the start of something more than just a visit. It felt like family.

The next day, Nati had a special plan for her parents: a trip to Paracas. This small village on the Peruvian coast, about three hours from Lima, offered the perfect blend of relaxation and adventure.

Paracas, with its sun-drenched shores like El Chaco, serves as the gateway to the Ballestas Islands. These rocky outcrops teem with life—sea lions bask on jagged cliffs, pelicans dive with precision, and Humboldt penguins waddle along the shore.

The rugged landscape of the Paracas National Reserve stretched across desert, ocean, and rocky islands, providing an ideal escape from city life. Their main activity was a two-hour boat tour around the Ballestas Islands; Krishna was captivated by the teeming wildlife. As the small vessel rocked gently, he took in the vibrant blue waters, watching dolphins leap and cormorants glide overhead.

For the first time, he saw dolphins leap playfully through the waves and birds like cormorants and Peruvian boobies darting through the sky. The guide pointed out the ancient Candelabra geoglyph etched into the hillside—a mysterious symbol not unlike the famous Nazca Lines. Krishna's eyes widened, taking in the beauty and history that Paracas had to offer.

After Paracas, they headed to Huacachina, an oasis surrounded by towering sand dunes—the largest in South America. It was a place unlike any other, a small paradise in the middle of the desert with lush palm trees encircling a green lagoon. Huacachina's dunes, towering over the oasis, stretched endlessly into the horizon, luring adventurers from across the world.

Nati and Krishna eagerly took part in sandboarding and a dune buggy ride. The adrenaline surged through them as the buggy driver expertly navigated the slopes, racing up steep hills and plummeting down the other side. At first, Krishna clenched his eyes shut, his knuckles white against the roll bar. But as the buggy plunged down the dunes, fear gave way to exhilaration. Laughter burst from his chest, mingling with Nati's delighted shrieks. It wasn't for the faint of heart, but the thrill was worth it. They took a break to soak in the views of the surrounding desert, glowed under the evening sun creating a golden spectacle that felt otherworldly.

The day's adventure ended with a mesmerizing sunset over the dunes, casting golden hues across the desert. They captured countless moments on camera, with Nati snapping pictures at every opportunity, preserving memories of the day's excitement.

The following day, they ventured to the nearby town of Ica, where Nati and Krishna signed up for skydiving. Freefalling through the sky, the world below blurred into a patchwork of sand and green. For a split second, fear clenched his chest—then came the rush, an electrifying mix of weightlessness and wild exhilaration.

The days with Nati's parents seemed to fly by, filled with adventure and the warmth of family bonding. In just a few days, Krishna had become more than Nati's friend—her parents had started treating him like a son. Her mother, especially, had grown close to him. She was a caring and emotional woman, always looking out for Nati's well-being.

Auntie confided in Krishna about her worries for Nati. "She's such a gentle-hearted girl," she said softly. "It's not easy being far from home. People have taken advantage of her kindness before, and she's been hurt." Krishna could see the pain in her eyes, the love and protectiveness that any mother would have. "But now that you're here, I feel more at peace," she added with a small smile.

Krishna's bond with Nati's father grew deeper too. They had countless conversations, often late into the night. Her father's stories from his time as a soldier revealed a man shaped by discipline, but also by compassion. Krishna could see that his concern for Nati was more than just paternal duty; it was an unyielding love forged through life's trials. It felt as though he had been welcomed into their family, these five days passed like a dream. He had stayed at Nati's apartment throughout, only going home once or twice to change clothes. Auntie noted that they hadn't stayed this long in Lima since Nati left home, yet this time, it truly felt like home.

At the airport, as they prepared to leave for Cusco, Krishna bent to touch their feet. The sincerity of the act was not lost on them.

Uncle and auntie were visibly moved. "Remember, Krishna," Auntie said earnestly, "even if Nati fights with you, don't take it to heart. She may be fiery, but she has the purest heart. She trusts easily, loves deeply. Please, don't ever let her go."

Her voice trembled slightly, revealing a mixture of worry and relief. Krishna nodded, touched by their openness and devotion to Nati.

Krishna could sense how deeply Nati's parents cared for her and why they were so protective. Auntie shared stories about Nati's childhood, one particular memory seemed to capture the essence of her daughter's generous heart. "When Nati was just a little girl," she began, "she once gave her entire tiffin away to a beggar on the street. She stayed hungry the rest of the day at school. That's just who she is—always thinking of others before herself."

There was a pause as auntie collected her thoughts, then she told Krishna something that made him sit up a little straighter. "You know," she said, "there was this fortune teller who once said that Nati's line of happiness crosses with someone else's lifeline. They spoke of it as a powerful connection, like destiny." She chuckled, though her eyes betrayed a wistful belief in the prediction. "It seems that kind of fortune-telling is everywhere, not just in India. It's funny, isn't it? People can look at your face, or the lines on your palm, and claim to know the future."

Krishna was intrigued. He had always been skeptical of such things, but he couldn't deny the weight auntie's words carried. It wasn't just about some prophecy; it was the way her parents viewed Nati's life, her happiness, and the need to shield her from a world that had, at times, been unkind. He saw now why they watched over her so closely, why every choice she made—every friend she kept—mattered to them.

Joshua was the reason. They had dreamed of forever, but reality chipped away at their bond. Love, once light and full of promise, became a weight that pulled her down instead of lifting her up. And in the end, Nati was the one left carrying the weight.

Auntie's voice softened as she glanced at Krishna. "Thank God Joshua didn't go on that cruise with her," she added. "If he had, I would never have met you." There was a warmth in her gaze that made Krishna feel welcomed in a way that went beyond words. She was genuinely comforted by his presence at Nati's side and even prayed that no arguments would come between them.

"Krishna responded with a reassuring smile. "Don't worry, auntie," he said gently.

"There's nothing in the world that Nati and I would ever fight about."

His words seemed to put her at ease, she pulled him into a hug before slipping a small envelope into his hand. Inside was a 100-sol note—a gesture that reminded Krishna of the small tokens of love his own mother would give him whenever he left home.

As they hugged one last time, Nati's father patted Krishna on the back. "See you soon, boy," he said. "Next time, come to Ollantaytambo. We'll be waiting to show you, our home."

"I'm looking forward to it," Krishna replied, smiling. "I've been waiting for Nati to take me to your place."

"Yes, Papa," Nati chimed in, "we'll definitely come next week."

As they walked towards the gate, Krishna couldn't help but feel grateful for the five days they had shared. It had been more than just a holiday; it had been a time of connection, deepening of bonds and the start of what felt like a new chapter. It wasn't just about him and Nati anymore—it was about becoming a part of each other's families and creating memories that would stay with them long after they had left Lima behind.

The next morning, the apartment felt strangely still. Krishna and Nati lay in bed, still drowsy from the whirlwind of the past five days.

Lima seemed quieter now, almost too calm without the lively presence of her parents. Yet, as they lingered in the silence, a newfound warmth lingered between them, a deeper bond formed through those shared days.

"I can't believe they're already gone," Nati murmured, rolling over to rest her head on Krishna's chest. "It feels like they just arrived."

Krishna wrapped his arm around her, drawing her closer. "I know," he murmured. "They made me feel like I belonged."

Nati's eyes met his, a glint of fondness in her gaze. "They adore you," she said with a smile. "Especially Mumma. She hasn't stopped talking about you since we got back from Paracas."

Krishna chuckled, a warm feeling spreading through him as he thought about the trip. Paracas had been a revelation. The moment they stepped off the bus, he had been enchanted by the tranquil charm of the coastal village, where time seemed to flow as gently as the waves on the beach. Nati had planned the entire itinerary with such care, making sure her parents would get to experience every bit of beauty the place had to offer.

From the boat ride to the Ballestas Islands, where sea lions barked from their rocky perches, penguins waddled by the shore, and dolphins danced in the shimmering blue waters, Krishna had been spellbound. He had never seen such wildlife up close; his awe was apparent as the tour guide pointed out the ancient geoglyph known as the Candelabra, etched on the desert hillside.

"That whole area felt like magic," Krishna said, as if reliving the view from the boat, the cool breeze carrying the scent of salt and sand. "And the Huacachina dunes… I've never experienced anything like that. It felt like we were in another world."

Nati grinned. "I was worried you'd chicken out on the buggy ride," she teased, playfully nudging his side. "You looked terrified when we first took off."

Krishna laughed; the memory vivid in his mind. The adrenaline rush of the buggy tearing across the endless dunes had been exhilarating. With the sun setting over the golden sands, the whole landscape had taken on an otherworldly glow. "I thought we were about to flip over at least three times," he admitted. "But then, it just felt… freeing. Like we were flying."

"Flying right into the sand," Nati teased. "You were covered head to toe after that sandboarding run."

Krishna shook his head with a chuckle, remembering how he'd struggled to stay balanced on the steep dunes, while Nati seemed to glide effortlessly. "You made it look so easy," he said, then added, "And your parents? I was amazed at how much energy they had. I could barely keep up."

Nati's eyes softened at the mention of her parents. "They were so happy to be there," she said quietly. "It was the first time they'd stayed in Lima for that long since I moved here. I think they felt at home because of you."

A moment of quiet passed between them as they thought back to the trip's final day in Ica, where Nati and Krishna had taken a leap of faith—quite literally—with their skydiving adventure. Soaring through the sky, feeling weightless and untethered, the world below seemed to dissolve into a patchwork of colors and textures. It was one of those rare moments when time seemed to stop, and all that mattered was the rush of the wind and the thudding of their hearts.

"I still can't believe we actually jumped," Krishna said, the thrill of the fall still echoing within him. "Your parents were probably more nervous than we were."

Nati chuckled. "Mumma told me she nearly fainted when she saw us falling through the air," she said. "But they were proud of us, especially you. She kept saying how brave you were and how grateful she was that you were there for me."

Krishna reflected on his conversations with Nati's mother. He now understood the depth of their concern for their daughter—how much they had worried and still did.

They had shared stories about Nati's past—about Joshua, the boy who had once been a significant part of her life. It wasn't lost on him how deep those wounds went, how much she had suffered, and why her parents were so protective.

Krishna promised her mother—and himself—that he would be there for Nati; he would cherish the light she brought into his life.

"They love you so much, Nati," he said, his voice tender. "And they just want you to be happy."

Nati's hand found his, squeezing gently. "I know," she whispered. "And I am happy, Krishna. With you."

Chapter 14

The Stranger's Story

Around 4:00 p.m., Krishna wandered through the crowded streets of Miraflores. The hustle and bustle were more intense than usual, with the long weekend approaching and people rushing to stock up on groceries before heading out of the city. Nati had gone to the university to submit a progress report for her project. She was supposed to be back by the afternoon, but it was already 4:00 p.m., and there was still no sign of her.

He called again. No answer. The silence was starting to bite. He told himself it was just university work, but the unease gnawed at him. Time seemed to slow, every minute stretching into an eternity, the hours expanding unbearable. He walked aimlessly through Miraflores, trying to distract himself with the sights and sounds of the bustling city. The colorful murals, the hum of conversations in cafes, the laughter of children playing in the park—it all seemed muted, as if the world had lost some of its vibrance without Nati beside him.

They hadn't been apart this long in months, and his unease only deepened with each passing hour.

He had stayed at the apartment until 3:00 p.m., waiting for Nati, the silence had grown unbearable. The thought of being confined indoors made him restless, so he headed out for a walk, hoping to clear his mind and find some distraction.

He cycled down to Larcomar, wandered along the beach, then circled back through the shopping mall before heading back to central Miraflores. His phone stayed glued to his palm, his eyes flicking to the screen every two minutes, waiting for something—anything—to ease the tension.

But as the hours dragged on, his surroundings began to feel suffocating.

He kept cycling through the same thoughts. What if something happened? What if she got stuck somewhere? What if she needed help? He knew it was irrational—Nati was an independent woman, perfectly capable of handling things on her own. But there was a tightness in his chest that wouldn't let go.

Krishna wandered past a small vendor selling churros and bought one without thinking. He took a bite, but the sugar and cinnamon did little to lift his spirits. Even the taste felt dull without her there to share it with. On any other day, he would've saved half for Nati—she loved them. Today, the idea only deepened the hollow in his chest.

By 5:30 p.m., he found himself standing at the Parque Kennedy, near the famous cat park. The sight of cats lounging in the shade or weaving around the legs of passersby brought a faint smile to his lips. He remembered how Nati would always try to pet each cat they passed, laughing as they either leaned into her touch or darted away. He crouched and reached out to a black-and-white stray cat that eyed him curiously. It sniffed his hand before padding away, leaving him with a lingering sense of solitude.

As the clock approached 6:00 p.m., Krishna walked back to the apartment, his heart heavy with worry. The thought of being inside, surrounded by the reminders of Nati—her books on the shelf, the framed photo from their trip to Paracas, her favorite mug on the kitchen counter, everything felt unbearable. He couldn't sit still, not while the hours crawled by without her. So, he kept moving, aimlessly wandering the streets, as if searching for something to fill the growing void within him.

The typically vibrant streets, full of life and energy, only seemed to emphasize his loneliness. The crowds flowed around him like an unending stream, but without Nati, there was no joy in the familiar sights and sounds. It was as if a layer of gloom had settled over everything. Each moment dragged, the time without her stretching unbearably, like a song stuck on repeat.

Eventually, Krishna found himself at the center of Miraflores, near the dance circle where a group of older people had gathered as usual. They were performing the zamacueca, their rhythmic steps and joyful expressions lighting up the space. But for Krishna, even the lively dance—normally a source of fascination—did little to lift his spirits. His thoughts kept drifting back to Nati, the emptiness of her absence deepening with every minute.

His phone buzzed in his hand, and his heart leapt, hoping it was Nati finally messaging to say she was on her way. But it was just a promotional text from one of the shops in Larcomar. He let out a frustrated sigh. Shoving the phone back into his pocket, he tried to shake off the disappointment.

The world without her felt strangely hollow. In that moment he realized just how much he had come to depend on her presence to feel whole.

It wasn't until the sky began to darken and the streetlights flickered to life that he felt his phone vibrate again. His heart raced as he pulled it from his pocket, a wave of relief washing over him when he saw Nati's name on the screen.

"Sorry, Krishna. Still caught up with a few things here. I'll leave as soon as I can. We'll have dinner together. Don't worry, okay? I'm safe."

He let out a long breath he hadn't realized he was holding. The reassurance helped, but it didn't dispel the emptiness completely. Krishna replied with a quick, "Take your time; just come home soon," then slipped the phone back into his pocket and relaxed.

Krishna was sitting on a nearby bench, watching the dance performance when he felt a light touch on his shoulder. He turned around and heard a familiar voice, speaking in his own language:

"Kaise ho, beta? " Krishna stood up and looked back with curiosity. Beside him was an elderly man with a saintly appearance. He had a long white beard, flowing hair, and wore a Punjabi kurta and a turban, resembling a traditional Sardarji. The man must have been in his seventies. Krishna instinctively greeted him with respect.

"Mai accha hu, Sir. Aap bhi India se ho?" Krishna asked, his hands folded in a Namaste.

"Haan ji, beta. I am from Punjab," the old man replied warmly. "Where are you from?"

"I'm from Maharashtra," Krishna answered.

"Ah, aamchi Mumbai," the silver-haired man said with a smile. "Why are you sitting like an old man? Come, walk with me. I'll show you something special about this place."

Without a second thought, Krishna followed the man. He seemed remarkably familiar with the streets, clearly not a tourist. His aura exuded wisdom, the kind that didn't need words or titles to make an impression; sometimes, a simple glance is enough to leave a lasting mark. As they walked, Krishna's curiosity grew.

"Are you a tourist?" He asked, although the question felt almost irrelevant. The man's demeanor suggested he was anything but.

"No, Puttar. Who would come here for tourism at my age?" The man chuckled. "If someone wanted to travel at this age, they'd visit the ancient places in India, not Miraflores."

Krishna's gaze landed on a couple kissing in the garden. Back home, such open affection would turn heads. Here, it was just another moment in the city's rhythm.

"I live here," the old man continued. "I worked hard in this place to fulfill my dreams. It's here that I want to take my last breath, surrounded by my family."

"How long have you been living here?" Krishna asked. "And why did you choose this country?"

The old man sidestepped the question, as if sensing that Krishna's curiosity ran deeper than his words. "Have you liked Peru so far?" He asked. "When did you arrive?"

"I've been here for just four weeks," Krishna replied. "I came with Nati, Natalia, my friend. Actually, she brought me here." He couldn't help but smile at the thought of her.

"And how do you find it?" The old man asked, his eyes twinkling with curiosity.

Krishna hesitated for a moment, then spoke honestly. "I'm surprised—maybe even a little shocked—by the culture. It's so different. People here are so... liberated. They kiss in public. It seems like there are no boundaries. Back home, things are so different."

The Sardarji listened patiently before responding, "Try to see it from another perspective. Here, people are free to live as they choose."

It's not like in India, where parents decide who their children will marry. Our traditions have their merits, but sometimes they come with limitations. Over here, at least, people can pursue their happiness without as many barriers." Krishna felt a bit taken aback but pressed on, "But doesn't that freedom come with a cost? Divorce rates are higher here. When people make the wrong choice, sometimes it's too late to go back."

The old man smiled gently. "Life is about choosing your own path and taking responsibility for it, even if you make mistakes along the way. It's better to make your own mistakes than to live a life of compromises and regrets because you were afraid to choose. Here, people live on their own terms. After all, life is about being happy, isn't it?"

Krishna fell silent, pondering the words. There was a truth to them, a wisdom that challenged his own views. Little did he realize he was in the presence of an ultimate master, someone who was pushing him to think beyond the known boundaries.

They walked on; Krishna kept glancing at the old man's face. His long white beard and hair flowed freely, giving him an air of timelessness. "Who are you?" Krishna finally asked. "And how did you end up here, far from home?"

The old man stopped and looked at him, as if deciding how much of his past to share. "Come, let's sit," he said, leading Krishna to a roadside bench.

"I'll tell you a little about my journey." The old man's voice took on a nostalgic tone as he spoke. "When I think back, I remember a young, intelligent student who had mastered ten languages before the age of fifteen. I came from a family of three—my father, my brother, and me. We inherited our intelligence from our parents; my father used to say it was a gift from our mother. At twenty-one, I was selected as a Spanish translator for an Indian government delegation visiting Latin America. It was during a time when India just begun to connect with the world. It was an opportunity I couldn't refuse."

As the old man reminisced, Krishna listened with rapt attention. "We were always busy with diplomats during the day," the man continued. "But at night, we used to explore the city. The city had a different charm after dark. I still remember one night vividly. We were in a nightclub, listening to Peruvian rock music. My Indian colleagues had let loose; the Pisco was flowing, for a moment, they had forgotten they were diplomats."

"That was the night I met Paula for the first time. She was dancing wildly, lost in the music. There was something about her spirit, her wildness, that drew me in. I had never felt that way before. I raised my glass in appreciation to a stranger, something I had never done before. We were complete strangers. Our eyes collide; there was an unspoken connection. She noticed me and raised her bottle in return. It was a moment when my heart took over my head. Instinct told me—we'd meet again."

"And you married her?" Krishna asked with curiosity.

"Eventually, yes. We were deeply in love, despite our differences."

The old man continued, sharing how he found his soulmate. A western girl who was nothing like the traditional Indian wives of his time. They had built a life together in Peru, balancing their cultural differences with mutual respect. They had made a promise to never try to rule over each other.

"We agreed that I would raise our first child in the Indian way. She would raise the second in her way," he said with a smile.

"Over time, she grew to understand India—not as a land of superstition, but as a place of deep family bonds and spirituality. She came to love India, we visited often."

Krishna was overwhelmed, his mind buzzing with questions, but it was already past 7:30. Nati had called him twice, Krishna had ignored the calls, engrossed in the old man's story. Before he could say anything else, the old man spoke. "I think it's time for you to go. Someone is waiting for you."

Krishna glanced at his phone. "Yes, Nati is waiting for dinner. Can we meet again sometime? I'd love to hear more about your journey."

The old man chuckled, eyes crinkling beneath his turban. "Haanji, why not? Here—" He reached into his vest pocket and pulled out a neatly kept card, handing it to Krishna with a steady hand. "This is my visiting card. Do visit us if time allows.

Sikh Seva Sabha
Vargas Machua, Lima, Peru

"Come to the Gurdwara when you have time," the old man said, with a gentle smile. "Waheguru will guide you."

Krishna promised to meet him again, then hurried to Nati. Her eyes held a trace of concern as she approached.

Chapter 15

The Night She Became a Star

"Where were you, Krishna? I called you so many times."

"Sorry, Nati. I met someone interesting today," he said, catching his breath. "I'll tell you all about it over dinner."

"Alright," she sighed, relief washing over her. "Let's meet near the church and then we'll go for dinner."

As walk towards the church, he couldn't help but glance back in the direction he had come from, wondering just how much more there was to learn from the old man with the flowing white beard.

Nati chose "De Aquí y De Allá", one of the most renowned restaurants in the area. The restaurant was her favorite spot near Miraflores, renowned for its romantic ambiance, sea view and soothing ocean breeze. Tonight, jazz music drifted through the air, setting the perfect mood for a celebration. The attentive service added to the allure, making it an ideal place for couples.

Krishna ordered his usual, ensalada de frutas con yogurt y frutos rojos.

Vegetarian options were scarce, as Latin America's definition of "vegetarian" often included anything without a heartbeat. But Krishna had grown accustomed to this, finding solace in his beloved fruit salad. Nati chose pollo a la brasa and a bottle of pisco. Being health-conscious, she often ate lightly, occasionally opting for a drink instead when she was with Krishna.

He, on the other hand, didn't start drinking on his own but never refused when she offered. It had become their little routine: minimal food, maximum conversation, and pisco.

As they settled into their familiar rhythm, Nati's eyes sparkled with excitement. "You know, Krishna, I got all the clearance for my thesis. I'm officially a psychologist now! I can start practicing." Her voice brimmed with pride. "Joshua wanted to celebrate together. But I wanted to share my best day with you."

Krishna's eyes widened with delight. He jumped up from his chair, wrapping her in a warm hug. "Wow, such amazing news! I'm so proud of you, Nati!" His enthusiasm echoed across the restaurant, drawing the attention of nearby patrons. It was a classy place, known for its upscale clientele; Krishna's outburst momentarily broke the polished calm. Nati noticed the curious gazes but didn't mind. For her, the world had paused, and all she could see was Krishna's pride and joy.

Krishna hugged her. A few curious glances flickered their way, but he didn't care. He decided to go all in. Grabbing a glass of wine, he tapped it with a fork to get everyone's focus. 'Ladies and gentlemen,' he began, only to realize that most of the crowd spoke little to no English. Quickly, he rushed over to the hotel manager, a young man who fortunately understood English, and requested a favor.

The manager agreed with a smile, and Krishna started again, this time in a mix of English and Spanish.

"Today is the happiest day of my life." He took Nati's hand.

The manager, with a friendly smile, took over.

"Señoras y señores, hoy es el día más feliz de mi vida."

"My girl completed her degree today!" Krishna continued, feeling the words tumble out in excitement.

With the manager echoing in Spanish, "Mi chica ha completado su licenciatura,"

! Por favor, un aplauso para la nueva psicóloga!" The manager's translation filled the room.

The room erupted in applause as the manager translated his words. Nati hugged him tightly as the crowd cheered. People around them raised their glasses, tapping them gently with spoons to show their approval. It was a magical moment, as if they had unintentionally stumbled into the spotlight. A couple approached to offer congratulations, followed by others. In an instant, the restaurant transformed into a celebration for Nati. She was overwhelmed by the affection, the applause, and Krishna's unique way of making the night special.

A glamorous couple came up to them, the woman congratulated and complimented Nati, "You have the best man by your side," the woman said. "Life has meaning when you're with someone who is happier for your success than their own. Don't let him go."

"Thank you, ma'am," Nati replied, kissing the woman's cheek in the traditional Spanish style. "I won't."

Just then, a waiter appeared with a bouquet, handing it to the manager, who presented it to them. "Congratulations," he said warmly, snapping a picture with them. "And welcome to our Wall of Fame."

The restaurant had a tradition known as "Fame of the Month," where they honored a special couple by displaying their picture on the Wall of Fame and offering a complimentary night's stay. It was a renowned trend in Latin America, where select couples were chosen each month for this honor, receiving free meals, drinks, and accommodation. Tonight, it was Krishna and Nati's turn to shine. They hadn't expected to find themselves being celebrated like celebrities. They felt like stars, graced by the night's serendipity.

The rest of the evening passed in a blissful blur. They ate, drank, and danced, embracing the freedom of the moment. In the nightclub section, the jazz music morphed into an energetic beat. Nati, swaying to the rhythm, grabbed Krishna's hand, pulling him to the center of the dance floor. They spun and moved until their legs grew weary, and the world around them seemed to pulse with the music. Nati kissed Krishna passionately, her lips pressing against his as if sealing the night's magic into a permanent memory. As she leaned into him, her eyes fluttered closed, and she went limp in his arms, fully relaxed.

Krishna wasn't faring much better—his legs wobbled, and the room tilted around him in slow motion. The lights blurred together, and the music felt distant. With Nati's weight on his shoulder, he stumbled toward the bar, trying to steady himself. Everything around him seemed like a dream—shadows moving through the haze.

A bouncer noticed their state and approached. "Sir, do you need help?"

Krishna fumbled in his pocket and pulled out the Fame of the Month card. The bouncer took it, recognizing the privilege it granted. With a nod, he guided them toward the private rooms reserved for honored guests.

Krishna blinked against the harsh sunlight streaming through the curtains. It was past noon; he felt the weight of exhaustion lingering from the previous night. He glanced down and saw Nati still asleep on his chest, her breathing slow and steady. Her hair spilled over his arm, she looked peaceful, almost angelic, as if in a deep, dreamless slumber.

The memories of the night before came rushing back—the applause, the dancing, the warmth of Nati's embrace and the swirling lights of the nightclub. The celebration had been nothing short of a whirlwind. He remembered the kiss Nati had given him on the dance floor just before she passed out in his arms, and how the world seemed to spin around them. It was as if they had stepped into a different realm where time slowed and reality blurred, leaving them with nothing but the sheer joy of being together. It wasn't often that they partied to such extremes, but then again, it wasn't every day that Nati became a certified psychologist. He glanced down at her peaceful face, then brushed a strand of hair away from her cheek.

Krishna exhaled, pressing his fingers to his temple as he glanced at the clock. It was already 2:30 p.m. Last night felt like a chaotic dream, its weight still pressing down on his limbs.

He gently shifted, trying not to wake Nati, but she stirred anyway, mumbling something under her breath before her eyes fluttered open. She blinked a few times, disoriented, then looked up at him with a sleepy smile.

"Hey," she whispered, her voice raspy. "What time is it?"

"Almost 2:30," Krishna replied, brushing a lock of hair away from her face. "We really went overboard last night."

Nati let out a soft laugh. "I don't even remember half of it. Everything feels... fuzzy." She sat up slowly, rubbing her temples. "What were we drinking?"

Krishna chuckled. "Probably more than we should have. That last bottle of pisco? Terrible idea."

She glanced around the room, taking in the unfamiliar surroundings. "Did we... end up in the Hall of Fame room?"

"Yeah, we did," Krishna said, grinning. "Apparently, we're "fame of the month" now. Complimentary stay and all."

Nati's eyes widened in surprise. "Are you serious?"

He nodded, reaching over to the bedside table and picking up the Fame of the Month card. "The manager gave us this last night. We're practically celebrities now."

Nati laughed, the sound bright and genuine. "Well, I guess we made an impression. I've never had anything like that happen before."

"Me neither," Krishna said. "But you deserved it. You're a newly minted psychologist now, officially."

She leaned in and kissed him softly on the lips. "Thank you, Krishna. For making it the best night of my life."

As he looked into her shimmering eyes, a rush of affection swept over him. He wrapped his arms around her and pulled her close, resting his chin on her head. "You make everything worth celebrating, Nati."

For a moment, they stayed like that, wrapped in each other's arms, letting the peace of the late afternoon envelop them. The chaos of the night had brought them closer, binding them together with an unspoken understanding. It was a day that would be etched in their memories forever—when they lived without restraint, when they allowed themselves to be vulnerable and free, when they realized just how much they meant to each other.

Eventually, Nati sighed and broke the silence. "We should probably freshen up and get some food. I'm starving."

Krishna nodded. "Good idea. Let's get out of here and find something to eat. And maybe some coffee, too."

As they got ready to leave, the events of the night seemed to blur into a fond memory, a moment where the world stood still just for them. They knew that life wouldn't always be filled with such spontaneous celebrations, but as they stepped out of the Hall of Fame room, hand in hand, they felt a renewed sense of connection. Some nights blurred into memories, leaving behind nothing but a quiet certainty—they were exactly where they belonged. Together.

Chapter 16

A Visit to Sikh Seva Sabha...

Krishna had planned to visit the old man on Sunday. He had hoped Nati would join him. But at the last minute, she had to meet Joshua to help with a submission. She promised to meet Krishna at Plaza de Armas later in the evening.

At the Sikha Seva Sabha, Krishna paused at the gate, reading the modest sign: "Sikha Seva Sabha – Vegas Machuka Lima Peru." It was a modest building, comprising a large hall and a smaller house behind it. As he rang the bell, A devotee swiftly opened the front door and welcomed him. A staircase led up to the first floor, He removed his shoes and ascended the staircase, following the soft murmur of voices upstairs.

The main hall, roughly 20 by 20 feet, had a large frame of Guru Darbar Sahib adorning the front wall. A few devotees were seated by the columns, while two or three women were busy in the kitchen, preparing food for the day's gathering. The aroma of Rasam rice filled the air. Their dedication to preserving their culture, thousands of miles from their homeland, was unmistakable.

Krishna offered a quiet prayer at the Guru Darbar Sahib and inquired about the old man.

"Excuse me, where can I find Sardarji?" Krishna asked.

One of the devotees gestured toward a woman in a Punjabi kurta orchestrating activity in the kitchen.

"You can ask Mataji," he replied, gesturing toward a woman overseeing the kitchen."

The woman, whom Krishna now knew as Mataji, was elderly, bright-eyed Peruvian overseeing the food preparations. She carried herself with a peaceful strength that felt deeply rooted in tradition, yet open to the world around her.

"Namaste, Mataji," Krishna greeted with folded hands. "I'm Krishna, from India. I came here to meet Sardarji."

"Namaste, beta. Como estás?" Mataji replied warmly. "Sardarji is out at a radio show. He broadcasts live every Sunday from 11 AM to 12 p.m. He should be back soon. Please wait." She instructed the women in the kitchen and then turned back to Krishna with a kind smile.

"Where did you meet Sardarji?" She asked, her tone affectionate.

Krishna smiled. "We met a few days ago in Miraflores."

Paula invited Krishna into the kitchen. It wasn't just a kitchen—it was the heart of the household, serving as a gurudwara, langar hall, and home. The blend of spaces, each fulfilling multiple roles, spoke volumes about the commitment to keeping their culture alive far from India.

They sat at the dining table with cups of coffee. As they talked, Krishna noticed a family photo on the wall, featuring a young boy and girl with Sardarji and Mata Ji.

"Are these your children?" He asked, pointing at the photo.

"Yes," she said, a fond smile gracing her face. "That's our daughter, Tally, and our son, Jovan."

In the picture, Tally looked modern and lively, while Jovan appeared traditional, sporting long hair like his father. "Your family is beautiful. I see Jovan has embraced Punjabi culture just like his father," Krishna observed.

Paula chuckled at his remark. "Yes, he resembles his father in many ways."

Curious about meeting the children, Krishna asked, "Are they here?"

"Tally is on vacation with friends, but Jovan is with Sardarji at the radio station. They'll be back soon," she replied.

Krishna continued his conversation with Mata Ji, learning how the couple had built a haven for their culture in Lima. They kept the community together through weekly gatherings, serving langar and sharing stories, making it more than just a place of worship.

A little past 1 p.m., the sound of voices filled the hall. Sardarji and Jovan had returned. The old man, with his white beard and serene aura, was a stark contrast to Jovan, who carried himself like a vibrant character from the 70s, with his long hair flowing freely.

"Ah, Krishna!" Sardarji greeted with a broad smile, embracing him warmly. "Meet Jovan, my son."

Before long, more people arrived for the prayer and langar.

Krishna and Jovan engaged in conversation while Sardarji went to help with serving the food. Jovan's curiosity about India was insatiable, Krishna found himself fascinated by the young man's deep connection to his cultural roots, even while living in a Western environment. The pictures on the wall told stories of a life dedicated to preserving Sikh values and teachings far from their homeland.

Soon, it was time for the prayer to conclude and the langar began. Krishna joined the others in serving rice and rasam. Though the gathering was modest, the spirit of seva filled the air. Sardarji's family worked tirelessly to make sure everything ran smoothly.

It was more than a meal—it was a gathering where people from all walks of life shared food, stories and wisdom.

When the meal was over, Sardarji approached Krishna. "Come, beta, have your langar." He handed Krishna a plate and took his place in line, just like everyone else.

After dinner, as the sun dipped lower in the sky, Sardarji and Krishna sat together. Krishna's mind was swirling with questions, not just about Sardarji's life but about how he had managed to shape his surroundings in such a profound way.

The old man seemed to sense his thoughts. "You're wondering how all this came to be," he said, his eyes twinkling.

"Whatever you do, give it your all. Let your actions shine so brightly that no one else's colors overshadow yours. Trust Rab to handle the rest." He used the Punjabi word.

He paused, his expression turning serious. "Aur ek baat yaad rakhna, beta. Jo bhi karo, jahan bhi jao, apna rang kabhi itna fika na rakhna ki koi dusra rang aake use zak de. If you stay firm in your ethics and values, others will come to revolve around you. But if you waver, you'll find yourself revolving around someone else."

Krishna listened intently, absorbing each word. Sardarji continued, "I've followed this all my life. Follow your heart, trust your gut, and keep pushing your limits. When you know what to do, the 'how' will come naturally."

As they talked, time seemed to pass effortlessly. It was already 4:30 when Krishna bid farewell to Sardarji, Mataji, and Jovan, promising to return. As he left, he couldn't shake the feeling that he had encountered not just a wise old man, but a living embodiment of the ideals he had always sought. He realized that Sardarji's life was a testament to his philosophy. A life defined by clarity, conviction, and the courage to follow his heart. It was how he had managed to leave his job, settle in Peru, and raise a family rooted in Indian traditions while adapting to a different culture.

The echoes of Sardarji's words followed him back to his hotel room, where Krishna found himself reflecting deeply on clarity and purpose. Sardarji's journey, leaving his life in India to settle in Peru, had been guided by an unyielding resolve. He had clarity about everything—his commitment to sobriety, raising Jovan with his culture's values, and building a community in a foreign land.

Krishna realized he had come across a true teacher, someone whose presence alone could change the way he saw the world. There were still many questions in his mind, questions that would undoubtedly bring him back to Sardarji's door again. But one thought had already taken root: When you have clarity about what to do, how to do will develops.

It was 8:30 when Nati finally arrived, looking weary and troubled. Her usual vibrant energy had faded, replaced by a heaviness that dragged at her shoulders. Guilt lingered in her eyes as she approached Krishna.

"I'm sorry, Krishna. I kept you waiting alone all day," she said, her voice tinged with exhaustion.

"Don't worry, Nati. I know you were busy," Krishna replied gently. "I spent time with Sardarji. I missed you, of course, but I enjoyed my day. I wish you could have been there with me. I'll take you next time."

"Yes, we will go," she said, trying to muster a smile. But it faded quickly. The upset expression returned.

"What happened? You seem upset," Krishna asked, concerned.

"It's that donkey, Joshua. You know how he is! Such an egotistical idiot," she vented, frustration spilling out as she spoke. "He thinks he's so smart, but he's a complete duffer. Because of him, he couldn't even finish the submissions. He kept finding things to nitpick, making everything more difficult."

Krishna listened patiently, his eyes steady and kind. He reached out, running his fingers through her hair in a soothing gesture. He knew she needed to vent, she needed to let it all out. Krishna gave her space to do so. When her words finally slowed, he rubbed her temples gently, easing away the tension.

"It's okay, Nati. Just let it go. Don't let Joshua ruin your mood," he said softly.

"I'm serious, Krishna. I'm done with him. I don't even want to talk to that duffer anymore," she declared, her irritation still palpable.

Krishna hugged her close, feeling the tension in her body slowly dissolve as he held her. This had become a familiar scene; every time Nati and Joshua spent any extended time together, they would end up fighting. It was almost predictable. Each time, it fell on Krishna to calm her and restore her usual lightheartedness.

Soon, the anger and frustration seemed to melt away, replaced by the comforting warmth of Krishna's embrace. They began to get ready for the evening, slipping into a familiar rhythm. It was time for their usual night out—first to the casino, then dinner. It had become a bit of a ritual; there were hardly any nights they skipped the casino.

At the casino, Krishna played his usual cautious game, knowing when to take risks and when to pull back. After losing three or four bets, he would step away from the table, resisting the urge to chase his losses.

He didn't believe in firefighting—a term he used to describe desperate attempts to recover from a losing streak. Some days, winning wasn't in the cards. He knew when to step away. He had seen too many people make that mistake when he worked as a blackjack dealer. They would refuse to accept a loss, letting their emotions take over until they lost everything. Krishna had learned to separate the thrill of the game from a desire to win at all costs. For him, it wasn't about defeat or victory. It was about the discipline to understand when to let go. It was about knowing the fine line between strategy and self-destruction.

Krishna's approach allowed him to enjoy the game without fear, experimenting and taking calculated risks. It wasn't just about the money for him; it was about mastering his mindset, embracing the highs and lows without letting them dictate his actions.

That night, like always, he stuck to his principles. When the cards weren't in his favor, he left the table, unburdened by losses and free to savor the rest of the night with Nati. The two of them headed out for dinner afterward, laughing and talking as if the day's frustrations had never happened.

Chapter 17

Beyond the Horizon

We spend most of our lives realizing that we can shape our destiny. It takes time to understand that nothing is impossible to a willing heart. We can shape our future the way we want, but only if we believe in ourselves and take the leap of faith. It all begins with a decision to jump, even if we don't see the wings that will carry us.

Days passed by. Nati grew increasingly occupied with securing an internship. She had a string of interviews lined up with some of the top psychologists in Lima. Occasionally, Krishna accompanied her, waiting nearby while she sat for interviews. In those quiet intervals, he would slip away to bring her a snack—a small gesture to keep her energy up.

Whenever he found himself with free time, Krishna would visit the old man, Sardarji. They would sit and talk for hours on end, their conversations weaving through stories, life lessons, and philosophies. With each visit, Krishna felt himself changing, like layers of his previous beliefs were being peeled away and something deeper was emerging. He had always lived by a simple philosophy: "Hum chalte gaye, raste milte gaye, manzilein banti gayi"—we kept walking, paths appeared, and destinations formed. Sardarji, however, wasn't convinced.

"What if you had never found these so-called paths?" Sardarji asked one day. "Would that mean you wouldn't be here? That you'd be lost?
Think about it. Has everything you've done so far been just an accident?

The old man's gaze was steady, challenging. "Stumbling onto a path once might be luck, maybe even coincidence. But when you must choose between two paths again and again, only sheer will and a clear vision of what you want will guide you."

Sardarji's emphasis on clarity was like a hammer striking at Krishna's doubts. Clarity. Will. The words felt foreign, yet the more time he spent with Sardarji, the more he questioned his own direction. For so long, he had drifted, going wherever life took him. Now, for the first time, he started to think about where he wanted his life to lead. But doubt clung to him—could he really make it happen? Did he have the strength to shape his own fate?

Krishna didn't know how to respond. He had always believed in going with the flow, trusting that life would sort itself out. But Sardarji was challenging that view, pointing out that sometimes the path doesn't just reveal itself. Sometimes, you must choose it—again and again, with a will strong enough to carve a way forward.

"It's not about stumbling upon the road by accident," Sardarji continued. "It's about having clarity. When you're faced with choices, you need to know which direction to take. Without that, life will carry you wherever it pleases—you'll have no say in where you end up."

Sardarji often said, "Those who don't dare to see a clear vision lack the confidence to bring it to life." He was certain that once you had a crystal-clear image of what you wanted, everything would align. His intent was unmistakable: he wanted Krishna to take charge of his own fate.

One evening, as they sat together, Sardarji asked Krishna a question that cut straight through his uncertainty. "Where do you see yourself, Krishna? What kind of life do you envision for yourself?"

A surge of anxiety rose in Krishna's chest. His hands trembled slightly, he clenched his jaw. "What do you mean?" What I think, does it even matter?" he blurted, his voice laced with frustration and fear. "This is life. We're just puppets on a stage, actors in a drama following a script that's already written and we—" His voice broke, he struggled to continue.

His voice softened as he continued, an unspoken longing surfacing.

I want to be here, where silence sings,
Where morning breaks with her laughter's wings.

I want to be close, to hold on tight,
To bask in her love from morning to night.

I want to be close, not far, not fading—
To hold her hand when the world feels grating.
To kiss her brow when the night is deep,
To watch her dream while I dare not sleep

But life—
Life quivers like a candle's flame,
And fate plays games with no face or name.

At any moment, the winds may change,
And pull me away like a whisper, estranged.

Still—
I wish, oh, I wish, for a future so near,
Where I'm not just a dreamer, but real and here.
I want to stay, to live where I've grown,
But I don't know if I'll ever call it my own.

I want to belong—not borrowed, not brief—
To root my soul in shared belief.
To build a home where her laughter rings,
And peace moves softly on unfolding wings.

Let me be here—
Where the sky leans low, where stars confess,
Where her name is the spell I never suppress.
Where love is not passing, but full and wide,
Where I no longer need to run or hide.

As long as she's near, I am wholly alive,
In the hush of her breath, I survive.
No clock can steal what the heart has known—
With her beside me, I am finally home.

Sardarji listened in silence, letting Krishna spill out the fears and uncertainties that had been weighing on him.

When Krishna finally fell silent, the old man spoke.

"You know, putter," he began after a moment, "we spend most of our lives realizing that we can shape our destiny. It takes time to understand that nothing is impossible to a willing heart. We can shape our future the way we want, but only if we believe in ourselves and take the leap of faith.

It all begins with a decision to jump, even if we don't see the wings that will carry us."

He paused, letting his words sink in. "I had my share of doubts about how I could find my own path. It seemed impossible at times, but when I made the decision to pursue it, doors began to open. This is the strangest secret in the world, Krishna. People get too caught up in worrying about how they will achieve something. In doing so, they forget to think about what they truly want. They end up like a dog chasing after a car, not knowing what to do when they catch it."

Krishna absorbed every word as though he were in a trance.

"You'll get what you want—if you know, without a doubt, exactly what that is. Prepare yourself. Take the first step toward what you seek. Visualize yourself already in possession of what you want, and things will start to change in your favor. Don't concern yourself too much with the 'how.' Leave that to the unknown powers. All you need to do is relax, dream, and see yourself living the life you desire."

For the first time, Krishna let himself dream without restraint. He envisioned a future where he wasn't merely drifting along, where he wasn't just reacting to life but actively shaping it. The image felt vivid and exhilarating— a life with Nati, chasing what set his soul on fire. It wasn't just a vague longing anymore. He was starting to see himself as the architect of his own destiny.

As he listened to the old man speak, Krishna felt something shift inside. For the first time, he wasn't just someone who would go wherever the current carried him; he was daring to chart his own course. He was daring to be where his heart wanted him to be.

"Kisna, I have an interview tomorrow with Mr. Ned," Nati said, stirring the pot absentmindedly. She was making dinner, but her mind was clearly elsewhere. "He's looking for an intern. Do you know he's among the top ten psychiatrists in Lima? I really hope I get this internship."

Krishna could sense the mix of excitement and anxiety in her voice. She was trying to stay upbeat, but it was clear she was nervous. After all, this wasn't just any interview; it was a potential turning point in her career. If she got this opportunity, it would be a significant step forward for her professional future. Krishna had seen her go through similar nerves before.

The next day, they left early. Krishna went with her, aware of her growing nerves. As they waited in the hospital parking lot, he took her hand, placing his palm gently on her cheek and stroking it soothingly. "You know, Nati," he said, his voice calm and reassuring, "today, you're going to get this job. Mark my words. I'm 100% sure. Do you know why?"

"Why?" Nati asked, looking up at him, searching his eyes for reassurance.

"Because I'm right here with you," he said, flashing a playful grin.

She managed a small, relieved smile. Somehow, Krishna always had a way of calming her down. Nati felt some of the tension leave her body. With Krishna around, everything seemed to fall into place. She often said that

Krishna completed her; together, they complemented each other perfectly. Good things always seemed to happen when they were together. She held onto that belief now.

To calm herself, she rehearsed how she'd talk about her passion for psychotherapy—her academic achievements and her ambitions. They arrived at Mr. Ned's hospital half an hour early, only to find five or six other candidates were already waiting in line for the interview. Seeing the competition made Nati even more nervous, but she held on to Krishna's words.

As they waited, Krishna could see Nati was growing more anxious with every minute that passed. They were the last to arrive, and by 4 p.m., Mr. Ned had completed only five interviews. The waiting stretched on, making her feel more restless. Krishna stepped out, returned with a couple of subs—he knew they hadn't eaten all day.

She was the last on the list, by the time they called her name, it was already 5:30. Krishna squeezed her hand for good luck. As she approached the door to the interview room, she glanced back at him one last time. He gave her a thumbs-up. Nati smiled nervously before walking in.

After forty-five minutes, Nati walked out, her face caught between relief and uncertainty. Krishna was already waiting by the reception, his eyes fixed on the door. As soon as she stepped out, the receptionist handed her an envelope containing some documents about the hospital. She mentioned that selected interns would receive a callback and the number in the envelope could be used for inquiries.

It wasn't long before Nati received a call from Mr. Ned's hospital. She was selected. The news was a burst of joy that left both ecstatic. Finally, her dream had come true, a chance to live it. There were no boundaries to their happiness that night. They celebrated with dinner and a trip to the casino, dancing and gambling the night away.

The excitement, however, got the better of Nati at the casino. She ended up losing almost everything Krishna had won earlier in the night. Krishna's personal rule was simple: whenever he lost 200 Sol or more, he'd walk away from the table. It was a principle that set him apart from the crowd, teaching him to balance calculated risks with self-control. When he played alongside Nati, he'd usually impose the same limit on her, but tonight was different. This was her day—her happiest moment. Before she realized it, she had lost three rounds totaling 600 sol.

The next day, as her hangover faded, she saw the humor in the whole thing, though the sting of the losses remained.

Few days later, Krishna received an email from Miami. His cruise was set to sail from Miami back to India. From this dreamlike chapter in Lima, he was returning to his birthplace.

The realization hit him hard—it had been two months. So much time had passed, yet so many plans were still unfulfilled. They had done so much together, yet countless things remained on their bucket list: visiting Machu Picchu, exploring Cusco and Ollantaytambo, meeting Nati's family. Even their dream of skydiving hung in the air, another adventure left unrealized.

The Unfinished Dream

So many things left behind, like whispers on the breeze,
Dreams still unspoken, drifting through the trees.

Time slipped away, as if yesterday had just begun,
And here he stood, not yet finished, not yet done.

He walked to the Old Man, eyes full of sky,
Searching for truths no book could supply.
A hunger lived in his chest, deep and wide—
A call to become, with no place to hide.

Lima whispered in moonlit tones,
A city of ghosts and sacred stones.
Something stirred—old and new—
A promise of life, unfiltered, true.

In Peru's breath, in her gentle grace,
He found his pulse, a sacred space.
He hadn't yet held her love full-grown,
Nor touched the warmth he longed to own.

He hadn't yet learned how hearts unfold,
How silence can shimmer brighter than gold.
Still stumbling through shadows of fear,
Still aching to pull her soul near.

So many things done, yet so much left to do,
Dreams half-lived, hopes still far from view.
The wildest wish? To stay, not roam—
To call her laughter, her arms, his home.

But life—uninvited—arrived with a note,
Its ink a tether, its message a moat.
He read the summons, eyes turned to glass,
As the world asked him to let it all pass.

Yet still the heart pounds, still the soul sings,
Of love not lost, but tethered with wings.

A story unwritten, a page yet to turn,
A fire still quiet, yet longing to burn.

So, he carries the dream in the hush of night,
An ember tucked close, out of the light.
Not finished. Not gone. Still burning bright—
An unfinished dream taking slow, steady flight.

Nati was silent, her expression mirroring the weight of Krishna's departure. She hadn't set foot in her apartment for fifteen days. Now, the reality of his imminent return loomed over them. They both knew that the day of parting would eventually come, but neither of them wanted to think about it. They clung to the hope that this moment would never arrive, that somehow time would stretch indefinitely in their favor. But reality was closing in: Krishna had to report to Miami in just four days.

Four days wasn't enough. The urgency gnawed at them; there was so much left unsaid, so many moments that still needed to be shared. Krishna scrambled to arrange his flights, but the timing was relentless.

Flights over the weekend were fully booked, even Friday was no longer an option. The only available seat was on a Thursday night flight, which meant they had barely two days left together. It wasn't enough, not for either of them, but they had no choice. With heavy hearts, they booked a 5 a.m. departure.

Krishna packed his belongings, cleared out his hotel room, and settled the bill in advance. Everything he had won at the casino over the past few weeks was tucked away in a locker. The locker was nearly full now. He converted the cash into dollars, totaling almost $8,000.

Among his preparations, he bought a diamond necklace for Nati, a rare and precious gift. Money had little meant when it came to her; his time and affection were priceless, Nati wasn't someone who measured love in material terms. Still, he wanted to give her something to remember him by.

For those final two days, they didn't go anywhere. Nati's face carried the strain of impending separation; her eyes glistened, barely holding back tears. Krishna couldn't find the words to comfort her—his own throat felt tight, suffocated by silence. When she finally spoke, her voice was fragile.

"Krishna, when will we meet again? When will you come back?" Her eyes pleaded with him. "Why don't you just stay here? You know you can find a job at the casino, and even if you don't, I'll be starting my therapy center in six months. You wouldn't even need to work. We'll have enough to live on. Just, don't go."

Krishna stroked her hair gently, his fingers tracing comforting circles. Her voice was full of innocence and desperation. She was grasping at any possibility, however impractical. But they both knew, deep down, that staying wasn't an option.

"We will meet again, Nati," Krishna assured her softly, his fingers gently combing through her hair. "Very soon."

"But how?" she asked, her voice barely above a whisper, laced with uncertainty. "I don't know how," he admitted. "But I know it will happen. I promise you." He spoke with a conviction that even he didn't fully understand. He didn't know when or how they would reunite, but he needed to believe it is possible.

"If I can't come back, then you'll come to India," he said, forcing a smile. "I'll show you, my country."

"You think India is not safe for women, that it's a male-dominated society with deep-rooted issues. But let me show you another side—the warmth of people who cherish lifelong love and loyalty, where kindness still thrives."

Nati's eyes shimmered with a mixture of hope and uncertainty. Krishna went on, trying to lighten the mood. "And in your spare time, you can run your therapy center there too. I'm sure I can find plenty of patients for you," he said with a mischievous grin.

They both laughed, but their smiles were tinged with a shared loneliness. Their laughter carried a hollow echo, the kind that lingers when you know a moment is slipping away, untouchable, no matter how many promises you make.

She hugged him tight, her tears flowed free,
"I love you, Krishna, how will I be?"
Her voice trembled, breaking, as she cried,
"How will I live without you by my side?"

He said nothing at first—only held her near,
His silence deep, carved out of fear.
"You know, Shona," he whispered low,
"The Old Man told, what the heart should know."

"If love is true—if it runs soul-deep,
The stars themselves will lose no sleep.
They'll move the heavens, bend the light,
To bring you back when the time is right."

"Oceans can stretch, cities divide,
But love—real love—won't be denied.

Even across the vast unknown,
You'll hear my voice. You won't be alone."

His words moved soft as candlelight flame,
Yet burned with a faith too wild to tame.
"The world is a circle, it bends back in time,
We'll return to the place where love crossed the line."

She drew a breath, slow and wide,
"I believe you," she said, tears still in her eyes.
"In every word, in every sky—
Love won't break. It only flies."

And there they stood, wrapped in the ache,
Two hearts trembling, too full to fake.
And though the road would wind and bend,
They believed in a love that would never end.
But hope kept singing what hadn't been said.
They believed in a love that would never end.

A vow on their lips no silence could shave.
A spark beneath waves no distance could cave.
And though morning would pull their hands apart,
Their souls still stitched with love's quiet art.

The sounds of music drifted through the room, as Krishna traced slow, deliberate circles on Nati's palm. Time seemed to move too quickly, carrying them inevitably towards the moment they dreaded. When morning came, they checked out, having already packed all Nati's things back into her apartment. It wasn't just a place—it held so many memories, moments they would carry for the rest of their lives. Room no 907 would always be a part of them.

They would miss that peculiar, haunting portrait of the woman on the bedroom wall, the sleepless nights spent curled together on the sofa listening to music, and all the little, crazy memories that room held.

The ride to the airport was quiet, the car carrying them through streets that seemed too familiar, too soon to be left behind. Nati rested her head on Krishna's lap, her face hidden, retreating from the reality of their impending separation. Krishna ran his fingers through her hair, but neither of them spoke. They both knew that if he said even one word, it would break the silence and release the flood of emotions they were struggling to contain. He was trying to stay composed, to be the strong one.

When the taxi stopped at the airport, Krishna drew in a deep breath. He looked down at Nati, still curled up in his lap. "Okay, Shona," he said softly, his voice just above a whisper. "Shall I say goodbye?"

She couldn't meet his gaze. Her eyes were glassy, glistening with unshed tears, and she nodded almost imperceptibly. There were no words left to say. The heaviness of the moment choked them both, leaving them with the sense that this parting was not just a temporary farewell but the closing of a chapter they might never return to.

Krishna turned to the driver, thanking him quietly before giving a final nod. "Good luck, Kisna." the driver said before pulling away to wait nearby for Nati.

He wrapped his arms around her one last time, pressing a kiss to her forehead. It felt as if he was leaving a part of himself behind with her. He lingered for a second longer, not wanting to let go, then turned away.

Krishna reached the entrance, his hand gripping the strap of his bag so tightly that his knuckles turned white. He knew he had to keep moving, but something inside him made him hesitate. Just one last look, he told himself. Just one more moment to see her standing there.

He turned back. What he saw tore at his heart. Nati was crying, her shoulders shaking with the kind of sobs that seemed to rise from somewhere deep within. She wasn't holding back anymore; she couldn't. Her tears fell freely, and before he could even process it, she was running toward him, her steps quick and desperate, like she needed to close the distance before it became too great.

She threw herself into his arms, pressing her face against his chest as if she could disappear into him, as if holding on long enough could keep him from leaving. Her grip tightened around his neck, her grief folded into his, raw and wordless.

"I can't do this, Krishna," she cried, her voice breaking. "I can't let you go." Her hands gripped the back of his shirt, refusing to let go, as if she could keep him here just a little longer.

He held her tightly, his fingers threading through her hair as his own tears escaped. "Shona…," he whispered, his voice trembling. "I don't want to leave either." His words came out in gasps, his breath ragged, as though speaking to them was tearing something from him. "I wish I could stay… I wish we could keep living this dream."

Their lips met in a desperate kiss—salted with tears, thick with the ache of goodbye. Their kiss ached with every word left unspoken, a fragile rebellion against the parting they couldn't stop. For a few stolen seconds, the world fell away. No airport, no looming departure—only them, locked in a kiss that carried every unspoken word, every promise they wished they could keep.

When they finally pulled back, Krishna cupped her face in his hands, brushing away the tears that stained her cheeks. "I'll come back to you," he said, his voice hoarse but full of a conviction that made his heart ache. "I swear, Nati. This is not the end for us."

She nodded, though her eyes told a different story, one of doubt, of fear that this was the last time they would see each other like this. "You promise?" She whispered, searching his eyes for the assurance she so desperately needed.

"I promise," he breathed. "I'll find my way back to you."

They held each other for a moment longer before Krishna gently loosened her grip and took a step back. He couldn't let himself hesitate anymore; the more he lingered, the harder it would be to leave. He turned and walked through the entrance, not daring to look back again. As the doors closed behind him, he heard her voice call out one last time, filled with all the love and heartbreak she could give: "I love you, Krishna."

And then he was gone, swallowed by the airport's bustle, leaving behind the girl he loved and the promise that one day, somehow, he would find his way back to her.

Nati stood frozen, as if stillness could halt time, could somehow keep Krishna from slipping away. Her vision blurred as tears spilled down, cascading over her cheeks. She wiped them away with the back of her hand, but they kept coming, refusing to be held back. She watched as Krishna reached the airport entrance, paused for a moment, and gave one last look over his shoulder. Their eyes met across the distance—hers filled with an unspoken plea, his with a sorrow that mirrored her own. Then, he disappeared, swallowed by the crowd and the inevitability of his departure. And yet, even as they parted, something sacred remained—an unspoken vow, carried in tears and memory. This wasn't the end. It was a pause. A quiet ache between chapters. One day, when the world was kinder, he would return—and they would begin again.

The emptiness hit her like a wave. It was a silence that filled every corner of her mind, a loneliness so profound that it seemed to echo in the space around her. The world moved on, oblivious to the quiet devastation left in his wake, as if the earth itself did not recognize that a piece of her heart had just walked away.

She took a trembling step forward, and then another, the reality of the separation crashing down on her all at once. She had always known this moment would come, yet nothing had prepared her for the heaviness of it—the unbearable finality. There were still so many things left unsaid, so many dreams they hadn't yet fulfilled, like unfinished chapters of a book she had hoped would never end.

Nati reached for her phone out of habit, her thumb hovering over Krishna's contact. But what could she say now that he was gone? She finally took a trembling breath and wiped her eyes, forcing herself to move, though each step felt heavy. Forcing herself to move, she headed toward the taxi, her legs feeling weak and unsteady beneath her. The driver glanced at her in the rearview mirror, perhaps seeing the red in her eyes, the unmistakable signs of a heart breaking.

As she got in, Nati glanced one more time at the airport entrance, half-expecting to see Krishna rushing back toward her. But there was only the flow of strangers, moving on with their lives.

"Back to your apartment, miss?" he asked, voice careful, almost hesitant.

She nodded; her voice caught in the weight of everything she couldn't say. As the car pulled away, she felt herself unraveling, each motion stealing a part of her. Lima blurred into a sea of memories, each one colored by Krishna's presence—every laughter shared, every quiet moment held between them. As the taxi wove through familiar streets, the city she once knew felt strange—hollow in his absence.

The driver's voice broke into her thoughts, asking if she was okay. She nodded faintly, not trusting her voice to answer. In truth, she wasn't sure how she would be without Krishna by her side. As they drove away from the airport, she realized that even though he was gone, there was a part of him that would always be with her—a part she would carry forward, wherever life took her next. And for now, that would have to be enough.

She didn't know how she'd step inside that apartment, how she'd face the silence, the echoes of him in every corner.

Room 907 had been their world, filled with love and laughter. Now, it was nothing more than a memory— a beautiful, bittersweet memory that would always haunt her, linger like a shadow over the days to come.

Nati closed her eyes', pretending Krishna was still there, whispering reassurances only he could give. But when she opened them, all that remained was an empty seat and the crushing weight of goodbye.

You ran to me, and the night seemed to shatter, Tears broke the silence, hearts spilled like rain.
We clung together as if the world might crumble, held each other close, aching through the pain.

To Krishna, it felt like an eternity. As soon as he settled into his seat, he shut his eyes, hoping sleep would offer a brief escape from the ache gripping his heart. But it didn't take long for Nati's face to come rushing back to him—her laughter, her playful teasing, the way she looked at him with those eyes full of light. His thoughts replayed all the memories they had made in Lima, vivid as an old film he couldn't stop watching.

He remembered them boarding the plane, their excitement bubbling over as they darted from window to window, eager for a glimpse of the Andes below. How they had laughed, snapped photos, and even caught the air hostesses sneaking amused glances at their antics. It had been one of those perfect moments that felt like it could last forever.

"Was destiny leading him to a better life—or merely testing his resolve?" or "Krishna couldn't ignore the unease creeping into his mind. Was this love enough to withstand the secrets he was yet to share—or the ones he was too afraid to uncover?"

In her presence, he felt invincible, as though love could mend anything. Krishna couldn't help but wonder: Was love enough to rewrite the chapters of their pasts, or were some stories destined to remain incomplete?

Little did he know, this journey would take them to places neither of them could have ever imagined, places that would test not only their love but their very identities.

What lay ahead would challenge them in ways he couldn't yet fathom—pushing not just their love, but who they were at their core.

The airport lights shimmered beneath him, fading into a blur of gold and shadow as the plane ascended. Krishna shut his eyes, but the ache refused to fade. For a breathless moment, he couldn't tell if it was the sting of goodbye—or the fear that it was goodbye for good.

Was this how it ended?

What if he never saw her again?

What if this was the final page of a story that had barely begun?

And then—like a whisper through the silence—Sardarji's words echoed in his mind, steady and sure, slicing through the doubt:

"Nothing is impossible for a willing heart."

As Krishna stood at the edge of a new horizon, the sea stretching infinitely before him, he understood that this wasn't a farewell—it was the first step toward everything that lay beyond.

This isn't the end. It's only the beginning.

Turn the page—but not just yet. Their story is far from finished.

Part Two coming soon …

www.ingramcontent.com/pod-product-compliance
Lightning Source LLC
LaVergne TN
LVHW091710070526
838199LV00050B/2337